# TUNGS OF DEATH

A Fantasy Adventure

## DANIEL MCCASLIN

The Plaga Chronicles - Part 1

info@minorflock.com
Minor Flock Publishing, LLC
1501 N Charlotte Ave Suite A104
Monroe, NC 28110
First paperback edition May 2023
Book design by Casey Fritz, Albatross Book Co.
ISBN 9798395294210 (paperback)
ISBN 978-8-89034-305-5 (ebook)

# ONE

Marian watched the sunset from a grassy hill outside the Steinigen fortress. Free from her father, and free from his warlocks and guards, the moment she carved out of time for herself was one of peace. She was surrounded by Harken Lilies, a rare flower whose seeds were prized elsewhere in the Kingdom of Ephorus. She whispered into the petals, a plea for rescue, and a tear rolled down her freckled cheek. Ancient texts told of pixies who could hear your cries through the delicate system the flower built beneath the earth with its roots, but no one had ever come. As the final ray of sunlight touched her, she snapped her fingers, and a bright spark arose on her fingertips, bobbing up and down in the wind. She smiled and concentrated on the flame, willing it to grow and spread across her hand. She didn't feel any pain; that had vanished years ago, along with her screams from being beaten by her father's men.

The sun was racing over the horizon, a cue for Marian to return to the fortress. She shoved her burning palm into the patch of Harken Lilies, and a puff of smoke and pollen burst forth. The smoke surrounded her as it drifted down to the ground. The first time she had tried to run away from her father, a similar cloud of smoke led his trackers right to her.

Marian gazed at the Logi Mountains as the sun dropped toward their jagged peaks. There was a volcanic fire raging inside those mountains, which made them impossible to cross. No one knew what lay beyond them. She had read once that her great-grandfather had sent a team of trackers to find a path off the isthmus, but they did not succeed. Marian felt a connection with the fire and sensed that it beckoned her. It gave her a feeling of warmth and belonging, something she never felt inside the walls of Steinigen.

Marian had never known a soul to call mother. No one ever mentioned who the woman may have been and Marian could find no images in her mind when she would search. She'd been raised by her father, a power-crazed maniac. The only female in her life had been her Aunt Maven, a wicked creature obsessed with death, who'd wandered the halls at night, shouting about the reign of darkness beyond the Logi Mountains, but she'd been sent away. Marian had never left Steinigen, though she knew her ancestors had destroyed vast swaths of the kingdom, and she doubted she would ever be welcomed alive by anyone south of the Morkere Forest. Perhaps, however, death wasn't the worst thing that could happen to her.

The sound of the massive fortress gates creaking open brought Marian's thoughts back to the present. Her father was heading east to the port of Valga. He always traveled after dark, boasting that he was the terror everyone feared in the night. Soon all Marian could hear was the pounding of horses' hooves. As the orange sun plunged behind the mountains, she knew the burning inside her was about to begin.

The ache began in her toes and crept up her legs. It felt like knives underneath her skin. After her last attempt at running away, her father had cast a spell on her: if she wasn't inside the fortress walls by sundown, her body would be engulfed in pain. He thought he had ended the possibility of her ever attempting to leave again, but it only made her remember every night why she must.

Racing the darkness, Marian climbed up the twenty-foot fortress wall. If she fell, she might die, but she was strong, and she gripped the unforgiving, gray stones with determination. She'd done it so many times that her fingers were calloused and her muscles hard, and she pulled herself up easily. When she reached the top, she lifted herself over and caught a guard by surprise. He quickly unsheathed his sword, but Marian raised her hands and snapped her fingers. Bright flames leapt from her hands, crawling up her arms. The guard looked terrified and backed away, tripping over the stones and tumbling backward as Marian walked past.

"Well done, Marian," she whispered to herself. "I know," she responded with a giggle, "but thank you for saying so."

Making her way to her quarters, Marian realized her father's departure meant she would have time for escape. It had been months since he had left the fortress grounds, but after a messenger arrived early that morning, his warlocks had begun to prepare his caravan of horses for a journey. She almost asked him where he was going, but she didn't want to hear his voice ever again.

She reached her door, smiling at its disheveled appearance. It was a heavy slab of oak covered with indentions from the guards who tried to force it open over the years. She leaned close and whispered into its cracks and crevices, her voice releasing the barrier she had created to prevent her father's guards from entering. Her father had taught her nothing about the world beyond Steinigen, but he did delight in seeing her develop her powers. Though he had no intention of ever dying or ceding his control, he dreamed of using her in his conquests; to what extent, he never said. Destruction brewed within their family's blood, and her father feasted on its potential. He'd be more than happy to watch her wither if it meant draining every last ounce of power from her body for his purpose.

The door responded to her voice and slowly opened to let her enter before slamming shut behind her. The room was dark, but she knew it well enough to find her way without the aid of light. When she got to her desk, she reached for the candle and brought it close to her mouth. She closed her eyes, inhaled deeply, and slowly exhaled on the wick. The scorching heat poured out from deep within her, and a tiny flame appeared on the candle. Her pale skin began to glow in its light. She smiled as the flame fought the drafts that permeated the entire fortress, admiring how it refused to surrender.

She put down the candle and sat on her bed, closing her eyes and taking slow, deep breaths as she steeled her courage for what would come next.

# Two

The sun was setting behind the Aurian Hills as Ian took a few puffs from his pipe. It was a peaceful evening. Birds were fluttering around the trees, dancing in the wind, enjoying the day's last bit of light. The nights had started getting colder, but he didn't need to start a fire yet. A slight chill at night gave him a chance to wrap an extra blanket around himself for comfort and security.

Taking a deep drag from his pipe, he exhaled a plume of smoke. The pipe had been his father's and was showing its age. When he smoked it, he felt much older than the two decades he had managed to survive. His father had picked up the habit as a young man, continuing through the years even though Ian's mom often chided him for it. She was convinced that Ian would emulate his father, clogging his body and mind with smoke.

Ian chuckled as he knocked the pipe against his boot and shook out the dried leaves. Only on rare occasions did he indulge in the ritual. His memories didn't let him enjoy it for too long, or too often.

Raucous laughter broke out from behind him in his shop. He turned and caught a glimpse of Benson showing off his magic tricks to a few drunken wanderers. Most likely, they were vagrants wanted for thievery or worse, but their money was good and Ian wasn't inclined to care. Benson wasn't concerned, so neither was he.

Ian placed the pipe in his shirt pocket and eased himself out of the chair, saying goodnight to the sun before making his way inside. As he entered, he saw that the table between Benson and the drunks was covered with stacks of cards and coins. They were playing Siyan, which Benson had learned only a few months earlier. The drunkard had been fascinated by Benson, a bear that could interact with humans, and spent hours teaching him the game. Ever since, Benson had become quite the savant, mastering Siyan quickly enough to defeat almost every challenger he faced.

Ian sidled up to the table, taking a seat beside his friend, and watched in fascination as Benson effortlessly demolished the hands of the men before him. As each man chose from the alliance, mischief, or war decks, Benson remained poised, his cards laid bare on the table taunting the three men. He countered an attack from the drunkard to his left while the other two joined forces through the alliance cards. Drawing a ne'er do well spell from the mischief deck, Benson combined it with a miscreant card he already had on the table. Laying the cards down together between the two men across from him sullied their alliance instantly, leaving them open for the shredding.

With their strategy in tatters, Benson continued to make mischief his aim as he confused his opponents and weakened their defenses. Then he swooped in and decimated all of them.

As the three men squabbled, insistent that they could have taken Benson down had the others not interfered, Ian motioned toward the window and the darkening sky. Benson nodded and groaned as he began picking the cards up from the deck.

"Sorry gentleman, but if you wish to win back your earnings you can return tomorrow. For now, though, the night is falling, and we're closing shop."

The men groaned. They had just settled on a new plan of attack to destroy Benson.

"Don't be a daisy, wee man," the drunk in the center scoffed as he took a swig from his mug. "The dark is when the fun begins!" He laughed as his drink dripped down his mustache onto his chest.

His friends snorted and hollered and began sorting the cards and shuffling the decks. Benson placed his paw on Ian's shoulder and smiled, eager to keep playing and take all of the money in the pockets of the three men.

"See. Even the bear wants to keep going. And you never argue with a bear."

The drunk in the middle appeared to be the mouthpiece of the group. Ian shrugged his shoulders and resigned himself to a long night of noise and debauchery.

"May he have mercy upon your coin, because he hasn't lost in weeks," Ian said as he walked away from the table.

Benson growled, pleased by the compliment and staring down the men as if to prove Ian's point. He squirmed in the chair, trying to get comfortable and its legs squeaked and whimpered under his hefty body. The men broke out in laughter. He ran his massive paw across his chest, the claws stretching out and scratching his dark brown fur. His smile of pleasure bared his glistening teeth.

"Never fear, wee boy," the man said as he took another swig from his cup and slammed it on the table. "I've changed my mind. It's not Siyan I wish to play now."

Ian and Benson sensed the shift in the man's mood, and so did his friends. As they stood up, Benson lifted himself upright, clearing Ian's head by several stones' length. The two backed away from the table. They had learned the value of separation and the avenues of defense it afforded over the years.

"Don't be going too far away now," the man said. "While we only plan to take your money and a few potions per request from our sponsor, we're also just a tad bored and would like to stomp on you for a while to lift our spirits. And maybe," the man sneered as he focused on Benson, "maybe we take home a new rug or jacket."

"Oh, no," Ian said, "that was a bad thing to say." He turned to see his furry friend becoming enraged. "Please apologize and leave before this gets worse."

A soft growl was coming from Benson as his mouth opened slowly, saliva dripping from his fangs.

"We leave when we're ready. And we never apologize," the man snapped.

His two friends charged Benson in unison, trying to flank him. Benson lunged at one of the men and smashed him with his head, sending him to the ground. Ian leaped onto the other man's back and pulled a vial from his pocket. He popped the top and shoved it to the man's nostril, forcing him to inhale it. Then Ian poured its contents down the man's shirt. In an instant the man began shouting as he violently tore at his clothes, ripping them off and running outside, naked.

"Might have gone a touch too far with the potion this ti—" Ian said, but he was cut off by a piercing scream. Benson was standing on top of his attacker, his saliva dripping down on the man's face.

"Please don't eat me," the man cried as he tried to wrench himself from beneath Benson.

"I told you not to—" Ian was cut off again as the naked man he had just dispatched came back inside screaming. "Oh, come on. Not in the shop!" Ian shouted as the man ran around, bumping into shelves before heading back out into the night.

Ian turned his attention to Benson, whose opponent was now passed out on the floor from fright. While Benson hoisted the unconscious man, Ian motioned for the trio's leader to make his way to the door.

"If you'd please leave, now. We can end this without any further acts of aggression."

The man placed his hand on the hilt of his sword as he backed away from the table.

"And if I don't?"

The man's words were meant to be menacing, but he was betrayed by his voice, which cracked as he spoke.

"Well, your friend running around naked in the dark might die of exposure. I'm not sure where I went wrong with the potion, but he got way too much of something, so you're going to need to check on him. This one," Ian pointed to the limp man on Benson's shoulder, "has shown you how well he can do in a fight with a bear, so that sucks for you," he paused as Benson raised the limp man's hand and waved it, easily holding the lifeless mass of human on his shoulder. "So feel free to take your chances, but we're not inclined to offer sanctuary after a fight's been started, and your little bear rug comment has done away with any leniency he may have shown."

"I..." the man began, his voice quivering. "I can't carry him. I got a bad back, you see. If I try to lift him, it's going to give out, and then I'll be laid out on the floor. I hired these guys to help me with the job, thinking I would just have to sound tough and have them do the fighting for me."

Puzzled, Ian replied, "But didn't you just threaten to beat up both of us without them?"

"I thought you guys might have backed down, intimidated by the gravitas of my voice."

"No. Not at all," Ian replied as Benson laughed and patted the man on his shoulder. "Follow us," Ian said to the man as he and Benson went out the door.

"To where?"

"To our wheelbarrow on the side of the shop. Benson will dump your buddy in it, and you can push it to the edge of the wood. The road will take you back to the heart of Cosen where you can find somewhere to dump your frie—" Ian stopped as he heard the naked man screaming in the distance, somewhere in the dark of night. "You are going to have a hard time finding him," he muttered.

As Ian stared into the dark with the man, Benson was already coming back with the limp man in the wheelbarrow. He rolled it up to the man and dropped the handles. The man spoke up again.

"Hate to ask, but could you lift it back up again? And then," he patted his hands against the small of his back, "and then I'll take it from there. My back, and all."

Benson sighed as Ian laughed. Their attackers were feeble. Benson lifted the wheelbarrow handles and gave them to the man, who groaned as he pushed the wheelbarrow forward.

"Many thanks," he said as he struggled to push the heavy load.

"Never come back," Ian said as he waved the man on, happy to see him out of the shop.

The feeble attacker slowly slipped away into the darkness of the night, and Ian and Benson headed back into the shop, ignoring the distant screams of the naked miscreant. The potion would wear off by morning, and it wasn't cold enough for him to freeze. This was their fourth attempted robbery in as many months, and they were exhausted. Ian slumped into a chair at the table. Benson sat beside him and grabbed the Siyan cards, growling happily.

Ian stared at his friend with amusement. Nothing ever seemed to faze Benson. But, when you're the biggest animal in the fight, you probably don't have to worry all that much. Ian nodded his consent and Benson began dealing the cards as they settled in for the night.

# THREE

A dollop of hot candle wax dripped onto Marian's bare toes as she leaned forward, perusing the books and journals scattered throughout her father's study. She muffled a shout by biting her lip. She wasn't supposed to be here, so she had to be discreet. But she opted to light a few more candles so that she could read without getting too close to the flame. The guards didn't patrol her father's quarters often, but would come running were they to notice the light and her unwelcomed presence there.

The flames flickered to life around her, and the room danced with shadows and filled with an orange glow. Her eyes went back to scanning the books, her inner voice coming back to life. It had woken her during the last several nights in the middle of nightmares about her father's impending campaign.

"You'll know it when you see it," she said softly. "But how? There are hundreds of dusty old journals in here." Her fingers ran across the books' spines. She closed her eyes, trying to focus. "You can do this, Marian," she whispered.

Her fingers trailed across a shelf nailed into the stone wall beneath the family crest. She stared at the insignia, a dragon surrounded by fire, set within a three-pronged shield. No love or kindness could come from such a thing.

"Focus!"

Marian spun around in fear, thinking she had been caught, but she found herself alone and realized that she had spoken aloud. She used to talk to herself for the company as a child but she thought she had moved past it by now. That voice was coming back even stronger now, though, leaving her to wonder if she was even in control of it. Her hand was still on the shelf, touching the books. Then her fingers slipped into a gap and felt like they'd gotten burned by fire.

She pushed the books aside to get a closer look. There was a small leather journal hidden between the ancestral tomes. She pulled it out and wiped the dust off, her heart skipping a beat when the leather tugged at her fingers, as if desperate to hold onto her. She felt excited when she saw the cover image was a meadow of Harken Lilies and clutched the journal as a voice rang through her head.

"Go, now," the voice called out.

She tried to get a hold of herself, desperate to control the voice inside her head. "It's just me. It's just me. It's just me," she whispered to herself as she wrapped her arms around herself as tight as she could, the journal pressing against her chest.

"And you are more than enough," the voice said with warmth and affection as if coming from the journal. "But you must go. Time is precious now."

Marian turned around to leave but knocked several books to the floor in her haste. As they crashed to the stones, she stood still, listening for footsteps. No one came, so she slipped the journal in a pocket in her cloak and put the books back in place.

She made quick work of blowing out the candles, letting the eyes of the dragon watching over the room disappear into the darkness. She inched the door open, hoping to see an empty hall indifferent to the noise she had caused.

She stepped out slowly, making sure no one saw her leaving her father's study. As she moved down the hallway toward her quarters, she began to relax, the warm presence of the journal resting tightly in her pocket. She raised her hands and let them run across the cool stone walls. The air outside was cold as it blew down from the Logi Mountains, unphased by the fire roiling deep beneath the black stones. The outside realm couldn't cross those mountains into Ephorus, but the icy wind did, a bleak reminder of the isolation the mountains imposed.

As her fingers began to grow numb, Marian imagined the fire from the candles igniting a flame within her hands. A cloud of smoke came from her lips, and a scent of sulfur filled the hall. Her hands began to glow, and the cold around her disappeared.

"You are stronger than you realize." The voice came out flat and stern, breaking her concentration and snapping her back into the moment. Burn marks appeared on the stones her hands were pressed against.

"I am stronger," she whispered to herself.

She hastened back to her quarters and whispered the incantation to the door. It opened and let her in. She removed the journal from her cloak, laid it on her bed, and began to gather her gear and provisions.

"I have no idea what I'm doing," she said, feeling her terror coming back.

"Why would you know what you're doing? You've never done this before," she answered herself.

Marian tried not to shout, "So why am I doing it?"

"Calm yourself," she snapped back. "You will not be left alone. They will help you."

The desire to scream out "who" was nearly unbearable, but she restrained every part of her body until she felt her sense of control return. Marian stared down at the journal and pressed her palms against the sides of her head, hoping the pressure would stabilize her thoughts. She stared at the Harken Lilies on the cover: she'd heard the old tale about pixies using the lilies to communicate, and she wondered if it were true. Marian flipped open the journal and saw a map of Ephorus. The artist cared not for cities and roads but focused on geography. Ephorus appeared as a large isthmus surrounded on three sides by an even larger sea. Landmasses arched around its eastern and western edges, nearly touching it at some points. According to legend, the First Walkers had designed all the lands as one, keeping the different peoples together. But their ambitious creation was no match for the chaos that bubbled under the surface of everything, and wrath and death had slowly consumed all the lands except for

Ephorus, their treasured home.

"Death is inevitable," Marian whispered to herself. She didn't want to believe it, but nothing she had seen in life offered her hope of anything else.

# Four

Nance's eyes turned up toward the stars above Valga, his eyes searching for the dreki constellation while he listened to the sea lash out at the shore. His ancestors owed their powers to the beast, a dragon resting beneath the Logi Mountains. Nance cared little for the tale, or the devotion his father and sister had given it. He wanted the power. He wanted to crush the world and the stars beyond if he could, scorching all existence beneath his reign.

They are quite beautiful, though, he thought to himself as he waited for the man before him to find his courage and speak. Telling the Master of Steinigen that something had gone wrong was a costly job, and this man's compatriot lay in a heap on the ground beside him.

"I'm sorry Master, but she would not take. Sir Garrin instructed us to halt our attempts and sail to you at once."

Turning away from the stars, Nance let the fire burn bright in his eyes as fury seeped through his skin. He grabbed the unconscious man from the ground and lifted him with one hand. Taking a few steps toward the poor soul left standing, staring into his eyes, Nance heaved his unconscious compatriot into the distance. They listened to the sound of the man's body tumbling down the hill until it ceased.

"Do you have the Hearthwood?" Nance's words seethed from his mouth.

The man stumbled over his answer as he muttered, "I was asked.... We were asked to inform you that it was not completed in the desired manner due to complications. Sir Garrin believes he can still make it powerful enough, but more time is needed."

"You're not answering my question," Nance snapped. As Master of Steinigen, he commanded complete obedience from his subjects, reserving the right to break, burn, or banish any or all parts of a transgressor.

"Would you like me to poke him a while, sir?" Sever asked as he ambled up.

Nance turned to his bodyguard, a creature made of enchanted volcanic stones, and saw him removing his sword from its sheath. He bore no armor but the insignia of Steinigen had been burned into his brittle chest by the Master. Sever stood unflinching, his unblinking emerald eyes casting an unnerving greenish glow. He stared at the broken man before them. The sword was unnecessary for him since he was strong enough to rip the man in half, but Nance preferred less splatter at times. And, although the thought of watching Sever torture this man would perk up his mood, it could also endanger his plans. After the Trofasthet were banished generations ago, they had made their way to Trension, a desolate and unwelcoming isle off the coast of Ephorus; recently, with the help of Sir Garrin, they'd come back to the mainland and taken refuge on the southern tip of Ephorus, in Crescent City, as far from Steinigen as one could go without drowning in the sea.

Steinigen had a death grip on the northern lands above the Morkere Forest, but its grip was more tenuous in the south. He blamed it on his predecessors. Because of their failings, he had been forced to assume creative tactics, such as engaging the likes of a banished religious cult like the Trofasthet. He loathed them, but, for the moment, he needed them.

"No, no. It is not a complete failure, I suppose." Nance's eyes locked on the man before him. "I'll just make a note to voice my displeasure." Feigning an attempt to find parchment to write on, Nance stepped close to the man. He could smell the sweat on the zealot's brow and sneered as he saw his legs shaking. "It appears you'll need to deliver this one personally," he said with a grin that revealed his blackened teeth, which had been scorched by the fire that burned inside him. "Do you enjoy the sights of Crescent City?"

"No, Master." The man answered meekly, closing his eyes and resigning himself to the pain that was to come.

"It is quite horrid with its mass of putrid and foul humans. Since Sir Garrin deemed it unnecessary to sail here himself, you'll need to return to that disgusting hovel once more."

With a flick of his wrist, a flame appeared on Nance's

right hand. Gripping the man's collar bone with his left, he squeezed until he heard the pop of bone breaking, then dropped the agonized man to the ground. Now that he had a more suitable writing space, he turned the man over and, using his fiery right hand, seared a message onto his back for Sir Garrin. The sound and stench of burning flesh sent a burst of joy through Nance's body as the man squirmed beneath him.

"Come, now!" Nance shouted. "You're only making this last longer. You know how neat I like to be in my writing."

Nance's finger swirled across the man's back and his clothing disintegrated and left his scarred flesh open to the air. Not wanting his message to be overlooked, Nance wrote in large letters, nearly covering the man's entire back with three words: DO NOT DISAPPOINT.

Nance let the man fall to the ground and kicked him out of his path. Sever snickered as he saw the words seared on the man's back.

"Beautiful writing, sir. You've grown gifted in your penmanship."

"Practice, Sever. One has but to practice something they enjoy, and over time they shall become a master at it."

"What would you like me to do with this one?" Sever asked as he nudged the man with his stone feet. "He's quite pitiful. Will most likely die, if we don't do the work of living for him."

Nance shook his head in frustration. "I grow weary

of the weakness in other humans." He took a few deep breaths as he looked at his guards sitting on their horses in the distance. "Toss him on one of their horses and have them deliver his body to Crescent City personally. I want to make sure Sir Garrin sees my message."

"And the other one, sir?" Sever nodded his head toward the hill Nance had tossed the man down.

"Oh, right," he laughed, scratching his head for a moment. "Forgot about that one." His shoulders sank as he grabbed the reins of his horse for support. "I'll be honest, Sever. I'm tired, I don't care, and the wolves need to eat too."

"What of their ship, sir?"

"Arrange for a few slaves to be brought here in the morning to make sure it's moored properly. If Sir Garrin does not complete the Hearthwood, we can use it to build a pyre to burn him on."

"Understood, sir."

Sever waved for the guards to come forward and hoisted the Trofasthet zealot onto the rear of a horse. He strapped him down tight, laughing as the man cried when the ropes dug into the fresh burns across his back, peeling the skin away as he cinched tight. Before the guard took off toward Crescent City, Nance held up his hand for him to halt.

"When you see Sir Garrin, let him know I expect you to return with the Hearthwood, or his head, immediately."

"Understood, sir," the guard answered before taking off at a gallop.

# FIVE

Marian's plan of escape had been simple. After gathering what food she needed from the galley, she would exit through a small door built in the iron gate. The guards were sparse on the lower levels when the Master was away, and she imagined a quick and painless departure. She had managed to avoid being seen in the hallways as she left the kitchen, her satchel packed with supplies for the journey. But the guards had gathered around the iron gate, in anticipation of her father's arrival, blocking any chance of exit.

"Well, shit," Marian sniped, a lot louder than she had intended.

The guards heard her, scrutinizing her as they assessed the situation. Marian was dressed for travel, her satchel weighing heavy on her shoulder. The captain of the guards began barking orders for his men to surround her as she backed away toward the kitchen.

"Sorry!" she shouted. "Thought this was my room," she shrugged her shoulders as she feigned laughter. "Argh, Marian, just light a candle next time." She wagged a finger at herself.

The guards cared little for her excuse and were moving quickly toward her now. She felt the kitchen door behind her and yanked it open, slid through, and slammed it closed. There was no lock, so she acted on instinct, lighting a flame in her palm and laying it on the door until it caught fire. As she ran toward the stairwell, she heard cries and shouts from the men who were unable to open the door. She smiled until she realized she was making her way up instead of out. There was only one way to exit the fortress from where she was headed.

Marian made quick work of the steps as she struggled to think of a better way to die than jumping off a thirty-foot wall, but nothing came to mind. As she emerged from the stairwell into the cool air of the night, she saw guards running down the ramparts toward her. She thought about heading back down the stairs but then she heard the echoing steps of guards charging up after her.

Jump little darling, and don't be afraid to fly, the voice said.

"Yeah, okay," Marian whispered to herself as she tightened her bag and ran toward the battlement.

She jumped. Her body felt weightless, but she knew that was an illusion. She closed her eyes and waited to die as she fell to the base of the fortress wall. She thought to look beneath her but was blinded by a light bursting forth from a patch of Harken Lilies.

When she landed, her breath shot out of her, and the pain was fierce. Her heart was pounding, and she could feel blood trickling down her cheeks. It had seemed like such a simple solution to jump. She made a mental note to avoid jumping from great heights ever again. She wriggled her legs and arms, pleased to find nothing broken, just in pain.

"You're an idiot," she murmured to herself as she took a few deep breaths. "Now, get up!"

She could hear the guards clamoring inside the fortress to open the gates. She looked up mockingly at the guards still staring down at her from the battlements. As intent as they were on capturing her, not one of them had been willing to follow her quick descent.

"What's wrong with you?" a guard shouted down at her.

"A lot!"

Marian had a brief head start if she could take advantage of it. Planting her hands on the ground, she lifted herself one knee at a time until she could stand. She picked up her bag and swung it over her arm, avoiding the thought of how she may have ruined the few rations she had brought. The world around her grew darker as the lights of Steinigen faded behind her, while the fiery pain of her fathers' spell began to burn its way through her feet as she trudged forward, heading to the Morkere Forest.

Her pace picked up when she heard the fortress gates creak open and the shouts of her father's guards coming through them. The land in front of the fortress was an open field, stretching for over a hundred yards until it reached the Morkere Forest, where the trees' dense canopy consumed everything. Even her fathers' trackers would have trouble finding her there if she left the trails behind.

Marian sprinted in a direct line toward the trees. She was desperate to control her breathing as her father's spell began to wreak havoc on her body. It burned relentlessly in her as she crept closer to the Morkere. She was only a few yards away when her legs locked up, and her mind filled with a memory of her Aunt Maven being dragged to the forest. She remembered her fathers' laughter as Aunt Maven was yanked across the rocky ground, screaming until her fury turned to a howling, frightening cackle. That had been the last time Marian saw her. Her father had given her to the Trofasthet as a reward for their loyalty.

"Into the woods she goes, never to be seen again," her father said. "A sacrifice to the ancient dragon of the Logi." Tears welled up in Marian's eyes as she remembered how helpless she had been, unable to help Aunt Maven. "I am not that weak anymore!" she shouted and turned to face the men who were charging toward her.

A feeling of rage surged through her entire body. Fire started pouring from her fingers and crept up her arms. She planted her feet, lifted her arms, and watched the men rush toward her. She waited until she could see the familiar dragon embroidered on their tunics, and then she let go.

Marian knew she was screaming, but she did not recognize her voice through the roar of the flames coming from her hands. The men scattered instantly. She could feel the power of her anger as the flames turned from orange to blue, burning brighter as she remembered all the years of torture and pain she had endured. The fire crept up her arms and shoulders and spread across the rest of her body.

"You must control the flames," she heard the voice whisper. "I can't," she answered, her voice breaking as she began to feel the heat of the flames. "You must!" the voice shouted from within her.

Marian screamed again as she forced her arms down, releasing the flames on the grasslands, which ignited immediately, blocking the guards in the distance who'd been afraid to attack. Turning to the forest, she ran to the safety of the trees, their dark canopy more than capable of consuming the remnants of the fire still burning within her.

She could hear only the crackling of the flames. The guards had stopped, unwilling to chase her for fear of their lives. Marian knew the power of fear—her father intended to build his kingdom on it—and she detested its very nature. She was beyond his control now; beyond any fear he could instill. Beyond his spells. The burning within her was gone, cast out with the flames, and he would never hold such power over her again.

"I'm free," she whispered to herself as she felt for the journal in her bag, relieved when her fingers found it unscathed. "Now, just don't die."

She waded deeper into the darkness of the Morkere, trying to summon the fleeting sense of hope that remained. Marian had spent her life struggling through the terrors she had been born into. Whatever the unknown ahead of her may offer, she would face it just the same.

# Six

A gigantic belch startled Ian from his sleep, and he tumbled to the floor. His hair was disheveled and his face was sticky with saliva. He stared through a groggy haze, trying to place himself.

He was on the main floor of the shop, which meant he never even made it to bed after closing the doors behind the thwarted robbers the night before. At some point during their game of Siyan, Benson had dared him to drink a new concoction he had made. It had been a bad idea to comply.

He could hear the rain drenching the shop. The Aurian Hills were shrouded in bleak, low-hanging clouds. Pulling the blanket Benson left for him tighter around his body, Ian let his mind wander to the beat of the raindrops. It eased the throbbing in his head as he began to hope that it would be a rather slow day for them if the rain kept up.

Ian wiped the crust out of his eyes and forced himself to stand up. As he got to his feet, he was whacked in the back, and he quickly dropped to his knees. Wincing, Ian turned to find his bear friend laughing and in good spirits.

"Well, I'm certainly glad the evening didn't leave you any worse for wear," Ian grumbled. Avoiding another swing, he used the chair to balance and lift himself to his feet.

Benson growled his approval of Ian's discomfort; he was happy he'd been able to goad his friend into downing his concoction. To make up for it, Benson placed a spread of cheese and bread in his hands to help soak up any remnants of the drink still sloshing through his body.

"And is this food laced with any of our potions as well?"

Feigning shock, Benson threw himself into the chair beside Ian. It rocked back violently, almost tipping over. As Benson flailed about, Ian managed to keep his food out of harm's way, digging in as soon as he was able.

"Here," Ian offered a piece of honeyed bread to his friend.

Grumbling, Benson snatched it out of Ian's hand and devoured it in one bite. Benson had already managed to finish two meals before Ian woke up, but he welcomed food at any point during the day.

"This is why you can't keep bears as pets," Ian joked as he pointed to the crumbs mingling with the drool dripping down Benson's jaw. "After all these years, you still haven't learned any manners."

Benson roared as he stood up from the chair. Stomping away on his hind legs, he went down to the basement and away from Ian.

"We do not!" Ian shouted as a knocking came from the shop's front door.

Benson grinned as Ian's fantasy of a quiet, rainy day disappeared. Shoving more food into his mouth, Ian sighed and tossed the plate on the counter. While he gnawed on the cheese still hanging from his mouth, he walked to the front door. A crowd of people had made their way to his shop at first light despite the rain, it would seem, and now he had to take their coin.

Swinging the door open, Ian opened his mouth to greet them with whatever politeness he could muster, but another gigantic belch came out, along with a terrible stench. A burst of laughter erupted from down the stairwell as Benson relished Ian's inability to act civilized.

"No one asked you, you furry mongrel!" Ian shouted at him. Turning to face the customers, he wiped his sleeve across his face, shrugged his shoulders, and motioned for them to come in.

He thought to ask for their patience so he could get a little fresh air, but that time had come and gone. The glances they had given him held little respect.

No matter, though, he thought to himself. They came to me. I didn't go to them.

He made his way to the stool at his counter and began eating his food again as the villagers meandered about his shop, scouring the aisles for some quick fix, some fleeting bit of happiness in their hardscrabble lives.

# SEVEN

"Shall I commence the execution, sir?" Sever asked as he stood in front of the guards who were kneeling on the ground before him. "I can do the plump one first if you like?" His sword moved swiftly from his sheath to over the guard's neck as he waited eagerly for his Master to command him.

After returning from the port in the early hours of the morning to find the southern range of his field scarred by flames, Nance had been trying to assess the damage his daughter had caused, and may still cause. This was not the first time she had tried to run away in his absence, but this one was successful. He had strived to stifle her powers until he could subdue them, but she had begun to break free, threatening his control.

Nance sat upon his throne with his elbows on his knees, his hands cupping his face as he pondered the ongoing incompetence he had come to expect from those around him. His ancestors had ruled Steinigen mercilessly through might and magic for generations. Some of them had not only plagued Ephorus but had journeyed into the world beyond the Logi. But Steinigen's halcyon days had slowly receded, an unforeseen consequence of a pact made generations before with the Vorkyre. Lost to time were the conquests his family hailed, and he needed more than a single lifetime to recover them.

Lifting his head from his hands, Nance cracked his neck, stretching his shoulders to release the tension caused by a long and hard ride from the port. He quietly chewed on a piece of sulfrite—a mixture of sulfur, sap, and flour—to keep his mind sharp. It was a rite of passage developed by his ancestors; to be able to hold in the heinous and vomit-inducing substance without losing your composure or wits would prepare you for commanding forces during battle as those around you fell. Standing from his throne, Nance swallowed and felt the sulfrite burn as it ran down his throat. He had grown to enjoy the pain.

"You imbecilic morons!"

Enraged, he lunged toward the men. Darkness fell upon the room as his anger absorbed the light from the torches placed around his dais and dimmed the torches lining the walls. His eyes were illuminated in a frightening orange haze. He reached out his hands and flames danced across his fingertips as he stood towering above the kneeling men. In the light of day, Nance was an impressive figure, standing tall with the broad shoulders of a laborer. But in the dark, there was no one more terrifying than the wraith that harnessed the power of fire.

"Sir!" Sever shouted, waving his hand to stop.

He stared at his stony friend with a brief sense of

confusion. Filled with the desire to kill, Nance's hands had clutched his hair in an attempt to avoid strangling the guards.

"I did that thing again," he said, pointing to his hair. "Killed it and turned it gray."

"Just a bit, sir," Sever nodded. "But, if I can be honest, I think it looks quite nice."

"Really," he said with a mixture of intrigue and incredulity. "I was so self-conscious the first time I did that, but I've always felt like I could do with a bit of gray."

Lifting his gaze from the ground, the plump guard decided to play his only hand. "It does look quite lovely, sir. You look a thousand times more wisdomery."

"Wisdomery?" Nance pinched the bridge of his nose as he fought to maintain composure. "Is this man important in any way, Sever? I held off killing him a moment ago, but I just don't think he deserves that courtesy to be extended again."

The fire had left Nance's eyes, returning to the candles around his dais as the torches sprang back to life. But the anger was still restless within him. Looking at Sever, he waited for the creature's dispassionate answer.

"Unfortunately, sir, these three men happen to be the illegitimate sons of Trofasthet members. You are most certainly right to kill them if you'd like, but it may prove problematic if the Trofasthet were to find out."

"Oh, it would just piss those old prattlers off, wouldn't it?" he shouted as he walked back and kicked his throne.

Before Nance usurped his father's reign, he had convinced the old man to sell off his older sister, Maven, to the Trofasthet. She was the bridge to an alliance he wanted to form with them. The Trofasthet had once been renowned for their cult of magic, but by the time they made their home on the island of Trension, in the last days of the Vorkyre, no one cared about them. Nance had ignored them for years until he realized their influence was growing in Crescent City. Building a coalition with them had been agonizing, but it was proving quite fruitful in his attempt to stealthily gain power throughout Ephorus.

"Okay, okay, okay."

"Okay," Sever said with a hint of glee, his sword swung high.

"Not okay, as in death and dismemberment," Nance said, throwing his hands up to halt the execution. "Okay as in, I'm forming a plan for these three to find a way to make themselves useful again so I don't have to kill them, which would then, in turn, make me have to kill all the Trofasthet before I want to. And I just do not have the time for that kind of a headache."

"Oh, well then. Okay, sir," Sever said. As he sheathed his sword, it scraped on his leg, causing a few stones on his upper thigh to break off.

"You there." Nance pointed to the disheveled man in the center. "You lead this trio of failures, correct?"

"Yes, sir," the man spoke softly, avoiding eye contact by staring at the crest in the center of the Master's chest. His skin was darkened by the sun, permanently tanned and tough as leather. "I am Lyco. My father was Lyran the Brave before he joined the order of the Trofasthet. He served your father as—"

Pointing to the man beside Lyco, Nance said, "Don't care. This plump fellow speaking out of turn, he's an idiot, yes?"

"Yes, sir. Ceril is an idiot, but we are part blood." He paused, hoping to add emphasis. "But, truly...he is an idiot."

"Fair enough," Ceril mumbled.

"Keeping my daughter's presence within these walls was your domain," Nance said, "and yet you let her escape the most impenetrable fort in this entire kingdom." He paused, catching his breath as his anger shot forth, flames leaping from his fingertips. "You now must find her and bring her to me. If you fail again, I will incinerate you and your brothers no matter your lineage!"

"Yes, Master," the three shouted as they hurried out of the throne room, escaping the reach of Nance's anger for the time being.

As the door slammed closed behind them, Nance collapsed into his throne, throwing his head back and releasing a long, deep moan.

"If my ancestors had not fallen so far into irrelevance, I would not have to put up with such stupidity. I just need a little bit of competency. Is that too much to ask?"

Sever took a knee by the Master, trying to find some thought to soothe him. "Cheer up, sir. Once the Hearthwood is complete, you'll be able to kill as many people as you'd like, related or not."

As he stared at Sever, Nance remembered the day he'd been created. Nance's father sought to ensure the safety of his son as his powers grew weaker, and he had river gnomes collect and assemble the volcanic stones that became Sever—Nance's enforcer—an unflinching life form who would kill without hesitation for him. Over time, Nance had grown to see Sever as his closest ally and advisor, keeping him at his side constantly.

"Ever the optimist, Sever. You always know how to cheer me up."

Standing at attention, Sever turned and asked, "Anything else I can do for you before you turn in for the night, sir?"

"Those idiots that just left here..."

"You'd like me to go kill them now," Sever said, reaching for his sword.

"No, no." Nance held up his hands. "It's kind of you to offer, but I need my daughter found. Make sure they take a set of experienced trackers with them. Marian has become crafty in recent years. I thought I had broken her spirits enough before, but now when she returns, we'll just have to break her legs. This will not work without her," his tone turned stark as his body stiffened. "Do not let them fail me."

"It will be done, sir."

As Sever plodded out of the throne room, Nance took a deep breath and slipped into thought. He saw the image of a young girl bathed in fire at the steps of their fortress. The powers his sister had wrested from within the Logi Mountains had provided him with the means to bring creation to its knees, and he would fulfill its desire.

# Eight

"Do you even hear yourself right now?" Marian snapped as she cinched her hood over her head.

Pacing back and forth in a patch of wildflowers amongst a clearing of trees, she had found a secluded spot to have a mental breakdown on the southern edge of the Morkere. It had been a hard night, and her body had taken a beating from low hanging limbs and roots as she ran recklessly. She ached and needed sleep, but time was too precious to waste. There were at least two more days of constant travel ahead of her to make it to Cosen.

"I hear just fine, and you should calm down," she muttered as she clamped her hands around her head. "You're not going to make it without food, though. It's kind of important." Marian leaned her head back and laughed. "Yeah, because I can just wander right into a town and buy supplies."

Marian carried on back and forth with herself as she began circling the patch of wildflowers. She was so preoccupied that she walked past two pixies sitting on a small shrub staring at her inquisitively.

They were each no bigger than a maple leaf, and they sat hand in hand as they watched Marian move about. They giggled and whispered in each other's ear, the smaller, raven-haired pixie mimicking Marian's obliviousness. Her partner, whose hair was bright and multicolored, doubled over, straining to hold in her laughter.

Fluttering into the air slowly, they made their way toward Marian.  As they came closer, the two could hear a rash of curses directed from Marian to herself; the scent of sulfur burning in the air.

The pixies carried on, whispering to each other, making their way toward Marian, unnoticed until one of them laughed loud enough for Marian to hear. The pixies hovered above the flowers and waved as Marian's eyes focused on them.

"Hi," the little raven-haired pixie started to speak but was cut off as Marian screamed, diving into the nearest bush.

This was not an elegant solution as the clearing was suffused in sunlight and Marian was in clear sight. Except now she had entangled herself in a holly bush and was grumbling, "Ow, ow, ow," as the prickly leaves pierced her tattered clothing.

The pixies placed their hands on their hips as they began fluttering down to a branch on the holly bush, the sun shimmering on their translucent wings. "This will not end well," the raven-haired pixie said as she landed, a look of disappointment in her eyes as she stared at Marian.

"A grim outlook does not suit your demeanor, my

love. We must trust in our old kook's plan," her partner answered. She smiled and began to pull back the twigs around Marian, helping her to find her way out with as few cuts as possible.

"I could not agree more," the pixie answered as she peered into the darkness of the bush and into the face of the groaning woman who was squirming her way out. "Except for the parts in which I don't. Namely, her, and the part where everyone hates us now."

"Some choices require sacrifices, my darling."

With a final push, Marian found herself on the open ground, the sunlight shining down on her face. She reached for her hood to pull it back over her head, but her hand was greeted with sharp leaves that were stuck to her cloak. She let out a sigh and let her shaggy hair flow free as she leaned against the trunk of a tall pine. Her face was flushed and scratched from her encounters with nature the night before.

"Hi, I'm Marian," she offered as the two pixies stared at her, hovering above the ground with their wings shimmering in the sunlight.

"I'm Pight, and this is Inibri," the raven-haired pixie answered with a smile as they took a seat on her knees. "Pleasure to make your acquaintance. We've never met someone from Steinigen who didn't try to kill us before."

Her friend, Inibri, let out a laugh as Pight smiled.

"The same, for us...me. Just me," Marian stumbled over her words. Her mind was racing, trying to figure out if she was more embarrassed about arguing with herself, jumping into a bush, or them knowing where she came from. Letting go of her embarrassment, she tried to focus on the most important issue. "How do you know where I'm from?

"We're happy to meet one, or both of you," Inibri said as she fluttered up to Marian's shoulder. She smiled as she took a seat, dusting off the remnants of a prickly leaf.

Marian's hand instinctively came off the ground slightly, as if to swat away an insect. But there was something about Inibri's touch and voice that calmed her nerves.

"We've been waiting for you since you called through the lilies. You've been quite vocal in your conversations with them, and I've learned a plethora of new words that would make our elders utterly furious," Pight said with a laugh.

"The Harken Lilies do work...," Marian's words trailed off. She remembered that she had seen a flash of light as she was falling from the top of the fortress. She'd felt like something was waiting for her on the ground to make sure she was okay, but she couldn't quite make sense of it.

While Marian sat lost in thought, Inibri examined her closely from her perch on Marian's shoulder. There were several small tears in her clothing, and she was surely covered in scrapes and bruises.

"You're not very good at this, are you dear?" Inibri asked as she and Pight smiled.

"No. No, I'm not."

Marian didn't try to lie, and she wasn't offended. Inibri's evaluation of Marian's abilities was accurate, and if these two were there to help, she would not refuse.

# NINE

An undulating groan could be heard inside the potion shop, springing from the mass of patrons. The windows were fogged by a rolling blue smoke that was seeping through cracks in the walls and ceilings. Ian made his way through the crowd and opened the front door to let the smoke billow out.

"I say again," Ian shouted through a bout of coughing. "Mind your children or the bear will be having them in his stew for dinner!"

The potion shop shook as Benson roared; his massive figure silhouetted by the sunlight and the blue smoke. A batch of miscreants had wandered in alongside their parents disregarding the 'No Children Allowed' policy hanging on the door. The kids screamed as they stared at his shadow and ran toward the door, their parents quickly following suit.

Ian took a deep breath of fresh air and turned his attention back to his shop. The smoke was still wafting through, and a layer of blue dust now coated his shelves, floor, and workbench. He sighed. It would take hours to meticulously clean the shop and make it safe for the mixing of potions.

"Pre-made potion sales only," he shouted as he walked back inside. "If you're wanting anything else, go chase down that family and berate them for contaminating my shop."

Benson eased himself into a chair beside Ian's workbench, a puff of blue dust billowing out from beneath him and clinging to his fur. Ian smiled as Benson fought fruitlessly to remove the dust. It clung to his fur and sank deeper the more he fought it. The few patrons left laughed openly at the bear until Benson let out another roar in frustration, emptying the shop as they ran out in fear. As Ian watched the last chance he had of making any coin run off into the fields in front of their shop, he smiled. He didn't feel like working much today anyway.

"All that tussling around is just going to get it deeper in your fur," Ian said as he patted Benson on the back. The bear turned to him with a pitiful expression, his eyes wide and his snout drooping as he held up his now blue paws. "Suck it up, buddy. You're just going to have to take a bath."

Benson roared angrily into Ian's face, his saliva splattering across Ian's cheeks.

"Take a bath, or become the first blue bear in Ephorus. Your choice," Ian snapped as he wiped his sleeve across his face to clean off the gunk.

Leaving his friend to fret over whether or not to bathe in the cold waters of the stream near their shop, Ian walked down the stairs to his study in the lower level. Kicking aside a few discarded vials, he placed his hand against the wall until he found the right spot and pressed on it.

There was a puff of smoke and a door opened into a darkened room. A simple potion can do amazing things if applied properly.

Walking into the darkness, he took a vial from his pocket and shook the contents until an orange light illuminated inside it. His hand could feel the warmth inside the glass, trying to free itself from its confines. Ian pulled the top off the vial and watched as the liquid turned to flame as it met the air.

The orange flame leaped from the container and swirled around the room touching the wicks of candles. As light filled the room, Ian took in the mess of papers and journals scattered across the tables and floor.

"Just as it was before," he said softly.

When his parents had failed to return home years ago, he had taken precautions to protect their work, and now his. Reaching inside his vest, Ian pulled out a smaller vial that was filled with an opaque white liquid. He let the liquid pour out from the vial to the stone floor. Smoke sprang up as the liquid transformed, and a wind rushed across Ian's face and sent papers and books flying off the ground, whirling throughout his study.

My study, Ian thought to himself, as he remembered playing amongst the books and bottles while his parents worked. He could still hear them laughing together at the desk if he tried hard enough.

Ian took a seat by the corner of the bookcase that covered two walls, finding comfort in the smell of old leather and ink that had been aging alongside him over the years. His father had spent so many hours peering through their pages, Ian couldn't tell if his father had smelled of the books or the books of his father.

Benson knocked at the door and grumbled a few words to Ian.

"Yes, it's okay now. You don't have to be scared of the books."

The door cracked open slightly, and Benson stuck his dusty blue snout inside and sniffed the air. Then he pushed the door wide enough to peer in.

"I feel like you don't trust me anymore," Ian said, feigning hurt feelings.

Benson moaned as he came in, his paws covering his face until he felt assured that there were no more flying books or journals.

"Just as I said?" Ian offered.

Benson dropped his paws and mumbled under his breath.

"I accept your apology," Ian said as he let his hand settle on the small table beside his chair, his fingers gripping the spine of the closest book.

As Benson shut the door behind him, Ian tossed the book across the room. It grazed Benson's forehead as he yelped and dropped to the floor. Before Benson could recover, the book ricocheted off the wall and landed on his back. His howl echoed across the room while he scampered back and forth.

Ian fell from his chair laughing until Benson regained control and charged toward him on his hind legs, the other chair gripped tightly by his front paws.

Benson swung the chair down, its legs slamming around Ian's head and chest. As Benson lowered himself to the floor with his fangs out and snarling, Ian's laughter ceased and he tried to smile.

"I'm realizing now that I may have gone too far. I apologize."

Benson snarled again but lifted the chair to let Ian up. When he dropped his hulking mass into the seat, a cloud of blue dust came off him. Ian coughed and said, "I see you have chosen to not take a bath."

Benson groaned as he grabbed for a bag of trinkets he kept in the study to amuse himself while Ian read.

"You're scared of the river gnomes!" Ian said. "That's why you won't take a bath."

Benson roared as he pulled a bubble pipe from his bag.

"I am not being a bully, and you're heading out there first thing in the morning to get cleaned up. You're not going to contaminate everything we have in the shop after I clean it because you think the river gnomes will get you."

Benson growled his disapproval but relinquished the fight as he began puffing away on his pipe.

"And must you play with that every night? You are not a child."

Puffing on the pipe, undisturbed by the insult, Benson watched as a stream of bubbles curled toward the ceiling.

# TEN

Pight sat in the open palms of Marian. They were laughing at another raunchy joke the pixie had picked up while spying on drunken travelers. Inibri tried to change the conversation, but Marian seemed desperate for laughs.

"Please, please, please. Just one more," Marian squeaked through her laughter as she fell backward into the dirt, taking Pight down with her.

Inibri grimaced as she watched Marian fall into the dirt, ruining her effort to clean up the girl's tousled appearance. It had been nearly two decades since Paramel had spoken gravely of Marian's arrival in Ephorus, but her spirit felt ancient.

"Another thought for another time," Inibri whispered to herself.

With the few provisions Marian had left, she would have to make her way to a village to resupply. Inibri wanted to help more, but, after generations of adoration, pixies were now unwelcome in most places. The Trofasthet had used them as an easy target on which to blame the downfall of man. Now pixies were killed for pleasure in Ephorus. Their presence had dissipated as many pixies feared venturing from their nestled cities tucked away from the outside world. Inibri had once envisioned a reconnection of the pixies with the world at large, rekindling the treaties they once had with even the goblins and ogres, but that desire led to her exile and the rainbow-colored hair. The mark on her hair meant she was a ghost to all who once knew her, except for Pight, who had an issue listening to anyone outside of her own thoughts.

Inibri's eyes lingered on her partner. Pight had chosen to disobey every elder to be with her, unwilling to sacrifice their relationship. Her support and compassion stood in stark contrast to the world they would be sending Marian into.

They were there to direct her to the nearby village of Redclave. Populated with an unforgiving collection of merchants and slave traders, Redclave did not take kindly to the downtrodden. It had been disreputable for years, and mud and excrement poured from its roadways and trails, its stench a woeful beacon to weary travelers.

"We need to talk about you," Pight began.

Marian shook her head and frowned. "I'm nobody special," she said.

"That may be your view, but we feel differently," Inibri spoke softly into Marian's ear as she settled on her shoulder. She placed her palm on Marian's cheek.

"Feeling as if you're alone in a world too vast to comprehend, but so small you never feel safe?" Pight asked.

Marian sat up, wrapping her arms around her knees, slowly rocking back and forth as she avoided their gaze. "It's a bit much sometimes."

"Especially when one is fighting against such great odds," Pight said as she fluttered to Inibri's side.

Marian stood up quickly and nearly flung them off her shoulder. As she paced back and forth, Pight and Inibri could feel her tension.

"Why should I trust words from either of you? What makes you think you know who I am?" Marian asked sharply, a light flickering in her eyes, the fire simmering within her causing her skin to heat up beneath her clothes.

Inibri and Pight traded glances, realizing they needed to calm her before they let her loose on the world around them. They lifted themselves into the air, hovering near Marian's face as they tried to get her to talk again, but Marian was growing more anxious and erratic.

"We only know what your body portrays," Inibri said softly.

"I think I should be going now," Marian said, refusing to look at them. Her eyes scanned the trees around her as she searched for a direction to run.

Inibri held out her hand to stop Pight from trying to talk her into staying. She knew Marian was no longer interested in a conversation with them. Inibri nodded to the trees, and a small bag dropped down from them, hitting Marian's head on its way down.

"Ow!" Marian shouted as she turned back to face the two pixies. "What was that for?"

On the ground between her and the pixies was a small blue bag. It had burst open, spilling some of its contents. Marian's anger diminished when she realized that the bronze coins alone would buy her enough food to travel around all of Ephorus.

"How did you...?" her question trailed off as she stared at the pixies and the bag of coin ten times their weight.

"Redclave will be your next destination for resources," Inibri said, fluttering back to Marian's shoulder, followed closely by Pight. "Are you familiar with the village?"

"No," Marian replied as she gathered the coins and set them in her bag. "I've never made it out of the Morkere Forest before."

"Keep the sun to your right as you travel today, and by nightfall, you'll find yourself near the Merchant's Road. These are not kind or forgiving people, so you must be cautious. Interact with only those you must and leave the town heading toward the setting sun when you have gathered what you need. Cosen lies to the west, a day's travel from Redclave."

Inibri and Pight flew up to her forehead together, kissing her gently before they swooped down and hugged her neck. Marian's face flushed at the affection.

"You're very kind," Marian whispered as she looked at the wildflowers sticking up between her feet.

"Yes, we are," Pight answered as she flew in front of Marian, motioning her to follow. "Now, let me tell you the one about the fungus, a hermit, and the baker's daughter."

"That sounds disgusting. Yes, please," Marian laughed and followed her, smiling at Inibri as she waved goodbye.

As Marian and Pight disappeared into the surroundings, Inibri flew up to the canopy to catch her last glimpse of the girl laughing as Pight landed her joke.

"I can see that went well," a sarcastic voice lamented.

"I believe you will be needed as he expected," Inibri replied to Erin's familiar voice while straining to see Marian's auburn hair stand out in the forest below. "Were you able to find any trackers coming for her?"

"A small group is on their way, less than a days' length behind her now. She's moving too slow on her own to stay ahead of them. She won't make it to Cosen without a little help behind her."

"She got past them before," Inibri offered with a smile.

"Yes, by surprising them and getting a head start. They know they're up for a fight now and have the certainty of death awaiting them if they fail," Erin answered coldly.

Pight fluttered up to the canopy, staring with confusion at the owl resting beside Inibri. "What's with the coloring?"

Inibri hadn't even looked at Erin. Her golden-blonde feathers were a far cry from the norm for their shape-shifting friend.

"I'm having trouble with the transition. I wasn't exactly given much time to prepare and the side effects are a little frustrating, and I've still got more work coming my way at Hallenberry when I'm done here, so I'd appreciate it if you used your ability to not speak in this situation," Erin sniped.

"Please let me watch you go talk to Marian like this," Pight laughed, unable and unwilling to comply with the request.

"I hate you," Erin replied as she focused her attention on Inibri. "I'll try to help Marian, but you need to find a way to slow the Master's men down, or she'll be cornered before she ever even sees the Aurian Hills on the horizon tomorrow."

"We'll cause a little mischief to slow their advance," Inibri nodded as Pight stared at Erin, aching to laugh at her appearance.

"Are you going to stare at me and laugh this whole time?" Erin snapped.

Smiling, Inibri lifted off the branch and motioned for Pight to follow. "It is understandable. Have you seen how you look?"

"I'm starting to think I might not like you as well," Erin said to Inibri.

"We're pixies," Inibri laughed. "Everyone loves us."

Erin stared angrily as the two flew away into the darkness of the woods. As soon as they were far enough away, she descended to the forest floor and shifted into her dwarven form. She gave herself a quick once-over in the small mirror she carried, from her blonde hair to her short and stout body. She hadn't been given much time to work on her appearance, so she would just have to hope it worked.

"You are the sexiest dwarf I have seen in all of my

years," Pight's voice shouted from somewhere in the canopy above her.

"I will hurt you the next time we meet." Erin refused to look back and instead began her slow march behind Marian, retracing her footsteps toward Redclave.

"Snarl that nostril for me," Pight screamed at her as Inibri laughed.

Making her way through the canopy of trees, Erin muttered under her breath. "I hate pixies."

# ELEVEN

Slouching behind his messy workbench, Ian sat motionless, trying to avoid the physical conflict that may lay before him. His shoulders slumped and he stared at the stains on his shirt.

Was that always there? he thought distractedly.

Ian was proud to have simply remained upright over the last few years. He took after his mother, never reaching the taller stature of his father, but Benson made up for his shortcomings. Ian also had the same tanned skin his mother had, the glow of someone who enjoyed his time outside, not stuck inside behind a counter getting yelled at by a drunken dwarf.

"What do yer mean yer not selling?" spat the angry dwarf.

Taking a moment to wipe the alcohol-laced saliva from his face, Ian took a look around the shop and realized it was just going to be one of those days. After he was done with the dwarf, he'd have to hold the hands of a lovesick gnome, and a reformed goblin. The off-the-shelf-potion business was an ordeal he had grown to loathe. It never seemed this tedious when his father was in charge.

Ian had dealt with many a day like this since inheriting the shop from his parents. After their disappearance, it was only natural for him to follow in their footsteps, whether he wanted to or not. In truth, he only kept the shop open to preserve his father's legacy as the best potion master and designer in the kingdom. His mother's enchantments were still talked about in reverential tones throughout Ephorus as well, although most women with her abilities these days were being rounded up and imprisoned by the Old King in Crescent City. His parents had been renowned for their talents before being summoned from Aurian Hills to the Towers of Crescent City to showcase their abilities.

Life changed very rapidly after their journey to see the Old King. When they returned, their light-hearted demeanor was shed for a more serious and purposeful attitude; immersed in their spell and potion development, they rarely took a break. Ian had begun to resent their work as he watched them delve even deeper into it with the help of ancient texts given to them by a decrepit being that dwelled alone in the Aurian Hills.

Feeling distant from his parents, Ian began pulling away as well, becoming detached from the shop and the knowledge his parents had amassed. The months passed by, his father spent more time in his workshop downstairs, and his mother made countless trips into the Aurian Hills to rendezvous with the Vorkyre. Ian had almost forgotten the life they had before the trip to Crescent City.

Ian snapped himself back to the present. He knew his next words had to be spoken politely and as concisely as possible to keep his shop from being destroyed by a drunk and angry dwarf. Oh, happy day...

"It's not that I'm not selling, Ryman. I'm just not selling," Ian paused for gentle emphasis, "to you." He tried his best to add a warm smile, though he quickly wished he could replace it with an iron shield.

Ryman's hands gripped the top of the workbench as he pulled himself up, carelessly knocking over vials and bottles, and looked Ian directly in his eyes. Ian held his breath, awaiting disaster, but none of the potions spilled out.

With drool running down his scraggly gray beard, Ryman seethed at Ian. "Rethink yer words, boy."

"Ryman, I'm not selling to you because," Ian began slowly, his voice soft. He dreaded having to say the next words, but he knew he must. "It's not going to work. Every week you come in here asking for me to give you some kind of potion to make you appear more handsome, debonair, or just slightly less ugly. But, let's be honest. It's not going to work. It's never worked. I can keep selling you quick fixes, but, again, it's not going to work."

Polite, concise, and screwed.

"This...this is an insult to my honor!" Ryman snapped, his body quivering as his stumpy legs tried to hold him steady. "And I shall have revenge!"

Launching himself on top of the workbench, the dwarf released a bellowing battle cry. Ian took a moment to give his customers a quick sign of reassurance that he would be with them momentarily, then rang the bell underneath the counter to call for backup. After Ryman finished his battle cry, he began reciting a list of grievances, a sad sonnet to all who had spurned his affections.

As he cursed an old friend for betrayal and an old hound for trying to sniff his rear, Ryman started to cry. At some point, Ian would have to stop him, but after seeing the other customers quietly making their way out the door, he abruptly decided to take advantage of the situation. Ian was growing accustomed to the idea of closing early.

With the last customer gone, and the howling dwarf still on top of his workbench, Ian wondered where his bumbling buffoon of a partner was. He angrily pressed the bell again but heard no sign of movement from the back of the shop.

It was, unfortunately, a common occurrence for Benson to find himself preoccupied when Ian required assistance. Despite Benson's many attributes, he could not be described as reliable. Not because he couldn't be trusted, but because he was as lazy as he was loyal—and he was very loyal.

"One job while we're open, Benson, just one job," Ian muttered until he grew impatient and backed away from the counter as Ryman carried on.

He opened up the door leading downstairs and sniffed the air.

"Is that? Oh yes, it is. I smell that honey. You sneaky little deviant."

Ian opened door after door, sure that his friend was

hiding behind one of them. Benson's animalistic side had gotten the best of him, and his shame was potent in the air. Ian stumbled over a box of discarded vials he'd placed in front of his study that morning, and his cursing momentarily overshadowed the howls of the dwarf upstairs. Ian wanted to make sure Benson heard his frustration.

"I know you're down here, and you know I'm going to find you, so you might as well come out of hiding and come help me upstairs. Which, by the way, is what you're supposed to be doing anyway!"

A rustling sound came from the end of the hall in the storage closet, followed by a whimper and a light growl.

"Yes, I know you're sorry. And yes, I know you can't always help it. But right now there is a crazy, drunken, and depressed dwarf on top of my workbench, and I need help getting him out of the shop!"

A roar of laughter burst out from the closet as Ian neared, followed by multiple grunts and snorts.

"Yes, it's Ryman again. And, no, it's still not funny. Every week, we go through this, but I'm not giving in this time. So get your oversized hide out of that closet and escort him out of the shop."

The hallway went silent except for the inane ramblings coming from above.

"Now, Benson!"

Pots and pans clamored as Benson tried to untangle himself from the jumbled mess of the closet. He found his way to the door and did his best to gracefully exit, but he failed quite fantastically, tripping over a broom handle and slamming into the wood floor.

Benson groaned with pain, but Ian ignored him and walked back to the stairs, shouting, "Get up and get moving. We've got more important things to do today. And wipe that honey off your snout. You're not a wild animal. Only civilized folk work in this establishment."

With a quiet moan, Benson wiped his snout and rambled down the hall and up the stairs toward the belligerent shouting of the angry dwarf.

As Benson made it to the top of the stairs, he saw the remaining bits of Ryman's dignity wash away in a trail of tears. He shuffled over and heaved the dwarf onto his shoulders, holding him down tightly as he headed toward the front door on his hind legs.

"I will not stand for this!" Ryman shouted.

"Don't worry, Ryman, you don't have to."

Benson plopped the angry dwarf in the field outside the shop, growling loud enough to penetrate Ryman's rage and make it clear that he was not welcome back in the shop. And for the first time that day, things seemed to go how Ian wanted. Locking the door behind him, Benson snarled through the window as Ryman came toward the door. The menacing jowls of the bear made him think twice, and he turned and stomped away from the shop.

"I'm sure we'll see you again tomorrow," Ian laughed to himself.

# Twelve

From the inner branch of a bush, Pight could see the trackers arguing; there were almost a dozen of them. She turned to catch Inibri's gaze so they could share a joke about them, but Inibri wasn't there. They'd both been disguising Marian's tracks as best they could, causing hours of frustration to the Master's trackers, who ended up wandering in circles.

"These are simple questions, Kato!" she could hear the leader shouting, his frustration boiling over. "Did she head west to the Aurian Hills or east to the Gallen River?"

The man being snarled at stared toward the east. Inibri had been advancing in that direction, hoping to attract their attention.

"Her scent still leads in multiple directions," the tracker said, his frustration obvious. He pointed to two paths, one heading to the Gallen River, the other to the Aurian Hills.

"This could work," Pight mumbled as she reached for Inibri's hand on instinct, releasing a whimper as her fingers gripped a prickly leaf instead. She froze when the tracker's eyes seemed to turn directly on her.

"Lyco, there," Kato said, pointing to a small trail nearly overgrown with shrubs and wildflowers. "It's heading down that path as well."

"Looks like the wolves must've done a number on her then," a rotund man resting on a fallen tree behind the two said. "Our work here is done."

"If it had been wolves, where is the blood, or the signs of a struggle, or anything else that would come along with such an altercation, you idiot?" Lyco snapped quickly.

Scratching his head, the rotund one looked around and struggled to give his best answer. "Ghost wolves."

Pight couldn't contain the spurt of laughter coming through her clenched teeth. She was fortunate the leader was even louder than she was as he ripped into the man at full volume. She watched gleefully as the fellow trackers tried to keep their leader from pummeling him with the tree stump he sat on. The more they argued, the less sunlight they would have.

Desperate to share this moment with Inibri, Pight climbed up through the bush and made her way toward the tree canopy. She knew Inibri wasn't far. Peering to the east as she darted up, she didn't see the tree limb until she'd slammed into it. The collision sent a cascade of acorns to the ground below.

Their yelling stopped abruptly as they turned to look in her direction. Pight didn't dare move, cursing herself while they searched for the source of the noise.

"Where does this path lead to, Kato? Would she find shelter at the end or closed doors and callous villagers?"

Lyco asked.

The tracker paused before speaking, gauging the sun above him to place his direction. He stared in Pight's direction, still trying to find the source of the commotion she'd caused. "It would head south to Redclave. It was most likely an old smuggler's route from years before their trade became sanctioned, allowing them to take the main road from Aurian Hills."

"Are there any obstacles she would face? Anything that may slow her pace?"

"Ghost wolves!" the rotund man shouted before ducking quickly to avoid the knife launched at his head.

"Anything real?" Lyco snapped.

"Redclave itself, if she were naïve enough to go there instead of following the Gallen River to Crescent City."

"No," Pight whispered to herself as Lyco's gaze rested on the path to Marian.

"Ceril and Arman, you'll follow me. Kato, take the others with you to the east until you meet the river, then make your way south. Spread word at the first town you reach that we may require mercenaries in Redclave should the situation call for it. Fan out from there to reach as many towns as possible until you reach the Towers in Crescent City. We will not return home without her."

The rotund man whined as he pulled the knife out of the tree behind him, testing its blade on an innocent leaf at his side. "Are you sure you want to take that path? It could simply be a distraction."

"Yes, it may be. And if my suspicions are correct,

it won't be the last. Marian doesn't have the skill or foresight in a situation like this to disguise her tracks. Someone else is helping her."

Pight's heart sank, realizing she had blown their best chance at diverting them.

"We'll be betting our lives on this," Kato answered softly, a look of trepidation growing on his face.

"Death will be the sweet release of what will happen to us if we fail."

Pight saw Kato wave for the remaining trackers to follow him, and they began to run east toward the Gallen River.

"You two," Lyco shouted at Ceril and Arman, "with me."

Pight could do nothing but watch as they split up, and she felt her frustration turning to despair as tears welled behind her eyes. The soft-touch of Inibri's hand came down on her shoulder as she cried.

"I'm sorry," she said.

"I know," Inibri answered, wrapping her arms around Pight, kissing her on the cheek as she wept.

# THIRTEEN

"Thief!" the shopkeeper shouted after Marian as she stepped out of the doorway.

"Liar!" Marian snapped in response, unperturbed by the accusation.

"Harlot!"

"Fat, beleaguered old man!" Marian shouted back, rousing a chorus of laughter from the growing number of onlookers intrigued by the discontent. "If you want to turn this into an insult fight, I guarantee I can keep this going all day!" The fire in her words matched the flame burning in her eyes.

Although Marian would have been willing to continue shouting down the rude shopkeeper, she heard the sound of rushing boots and clanging metal. She heard that combination enough as a child to know that guards were charging toward her. She glanced around, frantically searching for an escape route while clutching her bag—and the journal inside it. "Anytime now, Marian," she mumbled to herself. But as her anxiety rose, so did her voice. "I don't want to rush you, Marian, but I really don't want to go back!"

"A thief and a freak! Or do you consider talking to yourself to be an acceptable practice as well?" the grimy old man spat at her.

"It's a condition and I don't like to talk about it, so shut up!"

Her paths of escape had been cut off by the horde of onlookers surrounding them now, aching for a good show. Redclave had once been a peaceful village, and a refuge for those with magical powers, but as Ephorus grew more concerned with riches than the welfare of its people, wickedness took hold even here. Slave merchants and hawkers came from across the land, controlling the movement of goods throughout the kingdom. Gnomes, nymphs, and pixies once worked hand-in-hand in this very village to keep it bright and filled with wildflowers and fruit-bearing plants and trees, all as an homage to the First Walkers' original intent and creation. But the people walking these streets now cared little of the First Walkers' work, or that Redclave had turned into a muck-ridden and fruitless center of depravity. The rich earth had turned to mud, dirt, and sewage. The treasure of Ephorus was now its wretched core, spilling out to taint the land around it. Magic wasn't welcome anymore, only money.

Marian looked around for any means of support, but the horde cheered on the merchant and the guards gathered to watch as well, unwilling to intervene and unconcerned with her guilt. "Your intent remains to save these people," she scolded herself as her hand began to raise, the fire surging forth to her fingertips, "no matter how fat and stupid they are." She clamped her hand into a fist to keep from exposing the fire that could incinerate them all if she were to let it.

"Don't be thinking you're the good-looking one amongst this crowd either, little girly!" a golden-haired dwarf shouted out, making her way toward Marian.

Marian turned to see the new provider of verbal affronts. The dwarf was dressed in a finely beaded and embellished jacket with a blouse and pants to match. It was easy to tell who had money in this area, Marian realized; the less mud on someone's clothes, the more money and power they had. As the dwarf stepped before her, she could barely see any mud on her at all.

"I am not scared of you," Marian said, her voice firm and loud.

With a grunt and a laugh, the dwarf kicked the back of Marian's legs, grabbing her by the head as she stumbled to her knees.

Marian knelt speechless while the dwarf whispered in her ear.

"That's what concerns me. Stopping your father is more important than winning an argument with an idiot. Stop resisting and a way out will present itself in time."

"Hey! What are you doing with her?" the shopkeeper shouted. "She stole from me, and I will claim the reward."

Marian tried to lift her head to make a searing retort to the shopkeeper but, to her dismay, the dwarf yanked her down. "When you escape, you must seek the shop of Ori and Penelope just outside of Cosen, near the Aurian Hills. And sorry about this next part." With a shove, she pushed Marian into the mud in front of the shopkeeper, splashing him up to his waist in filth. "You can have your small change," the dwarf shouted. "With that much mud on you, you'll need it."

Laughter rocked the crowd as the dwarf side-stepped Marian, giving her a small nod as she passed. Looking at the shopkeeper, the dwarf let out a deep laugh and began to whistle a jaunty tune, leaving without another word. The shopkeeper began to respond, but couldn't seem to figure out what he was responding to. A look of puzzlement fell across his face, and Marian tried to make the best of the moment by jumping to her feet to run away.

Grabbing her bag from the ground, she kicked off the mud and started to dash away, only to run into the open arms of a town guardsman who had grown bored with the altercation. With his arms wrapped firmly around her, Marian could do nothing but give in to the inevitable. She muttered, "Well, at least you hugged me first. My dad used to kick me before he locked me up in a dark room."

A blank stare was all that the guardsman could muster as he gazed down at her. "Yeah, I don't know what to say to that, so I'm just going to ignore it." He tied her arms behind her and began to question her and the shopkeeper, trying to understand why they were causing such a ruckus. Taking what could be her only opportunity to speak for a long time, Marian proceeded to make her case as quickly as she could.

"Absolutely none of this is my fault," she started. "All I wanted was a little food, and some new linens to patch up a few tears in my clothes, and—"

"Those are more rags than clothes," the shopkeeper snorted.

"You're fat, you're ugly, and you'll probably die alone," Marian snapped before turning back to the guard. "Anyway, I had all my stuff in my bag and it was paid for, but as I was leaving the shop, he began shouting that I was stealing his merchandise."

"The little she-witch was stealing! Our laws clearly state that when demand goes up so does the price."

"Not after it's been purchased!" Marian was losing control over the absurdity of the situation.

Caring little for what she had to say, the guard simply waited until Marian was done talking to ask the shopkeeper, "Are you claiming this child..."

"I am not a child!" Marian shouted.

With a deep breath, the guard began again, "Are you claiming this person is a thief, sir?"

Straightening his shirt and standing as tall as the inserts in his boots would allow, the shopkeeper responded, "I do indeed. And I wish to accompany you to the jailors to claim my reward for apprehending her myself."

More annoyed than engaged, the guard gruffly responded, "If you must," then turned toward the crowd. "Make way!" he shouted, dragging Marian along with him.

The shopkeeper hurried along beside them and gave Marian a quick smack on her rear end and laughed. "Maybe if your father had done that more often, you wouldn't be going to jail now."

Yanking her hands away from the guard, Marian turned to face the shopkeeper and hissed, "I prefer men who bend a knee in front of a lady."

"Too bad you're not a la—"

A swift kick to the groin stopped him from finishing, sending him to his knees. The shopkeeper hunched over in agony, moaning in pain.

"I accept your apology," she said with a slight bow.

The guard grabbed her by her arms and forced her to the ground, shackling her legs. With the shopkeeper unable to speak, they shuffled on in silence, dispersing the crowd in the process.

Marian stared straight ahead, ignoring the glares and shouts of "thief" from the crowd. They might have hated her, and she might have hated them as well, but she would not be disheartened by any of them. By the rise of the moon, she would be on her way to Cosen, for better or worse.

But seriously, she thought to herself. Who was that dwarf?

# Fourteen

Pight and Inibri sat side by side on a branch in the glow of the moonlight, their foreheads touching ever so slightly. They had raced ahead of the trackers to Redclave, flying above the canopy to warn Erin of their impending arrival. As they whispered and giggled, Erin came toward them, climbing effortlessly through the branches until she rested beside the two. Seeing Pight's eyes light up, Erin remembered she had yet to shed her golden locks and dwarfish figure.

"You. Look. Amazing!" Pight shouted as she tried to maintain a sense of composure.

Erin immediately shed her form and slipped into the shifting, shadowy shape she was born into. Her form rested upon the branch, merging with the other shadows of the night. She was smaller now than she'd been as a dwarf, but her voice echoed around the pixies as if it were immense.

"I always look amazing," she whispered, and her words seemed to come from all sides.

Inibri placed her hand out to the shadow form. "I do believe you are right, my friend."

Inibri's hand disappeared for a moment into the black void, then reappeared along with Erin, who had shifted into her human form. Inibri fluttered up and kissed her on the forehead.

"Do not forget to do this form the honor it deserves," Inibri whispered into her ear before returning to Pight's side.

She spoke in a soft tone, but her words carried weight for Erin, whose irritation with Pight began to fade. Erin's other forms, including the dwarf, were based on beings she had no connection to and which could be adorned or shed without fuss. A deal had been made years ago, however, granting her this particular form, and it was important to her.

Pight flew toward Erin. She saw the supple face of a woman with raven hair as dark as Pight's; her skin was soft and delicate, shining in the moonlight. Pight gave her a quick kiss on the forehead, then leaned in to touch Erin's head with hers just as she had done with Inibri.

"An offering of peace?" Erin asked with a wry smile.

"I suppose it is." Pight smiled as she made her way back to the branch. "Now, how did our little friend do in Redclave?"

"Quite well, I suppose," Erin offered with a hint of sarcasm.

"How bad?" Inibri asked.

"She managed to get herself jailed, and she will be sent to the auction in the morning if she doesn't escape," Erin said flatly as she slipped back down to the ground, resting her back against the tree. Her eyes shut and her shoulders slumped, her lungs taking a deep breath before exhaling the cold night air back into the world around her.

Pight rolled off the branch and fluttered to the ground. Tucking her wings underneath her back, Pight lay flat on the earth and stared at the moon between the branches above them. Her head lay propped up on Erin's leg, and Inibri came to lie beside her.

"She's going to have even less time now, with an encroaching rank of trackers," Inibri lamented.

"I take it her father's men weren't fooled?" Erin asked.

"It would appear we are too far out of practice, or they have gotten much better at seeing through our deceptions," Inibri responded, gripping Pight's hand to keep her from talking.

"She might make mistakes, but I have a growing faith in her," Pight said softly, her face flushed with embarrassment while quietly reliving her mistake in her head.

"If only that were all she needed," Erin added as she let the pixies grasp her hand. "I'm beginning to fear it's a lot worse than the old kook lets on."

"What's wrong?" Inibri asked as she and Pight both shifted their heads to look at her.

"I can feel the old darkness surging. And not just from Steinigen." Erin's eyes had filled with tears and she was desperately fighting to hold them back. "I can feel the Plaga's presence."

Pight sat up and asked, "Have you talked to Paramel?"

Erin wiped away the tears that refused to leave her eyes. She nodded to give herself another moment to clear her throat and control her thoughts. "He doesn't have enough in him for both fights, and he knows it."

"We still have the others," Inibri added as she lay her head on Erin's leg. "If they can at least stop her father, we have a chance."

"I believe we should be on our way," Pight climbed onto Erin's hand and began walking up toward her shoulder. Inibri followed behind, and they each kissed her cheek goodbye. "If she's been stalled for the time being, we need to keep a constant eye on the trackers and do what we can to slow them until she reaches Cosen."

Erin leaned her head toward them and smiled as she watched them lift off and fly away. There would be no telling if their traps and tricks would work to buy Marian more time, but she knew they would give everything they could. As Erin stood, she let her mind drift back to Paramel. The old kook had been mumbling about these trials for years now, never letting her forget that the worst was yet to come. She often wondered if that was because he couldn't maintain his thoughts for too long. But now, with the growing fear of the darkness creeping toward her, she feared even he was underestimating the danger.

Taking one last glance at the moon, Erin breathed deeply and let the tense shape of her human form slip away while the rest of her crept into the shadows, heading toward Redclave.

# Fifteen

Upon reaching the ramshackle jail house, Marian had no doubt she would be able to break out. Her father had put many more obstacles in her way when he'd locked her up as a child. She tried and failed to hide her smirk, and the jailer knocked it away with the back of his hand. He was a gross and oafish ogre, and Marian could smell the remnants of food rotting in his jowls. Once a favored species of devastating power, the ogres, along with their goblin kin, were decimated by the campaigns of Masters of old to traverse the Logi Mountains. The few that remained in Ephorus used their bulky mass to work for anyone who would give them food and coin. Many were mercenaries, entrenching themselves with large bands of roaming vigilante armies, employed either directly by her father or through his counterparts in the Trofasthet. This one was either too lazy or too dim-witted to have earned that position.

"Keep smiling, thief!" Malice dripped from the ogre as it slapped her across the face for the second time.

Marian hadn't thought she would miss the town

guard who apprehended her, but now she longed for his apathetic temperament. The ogre proceeded to kick her in the back of the legs, causing her to fall to the ground, her knees scraping hard upon the stone floor, her tattered leggings ripping even more. She could see the empty cells as she lifted her head. It must have been a busy day at the stockyard for them to have such few tenants.

Her thoughts faded as a scrawny goblin approached, scraping a hot poker against the stone walls, sparks flying. The slovenly ogre swung its arm and struck her again. Its blow was a mere distraction compared to the torrent of pain that tore through her body as her right arm was seared by the hot poker. The smell of burning flesh surrounded her. When she screamed, she could hear the shopkeeper howling with laughter. The pain was nearly unbearable, and tears fell from her eyes to the floor. The goblin finally pulled the hot poker away from her skin, its eyes wide with pleasure, cackling and speaking in an ancient tongue as it waited for the ogre's approval. The ogre uttered its response in the same tongue with a hideous grin, and the goblin was pleased, hissing with joy as it ran from the cell.

Marian tried to fight back the pain coursing through her body. The wicked little monster had burned a crescent moon, the mark of a thief, on her forearm. She could barely muffle the scream that boiled up inside of her. As she held back her fury, a new freckle appeared on her face—like the many others she had given herself as a child.

"Just hold on. Not much longer and you'll be free,"

the voice broke through her thoughts, echoing off the walls to comfort her. She nodded, swallowing the rage that sought to decimate all life around her. Slowly rising to her feet, she watched as her tears dotted the stone floor beneath her. "You can do this, Marian," the voice said, easing her heart rate, taming the fire within her.

"Free is not a word little thieves like you will ever understand," the shopkeeper said as he walked up to get a closer look at her misery.

"Petty is the man who relishes another's pain," she replied, her bright eyes growing dark.

The shopkeeper recoiled, stumbling back into the jailor's chair and nearly tumbling to the ground. Marian stared emotionless at the man; her black eyes locked on him while he began to quiver.

"Enough!" the ogre spat out, releasing bits of saliva, its jowls losing the fight against age and decaying muscles.

The goblin came back with a few cohorts, and they began shoving Marian into her cell, while the shopkeeper was taken away to make a motion that she should be traded as a slave—an easy way to make a few more coins off her.

Marian's eyes fixed on the goblin shoving her violently; on their arms, she could see the inked insignia of the Trofasthet, an ancient religious sect bent on controlled annihilation. The ogre and his companion weren't exactly the pious type, but every religion needed enforcers to remind people how important their faith and leadership were. Her father had lured the

Trofasthet from the shadows of their island, beguiling them with the powers he drew from the volcanoes of the Logi Mountains. Desperate to harness such power, the Trofasthet willingly aligned with her father. Both were intent on destruction in different ways. They would not be satisfied until the world around them was abolished and rebuilt by their design.

As the goblins shoved her into the cell, her eyes lifted from their tattoos to see her drab new quarters. She thought of how right the dwarf had been. Marian had been careless.

Stumbling on the muddy floor of her cell, Marian tried steeling herself for the night to come. She ignored the hissing laughter of the goblins as they slunk back down the hall. When they were out of sight, she gingerly scraped together some mud and spread it over her burned arm, covering the crescent moon. The cold, damp soil eased the pain slightly, and she slid against the wall as tears rolled down her cheeks.

"They cannot break you," she whispered to herself.

"What if they already have?" she responded. Her body began to shake as the voice inside her head shouted, Despair is a tool of the wicked. Let it in, and it will control you.

Marian nodded, wiping the tears from her eyes with her sleeve, leaving bits of mud in their place. She took a deep breath, placed her left hand over the wound, and clamped down. She bit her lower lip hard to keep from screaming, and blood began to trickle down her chin. She began to chant softly, bringing the power within her to life. Her hand began to glow with a blue haze that flowed toward the wound.

Marian watched most of the mud disperse into vapor, and then she wiped away the rest of it to see if her skin had healed. The mark itself was still tender, but the wound would soon heal now. The scar would remain, a permanent reminder to be more cautious. The burn had lost its pain, and she could move her arm again without wanting to cry. The fire from the Logi Mountains offered the power to destroy as her ancestors had done. But fire could heal and purify with the right touch.

"One problem down," she sighed as her head lay back on the cold cell wall. "Many, many more to go."

# Sixteen

Marian didn't see her abusers after they abandoned her in the jail cell. They weren't paid for their intellect or reliability, and there was likely no mandate that prisoners should be given any attention outside of beatings. She took time to gather herself in solitude—as she had always done. It was a familiar scenario for her, and, as she stared at the crude containment system devised to keep her compliant, she nearly chuckled.

"How many times can one person be locked away in their life," she wondered. "I don't know Marian," she responded, "but you're pretty damn consistent at it."

Dusting the sand and mud off her clothes, Marian briefly longed for her sparse but clean wardrobe at home. But she knew this was nothing more than a longing to be free. As she looked more closely at the rotted wooden door and meager iron bars barring her escape, she laughed. When her father had sought to punish her, he had made sure she was locked behind at least three doors, each of which had an iron outer shell and a wooden inner to prevent her from using just one spell or enchantment to break through them.

Few people could contain the heat and fire that burned within Marian. In Steinigen, there was a tale passed down of how the ancients tamed a great dragon and buried it alive, forming the Logi Mountains. The beast raged within its confinement for millennia, burning the land and changing it into a fiery hellscape, melting the rock and roiling the earth beneath it until Ephorus was cut off from the world beyond. Her ancestors kept the raging beast alive, silencing its rage by siphoning its power.

With this great power, her ancestors had caused sorrow and fear to the people around them. Marian herself had witnessed the slaying of numerous villagers who were trapped in their hovels surrounding Steinigen, all for the amusement of her father. As a child, she didn't know why his guards called him the Jesting Master until she heard his terrible laughter while he decimated a young family for accidentally poaching too close to the fortress. Marian had wondered why the villagers never left, why they never ran away and rebuilt their homes somewhere else, but one day she found the treatise her father had signed with the Old King. To keep his power, Tomas McCordian, resting on his throne in Crescent City, had pledged to extradite any villagers from the Steinigen region who fled. In return, Marian's father would quell revolts and help extend the Trofasthet's reach. The dim-witted ruler didn't know of her father's pact with the Trofasthet or that his rule was by proxy, now at the mercy of more powerful forces.

Placing her palms on the door of her cell, Marian

pressed her forehead against the wood. With a flick of her wrists, her fingers ignited, a soft orange blaze springing from each fingertip. Marian began chanting a soft lullaby to the fire, feeling it spread out from her fingertips. She closed her eyes and saw the fire weakening the rotted wood. Her eyes turned black, and she pushed her hands against the door, slowly increasing the pressure until the wood splintered and turned to ash.

The iron bars inside the door fell to the ground. Marian stood motionless, a faint orange glow circling her black eyes as she drew the fire back inside, smoke flowing out of her mouth as her body quenched the flames. She briefly closed her eyes and smiled as she opened them to see no door, no guards, and nothing to stop her.

"You're getting pretty good at that," the voice said, echoing on the walls around her. "I know, thank you," she said. Then she blushed and clenched her fists. "Stop it, Marian. Please stop talking to yourself. Out loud at least."

With a light whack to the side of her head, Marian composed herself and went to retrieve her bag from the jailer's storage. She crept through the hallway and saw the ogre was passed out, lying motionless with his mouth open and drool dripping into a puddle on the floor; his goblin accomplice resting beside him, dangerously close to drowning. It smelled as if the ogre had soiled himself and Marian gagged, trying not to vomit. She stared at the two creatures who had hurt her so terribly without cause. She could kill them, incinerate them, and be gone before anyone knew where the smell of burning flesh was coming from.

A fire flickered in her hands as she thought of retribution. "That is his way! That is his way!" she snarled to herself. She knew she needed to get going, and death would eventually come here to find both of them—with or without her participation.

Marian looked around until she saw her bag hanging delicately on the door. It was surprising to think that even these ill-witted creatures would leave her bag in such an accessible place, but she wasn't going to waste time thinking about their stupidity until she was much farther away. Marian quickly crept past the two, grabbed her bag, and slipped out the door with only the slightest of creaks while the moonlight swept down to welcome her back to freedom.

Outside, Marian was all too happy to start putting Redclave behind her. The twinge of pain in her arm would be the only reminder. Tightening the straps of her bag, she hurried down the road leading west out of the town. She would only be exposed for a few minutes until she made it to the trail. She felt around in her bag and realized she also had the benefit of fresh supplies—they had not let the shopkeeper take back his goods.

It would take another day's journey on the trail to reach Cosen, and she would need to move quickly. Her exhilaration at leaving Redclave was palpable, but she also knew that by now her father's trackers would have gained a large amount of ground.

Marian hastened away from the main merchant's

road and took an old and overgrown path. This route would be difficult in the dark, but she had made it through similar terrain in the Morkere Forest, hadn't she? Her toes frequently slammed into rocks and roots, causing her to trip and stumble, but she couldn't risk stopping or slowing down. Sleep would be necessary at some point, but for now, the adrenaline was coursing through her veins and propelling her forward, and she wanted to take advantage of it. When she had used it up, then she would sleep.

The world was silent around her, as if all of Ephorus was in the throes of a dream, entranced and unwilling to wake. Her mind began to drift while she ran, musing on what her life may have been like had she just been born to a common family whose lot in life was merely to toil for peace and contentment. A soft lullaby sang in her head in the voice of a woman she wished she knew, a woman who could have coddled her and loved her.

The reverie lasted but a few short moments—Ephorus insisted on putting her in her place. Her foot snagged on a root, and losing her balance, she quickly plummeted to the ground. She caught a glimpse of the moon through the canopy while she laid in pain on the ground.

"Asshole," she murmured angrily, glaring at the root, her chest rising and falling spastically as she fought to catch her breath.

Aching from exhaustion, Marian turned from the root to the rest of the tree and found a rather welcoming oak, with wide branches that would be easy to reach and climb. With the moon fading fast, she knew she had only a few hours to rest before daylight, and she would find no better place. She rested against the tree, looking around the forest for any traces of life, and found herself staring into the large and judgmental eyes of a golden owl.

"You wouldn't happen to know how to stop my father from killing me and everyone else in Ephorus, would you?" she asked sheepishly.

The owl cooed, flapping its wings as its head turned from side to side.

"Well, it was worth a shot," Marian grumbled. "Maybe next time you could come up with an answer, though. Owls are supposed to be smart."

Marian turned her back as the owl screeched, focusing her attention on climbing the tree. She heard something rustling but paid it little attention. Then the owl managed to fly between her and the tree, dragging a young branch in its wake and letting it spring back to slap Marian in the face. She stumbled backward and tripped over the root again.

Grabbing whatever was in reach, Marian began throwing rocks and sticks at the owl until it disappeared into the canopy above her, letting out a loud hoot before disappearing. Realizing she was enraged at an owl, Marian forced herself to calm down and continue climbing up the tree so she could get some much-needed rest.

"Maybe I'll just burn all of Ephorus down myself," she muttered while hoisting her leg up and over a low limb. "Maybe you will, but then what?" she asked herself. "Oh, shut up," she snapped, wrapping her arms around her head to cover her mouth and ears as she found a nook large enough to curl up in. "Just go to sleep, Marian. Everything will be better with sleep."

# Seventeen

Bathed in the swaying light of a fire, the old man stared longingly into the flames as they danced back and forth, his hands moving along with them. The flames slowly formed a blazing tableau of the Vorkyre, his old companions and kinfolk, as they were when first put in charge of protecting Ephorus. He was the last of their kind. The First Walkers' creation, Ephorus and the world beyond the Logi Mountains, was never meant to last, but they dared to break the natural order and disobey the Pillars of Time. That is why the chaos and destruction came for them. Before the First Walkers sacrificed themselves, they entrusted the Vorkyres with their creation so they could keep guiding it through eternity.

Paramel looked at the wrinkles covering his hands, knowing they extended across his body and along his face. For each one he could count a memory that plagued him. For each one he could remember a friend he had come to know so deeply he felt they were an extension of himself. Disobeying the Pillars of time had caused more havoc than the First Walkers had anticipated, slowly dripping wickedness into the world around them. Many of his friends had fallen, succumbing to the evil that permeated throughout the world. He'd discovered that it is always hardest to face a foe you once loved deeply. One day he hoped to be rid of this mistake.

"To old friends and memories," he whispered into the fire.

As the flames became taller and more brilliant, he laid back against the Hearthwood, a red spruce tree that bore no cones nor shed its needles. The tree was a living tomb for his most beloved companion's spirit. Kareen had been by his side from time immemorial, laughing, dancing, and fighting through whatever the world thrust upon them. She had prevented him from losing his sanity, keeping him stable enough to hold his power within so that he could fight only when needed. Kareen was long gone, though. His truly better half had left to be with the others, but he could still feel her presence within the Hearthwood tree.

"It was all so long ago, yet it repeats itself now," he said, a wave of sadness pinning him to the ground.

The flapping of wings and a hoot from another dear friend brought his mind back to the present, and his smile reemerged from the depths.

"Ha, ha!" he clasped his hands together, jumping up from the ground. "Wonderful, wonderful! And how is our young lass doing on her journey?"

Erin flew down to the ground, her talons spread out, and a woman's legs took shape beneath her. Wobbling for a moment, she shook her body to cast off the last few feathers as her human form took over. Her raven-black hair fell upon her shoulders, her gray eyes staring into the night, a smile forming on her lips when she looked at Paramel and felt his exuberance at seeing her.

Paramel smiled too as Erin took the shape of Kareen. Her slender figure was hidden by a multicolored blouse and leggings, but strength poured from her eyes just as it had when Kareen and Paramel were young. Kareen had managed to help tame the venom within Erin, helping her break free of the darkness she was born in.

Old friends and memories, he thought to himself again. "Such wonderful colors you're wearing. Are you finally ready to let loose the black?"

"Those sneaky little bastards." Erin tugged at her blouse, which was usually black, desperate to remove the colors now shimmering in the light of the fire.

"By chance, did you happen to spend some time with Inibri and—"

"Pight," Erin spat through clenched teeth as she rubbed vigorously on her shirt to no avail.

"Such a sense of joy and laughter within them," Paramel smiled as he motioned for Erin to sit down with him.

"I cannot stand your little friends sometimes. It's almost as bad as having to shift into the form of a dwarf on little notice," Erin said pointedly.

"Yes, sorry for that request. But I had concerns that if you were recognized, you might lose your ability to help from Hallenberry Halls." Only slightly apologetic, he left Erin with no room for argument as he pressed on. "Now, to our main concern." He clapped his hands in excitement. "How was she?"

His eagerness was slightly odd, but Erin couldn't help being swept up in his enthusiasm. "She's so awkward!" Erin exclaimed as she recounted her story of the day's events. She regaled him with Marian's amusing inability to contain her inner monologue and her ability to use and contain her power.

Paramel sighed with relief. "I do believe that this one will not be like her father. We may have found a shred of good fortune for our future after all." He placed his arm over Erin's shoulder, pulling her in for a hug.

"Touching, touching!" she shouted as she pushed him away. "You know I don't like to be touched after I've shifted, so why do you always insist on hugging me?"

"Because it makes me laugh!" Falling backward into a bed of leaves, Paramel burst into raucous laughter while Erin stared at him, unamused.

"When you're done cackling like a crazy old magpie, would you like to tell me about the little 'present' that's supposed to be making its way to me at Hallenberry? I don't like surprises."

Pulling himself up, Paramel dusted off the leaves and dirt with a grin and sat with his back against the Hearthwood.

"She is the new emissary of Steinigen, sent there by the Master to collect whatever he or the Trofasthet may need."

"Is that all?" Erin's brow furrowed as she stared down at the old sorcerer.

"No. I believe the Master is planning to destroy the Halls this time, breaking the covenant between my people and this world."

"So why is he sending an emissary?"

"I'm not entirely sure," he offered with a shrug of his shoulders. "There is a slight trepidation in his moves as if he is lying in wait, keeping watch for me until he is ready to rain down his fire."

"If she's there to warn him of your presence, can she to be trusted?" Erin asked.

"I believe so. What I have seen from her aura is sorrow and grief from oppression and loss. She does not hold hate for the world, just for the life she has been forced to accept."

"What place does she hold that makes him trust her?"

Paramel's eyes turned dark as he looked at Erin, "There is no trust. But he keeps his warlocks and guards close. She was a villager in the Morkere, and one of the last of the elves. She was also the one who found Marian among the flames of the Logi Mountains."

"An elf?" Erin asked, her hand reaching up to cover her surprised expression.

"Indeed," he said, standing wearily, his energy expelled and his age showing. Placing his hands on Erin's shoulders, Paramel pulled her in close again. "Let us not be foolish and waste this opportunity."

# EIGHTEEN

It wasn't the most profitable thing to do, but closing up shop was all Ian could think about. Night had fallen on an uneventful day without the return of Ryman, or much of any other business. Sometimes they earned a few coins from the desperate or drunk souls rambling around after dark, but it rarely paid enough to justify missing out on a night of leisure. And they still had to decide to not go out to the tree line to retrieve their wheelbarrow, which could prove problematic if scoundrels were to try and relieve them of their goods again. But, it would be dark and they wouldn't care.

Benson carried on with his chores, cleaning up the shop while Ian put away the utensils on his work-bench. He had spent the better part of the sunset hours replenishing the shelves and mindlessly mixing potions for stock use. Harnessing the power of new concoctions often exhilarated him, but sometimes it caused him to recall painful memories. He sat back in his chair and listened to Benson growling away as he sang some bawdy tune he had learned from a customer. Ian tried making out the words as best he could, "Away we sail to shores more fair, where the women serve beer with their plump..."

"Hey! Benson!"

The bear stopped abruptly, looking at Ian with a grin of satisfaction.

"Keep it clean, buddy. This isn't a fisherman's wharf! We get respectable customers in here, and I don't want them having to hear that."

Benson groaned and dismissed Ian with a wave of his paw.

"I don't care if they can't understand you. You can't just talk like a dirty old lecher whenever you so please."

Snarling, Benson walked up to Ian, bumping him as he went past.

"Well, maybe I don't want to hear that kind of song."

Benson mumbled an insult at Ian in response.

"Who are you calling a pixie, you fluffy, vulgar piece of..."

A sharp growl and raised paw cut Ian off as Benson walked toward the door and sniffed the air.

"How far away?"

Benson sniffed again to narrow in on the smell.

"I guess we won't be having an early day, after all, my friend." Ian took a moment to consider their options. Someone or something was trying hard to not be seen. And that never went well for them or their shop. "Well, Benson," Ian said. "What do you say we get prepared for our guest of honor?"

In the years prior, the two had concocted an elaborate ruse to outsmart any potential attackers, but eventually, they learned it was just easier to set a trap at the door and wait. As they dimmed the lights in the shop, Ian lit two small candles by the front door, releasing a potion that was dangerous to an unprepared target. Then he took a seat beside Benson, crossing his arms and doing his best to look menacing. Looking to his left he saw Benson sitting with crossed legs while blowing bubbles from his wooden pipe.

"Just once," Ian moaned. "Just once could we strike fear into the heart of an intruder and make them think twice about trying to come here to rob us of our livelihoods?"

Benson shrugged and made a slight grumble as he continued to puff on his pipe and swat at the bubbles drifting toward his snout. The two fell into a silence that was filled with anticipation of the excitement to come.

The creak of the doorknob was almost inaudible, and the door slowly began opening. Ian and Benson sat back farther in their seats, their grins growing wider by the moment.

# Nineteen

A mist flowed gently around Steinigen, and the guards were pacing the ramparts as they had done for generations, ever watchful of the world around the fortress.

These walls had stood for ages now, built by those who raised Steinigen from the ground up, sealing their livelihoods to the power sourced from the Logi Mountains. The fire that burned within the mountains craved destruction and pushed Nance's ancestors to try and conquer the world around them, to one day have their throne be the seat of all power. Yet for centuries, Steinigen's reach had diminished amongst his addled forebearers, and the power of the Logi had retreated behind their fortress walls. Nance, however, planned to change that. He knew the terrible power was untapped, and he would wield it across all of Ephorus, but he could not do it alone.

Nance stood atop his dais, one hand clutching the throne he would reign from as the other gripped the pommel of his sword. The weapon was just for show: he preferred to use his hands in battle, but the fear it caused in the peasantry was gratifying and palpable. He gazed across the hall at the assembled masses: a smattering of slaves, cooks, and maids he had summoned from their hovels on the edges of the Morkere.

With a deep breath, Nance assessed each filthy person displayed before him. Dogs, he thought to himself. Nothing more than broken dogs.

He turned to Sever, "Kill them all."

The mass of people cried out in horror, their eyes darting around to try and find a way to escape. A few began frantically clawing the floor in front of them, howling for mercy from their Master.

"Enough!" Sever shouted as Nance held up his hand.

"What do you say, Sever, did I nail it...or did I nail it?" he asked.

The frightened mass grew quiet as they began to realize this was not an execution but a game. Thankful for the sparing of their lives, they awaited permission to leave the Master's presence, hoping he would not grow displeased. For weeks, he had been preparing speeches and death sentences to help him get ready for his eventual campaign of conquering and commanding all of Ephorus, and they had seen many of their kinsfolk enter the throne room and leave in a bloody heap.

"Definitely, sir," Sever said. "Couldn't have been better!" As he smiled at his Master's happiness the stones of his face shifted, the black rocks audibly scraping against one another. "Would you like to kill any of these miscreants to celebrate?" Sever asked as he began to draw his sword.

"No, no," Nance waved off the idea. "We have to leave some of them alive to cook and clean," Nance said, clapping his hands together. "I just wanted to make sure I could still get into the mood for slaughter!"

While Nance carried on, Sever started moving people out of the hall. The villagers filed out of the room, many crying, desperate to return to the seeming safety of their own homes. Nance ignored them until he heard an angry voice shout, "Monster!"

"What was that?" Nance asked, his eyes darkening.

A young woman stepped forward, clutching her child and pushing away the hands of her neighbors who were urging her to show caution. "I called you a monster," she shouted through tears.

Sever's hand moved quickly as he released his sword from its sheath and bore down on the woman.

"Hold," Nance spoke gently, his hand raised to keep Sever from ending the woman's life. "Let's hear her out."

"You don't have to do this to us. What kind of a life do you think we live, waiting to die at your whim?"

Her neighbors had given up on saving her and were reaching for the child in her arms, hoping they could spare it from her inescapable fate, but the woman refused to relinquish her babe. Nance moved closer, his laughter echoing off the walls as the room grew dark, his body absorbing light from the torches. His arms lit up with fire, and his eyes got hollow as flames flowed out, lapping at his eyelashes. Smoke billowed from his nose and mouth as he stood in front of the woman.

"You have such a strong spirit," Nance whispered, placing his hand on her chest. "I do not find that appealing in a dog."

She screamed and tried to run, but Nance would not let go, his hand searing her flesh as it sank deeper into it. His fingers wrapped around her heart, and her eyes turned toward his, her mouth trying to form words of sorrow to appease him, but none would come. Nance gripped her heart even tighter, stopping its beat as blood poured over his fingers. Her legs gave way, and he held her upright. Her eyes filled with tears in the last moment of her life, and he let her fall to the floor. The villagers rushed forward to grab the screaming babe, leaving the mother alone in death.

Staring down at her, Nance cackled loudly. "You were wrong. I am a savior, not a monster."

He studied her lifeless eyes for a moment, the adrenaline from an unexpected execution coursing through his body. His smile was wide and his spirit exhilarated as two of his guards dragged her body from his chamber.

"You know, Sever, it wasn't even in my original speech."

"What wasn't, sir? In the speech, I mean," Sever answered, his stony face scrunching in puzzlement.

"Almost all of it. I improvised it as I went along, and I thought that it might be something special, and it was. I didn't even intend to kill anyone tonight, but I aroused such ferocious anger in that dog that she couldn't help but bark at me until I ended her. Amazing!"

"It will go down in history when you stand atop your throne and shout it to the masses, sir."

As they continued talking, Nance's servant, Phillip,

slipped into the hall, the hood of his black cloak pulled over his head. Stealthy by nature, he slipped in and out of the shadows offered by the flickering torches.

"My apologies for the intrusion, Master," Phillip spoke softly.

Caught off-guard, Nance whipped around and raised his hand, ready to strike as a flame erupted from his palm.

"Every time, Phillip!" Nance shouted. "Every time you do this, even though I've told you, 'Do not sneak up on me!'" Nance came close enough to Phillip to singe the hair on his chin with his fiery hand. "If you keep creeping around here, I will have a bell sewn into your nostrils that you'll never be able to take out!"

Both Sever and Phillip stood silently until their Master spoke again. "A tad too much?" he asked, turning to Sever and letting the flame die out, his arm dropping to his side.

"Not at all, sir," Sever said. "Spot on again." Sever didn't care for the quiet types. The ones who could cause the most damage were the ones who were hardest to track.

"Truly excellent, sir. No one is quite as evil as you," Phillip added, touching the edges of his beard to make sure it was not on fire.

"You know I know you're just sucking up, Phillip. But it is still wonderful to hear." Nance patted him on his cloaked head and walked back to his throne. "My predecessors before me," he paused, staring at the painted portraits that hung high on the walls. "They were truly and devoutly evil. But what they lacked, what they could never understand, was how to have fun with it." Nance dropped into his throne and kicked his feet up. He motioned for the other two to come over and stand beside him. "You see, for the common person, showmanship or skill in theatrics is simply a luxury. But for a master of evil, such as myself, it is an absolute necessity."

"Right you are, sir," Sever said. "No one deserves the title Jesting Master more than you."

"Yes, I know," the Master said, patting Sever on the back as if he were a dog that had performed a trick.

Relishing the moment, Nance delayed asking his servant what he had come for. But he knew Phillip would linger if he didn't. He toyed with the idea of having Sever execute the man on the spot for fun, but he didn't want to have to go through the exhausting process of beating and training another servant. So he merely imagined Phillip being tortured while he asked him to proceed with his news.

"We've received word from Sir Garrin that he has had more success with the Hearthwood since your last round of encouragement. They have also acquired the remains of your sister, Maven, to study its effects on her more closely in Crescent City, where he will continue to work on this matter."

"It seems our dear Sir Garrin has grown fond of his new home in the Old King's company," Nance mused.

"Do you think he plans to betray you?" Sever asked.

"No, no. He hates that old moron more than I. What I think is that he plans on bringing the Trofas-thet back to the heart of Ephorus so he can control the people with his cult."

"What should we do, sir?" Sever instinctively gripped the pommel of his sword.

"We let him play his trivial game," Nance answered. "There is more at stake here than the ambitions of a religious fanatic." Nance waved for Phillip to carry on so he could be relieved of his presence.

"We have also received word from your tracker Lyco that they are very near to catching your daughter. After tracing her steps, they found that she made her way, rather unwisely, to Redclave. She was unaware of the dangers of shopping in the markets and was almost sold into servitude by a local merchant. She found her way out, but she was not very careful in covering her tracks. They are following her toward a small, scattered settlement to the west of Cosen, near the Aurian Hills. They believe they will be able to overtake her there and head back within a few days."

Although pleased to hear this annoying matter would soon be over, Nance sensed something troubling in Phillip's words.

"Are you alright, sir?" Sever asked. "I thought you would be a little more enthusiastic about retrieving your daughter."

Nance sat quietly for a moment, replaying the words in his mind again until something clicked. "Cosen," he said softly.

"I'm sorry, sir?" Sever said, confused.

"Marian has gone to betray me."

"Not sure I follow, sir. I thought she just ran away again."

"As did I, but her actions say otherwise. After every-thing I did for that wretched mass of fire, this is how she repays me."

Nance dismissed both men and contemplated this new, unfortunate development. The idea that Marian would have to die for him to advance his throne didn't bother him. But that she would betray him, and up-end the advancement of their people, of Steinigen and the Logi Mountains from whence she came, lit a fury within him that he would unleash on the world. He would ensure she felt his wrath.

# TWENTY

For the young woman, it all happened in an instant. She walked into the shop, a light flashed as bright as a new star, and a strange smell surrounded her and unleashed her most precious and horrid memories. She fell into a lump on the shop's floor. She wouldn't remember any of it.

For Ian and Benson, after nearly a half-hour, they quickly became bored with their unwanted guest. They had shielded their eyes from the flash and protected themselves from the fumes by wearing their potion-making masks. Bickering back and forth about who would interrogate the person passed out on their floor, they settled on handling it together and gathered up the intruder, tying her to an old wingback chair they let customers use as they waited for their elixirs.

This one was younger than most of the criminals they had the displeasure of dealing with. But she wasn't a lost child, at least, like some of the kids who'd had been left behind before. Her clothes were worn, and Ian could spot multiple areas where rips were beginning to spread. And the dirt. He hoped it was the dirt that made her smell, or he might have to lecture her on hygiene before he lectured her on thievery.

He turned to ask Benson to take a whiff then realized from the shame on his friend's face that he was the source of the foul stench. "You disgust me," Ian said.

Turning back to the captive, Ian pulled up the sleeves of her cloak to make sure she wasn't hiding any weapons or potions. It was there on her forearm that he saw why she was likely on the run. "The mark of a thief. Most likely from Redclave," Ian said, saddened. "If we send her back, they'll torture her for escaping."

Benson nodded in agreement and growled a few times. "I'm sure she's hungry," Ian said, "but I'm not going to give her shelter if she's trying to rob us." Benson didn't argue but grumbled that he was going to give her some food before they sent her away.

Trying to wake her up, the two poked at her face, pinching her cheeks and lifting her eyelids. Getting no response, they challenged one another to connect the freckles on her face to make different pictures. Benson was contorting her cheek with his paw, trying to make a unicorn, when she snorted, but she didn't wake up. They soon gave up, staring frustrated at her gaping mouth as it gathered an unflattering amount of drool on the lower lip. Benson grunted at Ian and pointed his paw at her mouth.

"No, it is not the same thing. She's hopped up on a potion, not wandering around the kitchen drooling all over the floor because she can't decide what to eat!"

The two carried on a heated debate about Benson's animalistic tendencies, their insults flying back and forth with none landing a decisive blow. There was only one way to solve their dilemma.

"Swordfight!"

Ian's shout rang through the shop as Benson tilted his head and let out the mightiest of roars while beating his paws against his chest. Racing to their leather scabbards, they continued hurling insults at one another until they met face to face in the center of the shop.

"I'll give you one last chance to surrender and admit defeat, you overgrown, foul-smelling, pot-bellied pig."

Benson leaned in, standing tall on his hind legs, a menacing glare on his face as he stared into Ian's eyes, his teeth bared and saliva dripping from his fangs. They each waited for the other to make the first move.

"Did you kiss your mother with that rotten mouth?" In hindsight, Ian would regret saying those words.

Without hesitation, Benson grabbed Ian and licked him from his chin to his forehead. The drool was everywhere. It blocked his vision and clogged his nose, filling his senses with a cadre of unwanted smells. Ian tried wiping it away, but there was too much of it.

"You are disgusting!" Ian moaned, trying to resist the urge to vomit.

A great roar echoed through the room as Benson fell on his hind end, laughing hysterically, by turns pointing at Ian's face with pleasure and pounding the floor in delight. He could have carried on for some time were it not for the sound of whimpering behind them. They tried to gather their composure and went to stand in front of the awakening young woman, unsheathing their swords and pointing them at her neck.

# TWENTY-ONE

The three stared at one another in silence. Neither Ian nor Benson altered their stance, but they lowered their swords as they realized the knots they'd tied appeared to be holding.

Marian's eyes went back and forth, scanning the man and then the very peculiar bear beside him. Though she was still trying to assess the situation, she sensed her best option would be to try to talk her way out of whatever she'd gotten herself into. Not that she had ever been successful at that before, but there was always a chance it could work.

"So," she began, trying to talk as an enormous yawn overtook her, "my name is Marian." She looked around to try and get a sense of the hour, but the moonlight was too faint through the window. "How are you?"

Ian and Benson glanced at each other before responding, each of them doing their best impression of an intimidating authority figure. They had developed a routine, but it was still a little clumsy.

"Should we kill her now Benson, or save her for the wolves when they come roaming later tonight?"

Benson growled, baring a few of his fangs.

"Interesting." Ian looked at Benson and then back at Marian. "My friend here would like to kill you now. Typically, he prefers to not get his hands dirty. But I guess there's just something about you he doesn't like."

Marian had spent her childhood in the presence of warlocks and torturers—true villains these two could never equate themselves with no matter how hard they tried. She could slip out of their knots and assert her dominance in an instant, but she needed them to help her, not fear her. The dwarf had told her to seek assistance here, and if she kept things civil enough, maybe she would even have a warm place to sleep for the night. They were ripe for the picking, though.

"Well, I guess if your friend wants to kill me, he should go ahead and do it. It's pretty dark outside, so his bedtime has probably already gone by already," she mused.

"Don't worry. He will—" Ian began, but he was cut off by the grumblings of his companion. "No, you don't have a bed—" he tried to speak but was cut short by Benson again. "Shut up and look mean," he said to Benson.

"If you are going to kill me, at least show me some decency and do it quickly." Marian could hear the voice in her head disapproving of her tactics, but she was having fun.

Confusion crept into Ian's face while he tried to comprehend the transformation in their captive's demeanor. If they were going to maintain control, they would need to act quickly.

"This isn't a pick and choose kind of place, lady. We tell you when things happen, how they happen, and by which one of us it happens. Understand?" Ian asked, feigning confidence.

"Not really. This is a potion shop, and customers come in here every day on their own time to pick and choose. So, not a strong statement on your part."

Benson roared at Marian, letting saliva drip down from his teeth to scare her. All he got in return was laughter. Ian scratched his head, unable to understand where everything went wrong. At least she hadn't slipped out of the rope and escaped. And, as irritating as she was, he was finding her company far more entertaining than their usual fare.

"Is there a particular reason," he said in his deepest, darkest tone, "that you would act so arrogantly to those who hold your fate in their hands?"

Marian hummed for a moment as she took in the awkward sight before her. They were desperately trying to intimidate her but were failing so majestically she found it endearing. "Just one? I could name quite a few if you'd like."

Benson perked up at the offer and started growling at Ian.

"No! We do not need any extra input. I only asked for one and that's not even the point!"

Benson crossed his arms in frustration, turning his head away from Ian.

"I don't care that she offered. I said one, which by the way," he turned to face Marian, "we don't need. Besides, I'm the one in control of this conversation. So if I say just one, then just one!"

Benson huffed, turning his back completely to Ian and mumbling softly under his breath. Marian chuckled and snorted, trying to hold back her laughter while the two bickered.

"Fine!" Ian shouted. "If the pouty little bear would like to hear the multiple reasons, then let's just ask the nice lady who broke into our shop to list them all."

Ian turned toward Marian, who was having a very hard time keeping her laughter inside.

"Please proceed with your list so my cohort and I can acknowledge our mistakes and adjust our strategies to more effectively make you tremble in fear."

"Okay, but I'll go ahead and leave off this last bit of the conversation since you seem a little agitated by it."

"Your kindness is overwhelming," Ian said between clenched teeth, seething.

"But of course," Marian said with a smile and a flip of her hair, cracking a few tight spots in her neck in the process. "First, let's start with your swords." Marian was growing more confident in her decision to listen to the dwarf's command to seek out the potion shop and was eager to carry on this shamble of a shakedown. If nothing else came of it, it was at least an entertaining reprieve from running through the forest alone at night.

"What's wrong with our swords?" Ian shot back.

"They're wooden."

After a derisive smirk, Ian held up his sword to Benson so they could laugh at her remarks. This was his sword, the sword his mother taught him to defend himself with, and he knew it quite well. But, as he caught Benson avoiding eye contact, he slowly looked over his sword and noticed that its shiny metal was now dull and brown.

"Benson," Ian said softly.

Benson gave a quiet mumble of acknowledgment.

"Why is the blade of my sword made of wood?"

Benson mumbled under his breath and stared at the floor.

"You put..." Ian paused to catch his breath, a combination of anxiety and anger forcing the air from his lungs. "You put a mood shifter on my sword? You put a.... Why would you put a mood shifter on my sword?"

Benson growled an explanation, focusing on the grain of the wood planks beneath him and avoiding eye contact with Ian.

"What good is a sword if the blade turns to wood when I get angry?"

Benson responded by poking Ian in the chest with a single claw, now more dangerous than either of their swords.

"It's supposed to be a lethal weapon! What happens if I need to attack or defend myself against someone, and I swing this at them?" Ian's arm waved in front of Benson's face as he contemplated smacking the wooden sword against Benson's head.

Benson's mouth curled up in a smirk as he locked eyes with Ian, unabashedly uttering his response.

"A dusting feather?" Ian cried out.

Ian lunged at Benson and swung the wooden sword at him, bringing his arm down for a crushing blow.

A feather gently fell atop Benson's head. Their eyes locked on one another until Benson broke the tension, opening his arms for a hug.

Marian could no longer hold back her laughter, letting it ring through the shop as she marveled at the innocence and idiocy of her captors. It had been quite some time since she had an opportunity to laugh. Her amusement didn't last long though, because, as she shook with laughter, the chair rocked backward, and she landed in a lump on the floor again.

Benson moved quickly to her side, righting her chair, and giving her a gentle tap on the head before he returned to his position beside Ian, replacing his pleasant smile with a fierce expression. It was all Ian could do to keep himself from swinging at Benson again. Knowing the futility of this ever so desirable of actions, he took a moment to calm himself, then proceeded with his interrogation.

"Frivolities and idiocies aside," he paused, glaring at Benson, "why are you trying to sneak into our shop?"

Marian collected herself and was about to answer, but she couldn't pass up the opportunity he'd left open for her. "I thought you wanted me to list the reasons for not taking you so," she paused for dramatic effect, lowering her voice to help emphasize every syllable, "seriously."

Benson perked up but was immediately tempered by the scathing disdain in Ian's eyes. He'd had enough of this miscreant who had tried to sneak into their shop and potentially do them harm. It was time for some answers.

"No. But thank you," Ian said.

As a show of solidarity with Ian, Benson went and got two chairs and placed them directly in front of Marian. He and Ian sat down in unison, intent on getting the truth from their captive.

Ian was feeling more in control now, even if Marian wasn't showing any signs of concern. It wasn't often that a captive smiled and talked to him and Benson as if they were friends. He was almost proud of Benson until he realized Marian was snorting and holding back her laughter. He looked at Benson and realized why: the bear had begun puffing on his bubble pipe again. Ian mumbled contemptuously under his breath but did not tell him to put the pipe down. It was keeping him quiet, and for the moment, Ian needed that.

"Now, where were we? Oh yes. What we need to know is why you came sneaking around our shop and broke in after hours. We don't take very kindly to that sort of thing."

Marian was caught on that account. She was hesitant to tell them her reasons for being there but started to work her way toward it. The bear was amusing and the young man was sort of adorable in a moronic way, but she wasn't quite convinced they were the ones she'd been sent to find.

"I've been in disguise for days, struggling to get here to see Ori and Penelope. I learned of their mastery of potions and enchantments during my travels and was instructed to study under their tutelage so I could succeed in my mission."

"Sounds delightful. Unfortunately, you'll only find

Ian and Benson here," Ian said, pointing at himself and his friend. He was upset at the mention of his parent's names. "I'm not sure how much good looking for the dead will do for you, and I'm not inclined to let you stay here much longer," he said.

"Please," Marian said softly, realizing her gamble was quickly trending badly. "I'm here for a good reason, a good cause," she said, trying to maintain her composure. She was confused, and even her contrarian inner voice had gone quiet. If Ori and Penelope were dead, why was she sent here?

# Twenty-Two

Standing alone in a meadow cut within the woods on the southern edge of the Aurian Hills stood Hallenberry Halls. Isolated from civilization, the building presented a stark contrast to the surrounding world. It was designed and built by the Vorkyre ages before as a bastion of knowledge to aid the people of Ephorus and to cloak their land in protection from the Pillars of Time and their darkness and chaos. It was the Vorkyres' last united act of obedience to the First Walkers' desires. All the wisdom that had been granted to them by the First Walkers was collected in journals and scrolls on the shelves of the great library.

The Vorkyre had established a council of Elders amongst all sentient life on Ephorus to watch over Hallenberry Halls. For centuries, the Elders were revered by the people, a compiled class of learned scholars guiding the different inhabitants of the land until the Trofasthet poisoned the mind of the people in their first attempt to spread across Ephorus. The will of the people weakened the resolve of the humans on the board of Elders as they forced out the pixies, gnomes, elves, and dwarves. As time passed during the religious revolt, none but human men roamed these halls, a far cry from the symbol of peace and unity it had been created for. The most powerful people in Ephorus chose to make the Elders a target for their own insecurities, mocking and deriding their intellect and elitism. The Elders became meek and aloof, choosing to shrink behind their walls instead of rebuking the divisive claims about them. Hallenberry Halls never returned to its intended stature and was no longer a bastion for peace and knowledge. The Elders, in their weakened state, were now easy prey for Nance to strangle what little life remained, and his emissary would serve as his only warning for the destruction bound to come.

Born a servant in Steinigen, Artimus knew little of the world beyond the Logi Mountains and the Morkere. The mountains had always stood tall in the sky above her as she toiled away in the muck, subject to the whims and frivolities of the Master. One such whim now brought her to the Halls with armed escorts who looked more likely to burn scrolls rather than read them. At the Halls, she was met with disdain and mistrust because of the emblem on her tunic. She longed to remove it but wondered if it were the only thing still keeping her alive. When she was a child, she had lost hope as she watched her parents toil to death on the outskirts of hell, exiled from what remained of their people. When she had found the girl born of fire, she felt hope again, for a reward at least. But then she'd been shackled and put into service inside the fortress walls, and all notion of hope had faded away.

For several days after arriving at Hallenberry Halls, Artimus was ignored and left to wander on her own. The old stone walls were grimy with layers of soot from ages of burning candles. Her eyes traced the shapes on the walls where the dust lay unevenly, leaving her to wonder whose portrait once hung for everyone to see. These shadows of the past were apparent in every hallway of her new home.

Artimus knew she was not to speak to the scribes or Elders. She felt the same stares and awkward glances she had felt all her life as she waited for people's fascination with her appearance to abate. As an elf, she expected it; there were so few elves left that people rarely saw them anymore. The soft blue pigment of her skin looked like it was cut from the sky. Her white hair swept down her back to the base of her spine. Her ears were rigid and pointed and serrated on the bottom. Her eyes stood in contrast to her skin, a soft lavender, desperate to see something worth remembering at night. She was always waiting for the next person to judge her. The scar tissue covering her arms spoke of the fear and anger she'd endured; her self-inflicted wounds an attempt to abate the hatred others poured onto her. It hadn't worked. The pain only eased when she relinquished her desire for people's approval.

Spending many nights in a cold, dark room alone in the Halls somehow felt worse to her than living in the tattered cells within Steinigen's walls, where at least she had the support of other families—when she wasn't being teased or tormented. They still asked her questions about the girl born of fire she'd found in the mountains. That story had a painful ending for her, but she had grown to enjoy the attention. In the Halls, however, she was simply ignored; a ghost left to its intentions, never to be seen or heard from. She tried to see how far she could wander amongst those who chose not to acknowledge her, and, to Artimus's surprise, she was not denied access anywhere except the Elders' private studies.

With little to do, Artimus continued meandering through the Halls, finding a rather quiet corridor with what appeared to be a maze of doorways in the upper walkway of the northeast corner. No soot, no dust, and no forgotten memories could be found on the walls or floors. Intrigued, she made a few notations on a makeshift map she had drawn in a notebook before placing it back within her tunic. She wandered through a series of doors and ended up on a strange pathway between rooms that appeared to lead nowhere.

It was an irritating, yet entertaining waste of time, but she still had plenty of it left with no instructions given other than to standby for word from the Master. Artimus decided to take the door opposite to the one that common sense told her was correct. Stumbling forward, frightened and exhilarated, Artimus went through a few more doors until she arrived in an empty room.

"Is there no sense of privacy where you're from?" a voice shouted from above.

Artimus looked around the room in fear, but there was no one that she could see and nowhere to hide.

"Up here," the voice said, exasperated.

When she tilted her head, Artimus saw an owl perched atop the crossbeam, staring at her with disapproval. Artimus tried to speak, but the words were caught in her throat. She watched the owl spread its wings and descend to the floor, where it promptly turned into a rather large terrier. Reaching its front legs forward and raising its rear high, the terrier stretched as far as it could and shook the remnants of a peaceful sleep out of its head.

The terrier sat down and, turning its attention to Artimus, looked into her eyes. Unsure of what to say, and wondering if she was even awake and not in a fever dream, Artimus reached out to pet it.

"Do not presume you get to touch me! I get enough of that from the drunkards down the hall when they stay up past their bedtime. I'd appreciate a little space, seeing how we don't know each other."

"I'm sorry?" Artimus pulled her hand back and hoped she would wake up before she lost all her mental faculties.

"Yes." The terrier paused as it stretched out, licking its lips with satisfaction. "Yes, you are sorry. And let's run through the rest of the gambit to save time. No, you're not dreaming. Yes, I am speaking. Yes, other people can hear me too. And yes"—the terrier hopped on its hind legs and transformed into a woman, standing several inches above Artimus—"I am a shifter."

"Hmmph," Artimus muttered as she gave up on controlling the situation. She began to chuckle under her breath.

"What is it you find so funny?" the woman asked angrily.

"I think you might be cuter as a dog," Artimus said, a coy smile curling her lips.

"First of all, I'm cute no matter what form I take, especially this one. And second," she slumped to the ground, turning back into the terrier, "I know who you are."

"Great," Artimus muttered against her knees. "If you want to ignore me like everyone else, could you at least leave this part out? It's been a bit of a disastrous week so far."

"They're scared of you," the terrier said, winding her way between Artimus's legs. "You are now surrounded by a group of scared old men afraid that they have no control over their future or the knowledge they have pledged to protect. Nothing can be sadder than a group of scared old men being forced to reckon with their failures."

"And you?"

"I was dropped off years ago, much the same. Just by a slightly less hateful person than the Jesting Master. It took time, but after repeated bouts of isolation, we found a way for me to be accepted," she said, raising her snout and wagging her tail.

"What do you mean?" Artimus asked as she sat on the floor so she and the canine would be on the same level.

"I mean it'll get better," the terrier said.

"I don't think anyone else here sees it that way. I think they'd rather kill me than welcome me."

"Even in the moments when they think they are free to study and write whatever they desire, there's this tinge of doubt that overshadows them, as if it may be the last thing they do. And when you showed up at the front door, many of them thought you and that group of mongrels were here to bring death upon them."

"You don't think that?" Artimus was hoping her innocence would shine through as she watched the terrier shift back into the form of the woman, now sitting cross-legged before her. Artimus was becoming entranced with the being's soft pale skin and gray irises staring back at her.

"The stew here can be more deadly at times than you could ever be to us," she laughed. "I mean no disrespect, but for an elf, you seem utterly incapable of fighting."

Pleased though somewhat offended, Artimus managed to smile again. "Thank you."

"My name is Erin," the woman said, offering her hand to Artimus.

"Artimus," she answered, hesitantly shaking her hand. Her trepidation lingered, but as she took hold of Erin's hand she felt a spark erupt in her heart.

"Give me a little time with the Elders," Erin began. "I've managed to carve out a nice little home here and have even garnered some sway from my friend who brought me here. Things will not be easy, but if you do what is asked then you may come to find some modicum of peace within these walls."

Artimus lunged at Erin, awkwardly wrapping her arms around the shifter before realizing what she was doing. It had been ages since Erin had even attempted to embrace another person, and her body stiffened, though she did her best not to turn away from the unsolicited affection. She held out her arms and gently patted Artimus on the back without embracing her, and Artimus slowly pulled away.

"You don't like to be touched, huh?" Artimus asked, hoping her ill-advised affection hadn't cost her an ally.

"It's not necessarily the touching that's the problem." Erin paused, trying to find a delicate way to explain it, but nothing came to mind. "It's just, you people smell. And I don't think they've been giving you a lot of wash time, because, and I say this with good intention, your stench is rancid."

Artimus swung her arm, hitting Erin in the shoulder before she realized she was attacking the only person who'd spoken to her in weeks. "Sorry," Artimus muttered, her eyes widening as Erin shifted back to a terrier, her jaws open and fangs dripping with saliva.

"Yes," Erin said, "you will be."

Artimus jumped to her feet and tried to pat Erin on the head. "Good doggy," she shouted, her voice nervous as she backed her way to the door.

"Nope, not right now."

Leaping forward, Erin knocked Artimus on her back and began licking her face and gnawing on her clothes.

"This is weird on so many different levels!" Artimus shouted.

"No, this is what peers do!" Erin shot back as she placed her paws on Artimus's head and shouted, "Stay!" Erin tried to make herself comfortable on

Artimus's back, kneading her clothes into the perfect array of lumps to lie on.

"This isn't comfortable for me!"

"That would be my intention," Erin yawned. "But, besides the stench, it's quite cozy for me."

# Twenty-Three

Marian was at a loss. She was given no more information than to come to this shop and seek help, and the once-constant voice in her head had gone silent. Ian's unkempt appearance belied his focused gaze that bore right through her. He wasn't stupid; he just liked to play the part. She had no choice but to move forward; were she to backtrack, he would most likely try to kick her back into the dark or, worse, pick a fight.

"I am sorry for your parents passing, but I am compelled to complete my journey. I was sent here to seek their guidance, and if you have anything of theirs that might help, I'd be grateful to see it."

Scoffing at her words, Ian turned to Benson, who growled a few words in a high pitch, mocking her. The two chuckled briefly before falling silent. She could feel the tension building as Ian studied her from head to toe, growing less patient with her by the moment.

"Well," Ian began, "Then I must regretfully inform you that all access to their work is under strict lock and key and cannot be accessed. My colleague and I take great pride in what we offer and cannot let the name be sullied by someone we don't even know."

Benson made a slight nod of his head and took a strong puff on his pipe, sending a few errant bubbles into his nose that made him sneeze. Ian sighed as Benson pawed at his nose to rid himself of the bubble residue.

Trust had not been valuable to Marian as a child. No one in the Master's circle could ever trust anyone, nor did her father want them to. He craved fear and submission and sought to instill nothing else in Marian. But now she needed to take a chance, no matter how anxious it made her. She needed someone else to help carry the burden. "I know you have no reason to trust me," she blurted out, "but I promise I'm not here to intentionally cause you or your friend harm."

Ian shrugged at her remark. He waited and watched her, letting her discomfort grow. She wondered if he was looking at her messy clothes—her dirty black cloak, her mud-stained silk blouse and boots. Her leggings were worn out and shapeless. When was the last time you ate? she asked herself. His gaze was now fixed on her right arm. The scar was still tender underneath her sleeve—he must have seen it while tying her to the chair.

"How long?" Ian said wearily.

"What do you mean?" Marian responded.

"Let's start with how long you've been prancing around the forest on the run, and then we'll move on to some of the other, more interesting questions."

"I told you, I just came to see Ori and Penel—"

"Not the answer to my question." Ian leaned over

to Benson and whispered in his ear. Marian could hear him instructing the bear to grab the bottle from underneath the counter. Benson nodded casually and set his pipe down before walking to the other side of the shop.

"What's the bear doing?" Marian said, trying to buy more time.

"My friend," Ian paused for emphasis, "is grabbing a special concoction I worked up to assist in situations like these when people refuse to tell the truth. So, before I need to use it, maybe you could rethink your answer and tell me how long you've been on the run."

Marian was at an impasse; she had hoped they were as dim-witted as they first appeared, but that impression wore off quickly. Tied to a chair in a potion shop would not be how her journey ended. She had to switch paths. She couldn't run away.

"I've been on my way here for a few days; I didn't lie about that. But I am not on the run. The only reason I've been hiding is that I didn't want to get accosted by a drifter on the way."

Returning to his seat, Benson tossed his paw up to cover his face and feigned fear, throwing his other paw out to ward off a nonexistent attacker. Then he dipped his paw into a jar of honey.

"That's not.... You were supposed to grab the thing," Ian said irritably. Benson grumbled a retort, but Ian waved it off.

Marian had finally lost her desire to laugh; anxiety and fear were weakening the control she had over her emotions, and bad memories of her recent experiences were starting to catch up with her.

"Well," Ian said. "It sounds like we might be getting somewhat closer to the truth. But I'd like to move things forward a little faster, so let me take a stab. You're on the run, and we know that because of the mark you were branded with. That crescent moon is the sign of a thief, and it's too fresh and tender to have been handed down by the King's guard in Crescent City. You've been claimed as Redclave property, a runaway thief soon to be a slave. Now, neither Benson nor I approve of the Old King's laws granting such disgusting activities, but you have been marked as a criminal. That would lead me to hold on to the notion that you were trying to steal from us, and your talk of having business with my parents was an attempt to get yourself out of trouble. And a horribly misplayed one at that," he scolded as his eyes tightened.

Marian was fidgeting in her chair as Ian carried on, a growing sense of urgency building within her while she sensed the approach of her father—or his trackers. Benson seemed to sense what she was thinking, holding up his paw to Ian while he sniffed the air. Ian took the displeased grunts of his friend in stride and carried on.

"Not to mention the fact that the people who followed you here are hiding out by the tree line. Kind of makes me wonder if I should help you avoid being captured by them, or if I should just throw you out and let them have you."

"What do you mean?" she asked apprehensively. "How long was I unconscious?"

"Several hours, I suppose. You're quite small in

comparison to the scum we usually get trying to steal from us so I overdid the potion a little."

"They caught up to me," Marian's voice was soft.

"They did. Benson, how many people can you smell? And, Marian, would you like to tell us who's creepily hanging out on the outskirts of our shop because of you?"

Benson grunted at Ian.

"A trio of new friends," Ian said.

Marian had become annoyed that these two might destroy any chance she had of stopping her father. She had to speak up and hope that they would listen, otherwise, she would have to use force.

"You must listen to me now—" she started but was cut off.

"Oh," Ian said to Benson. "I've never been given orders by a captive before. This certainly is new."

As the two began laughing, Marian's startled expression turned to anger. Her hands were still tied behind her, but she lit a flame in her palms.

"If they catch me, they will take me back to my father, leaving no one to stand in his way. I cannot be stopped here, and I don't want to go back, knowing you were killed because of me as well. You must—"

"Hold on! Let's clarify the whole 'we're going to get killed' thing before we just quickly move on," Ian chimed in as Benson leaned closer, nodding his head and trying to hide his sudden urge to hide.

"These men were sent by my father to bring me back. They do not care to leave people alive whom they find burdensome, and they have no qualms about killing the innocent."

"And so they'll decide to give us an early escape from our earthly troubles and blah, blah, blah," Ian said. "Why is knowing who you are such a bad thing, and who..." The smell of burning rope filled the air, and his voice trailed off.

Marian yanked her arms free from the burning rope. She handed the remnants to Benson, the flames continuing to dance on the tips of her fingers.

# Twenty-Four

"Stop staring at my ears," Artimus snapped.

"I'm not, but if I were, it's because they're weird," Erin said, unabashedly staring at the side of Artimus's head. "But seriously though, are you able to fly with those? It could prove quite helpful."

"I'd like to hit you."

"Understandable, but certainly unadvisable," Erin proclaimed, a wry smile forming on her narrow lips.

Laughing off her indignation, Artimus attended to her newfound chores of tidying the library with her shadow in tow. She was grateful Erin had been able to convince the Elders to let her do more than wait quietly for a message from Steinigen. She dragged Erin along while rolling her cart down the aisles, returning books and journals to their proper homes, and grabbing any new items that had been requested.

It was a meager responsibility, but Artimus wasn't complaining. She had spent the last two days without any sense of fear, roaming peacefully through the aisles of Hallenberry Halls with Erin and resting in the meadow amongst the wildflowers at dawn and dusk to watch the sun illuminate the life she never got to enjoy.

"How old do you think I am?" Erin asked Artimus as the two lazily walked together, arms locked tightly.

"Would that be in dog, owl, or pretend human years?" Artimus asked sarcastically.

"Let's say in, 'answer-or-I-beat-you-with-that-book' years."

"Oh, well, in that case," Artimus chuckled, laughing off the threat. "I'd say, too old to look so young, but young enough to hurt me if I say you're old and decrepit."

"I will always be young enough to beat you for saying that," Erin said, glaring at Artimus as she cackled loudly. The two stood motionless and waited for the echo of her laughter to dissipate.

"Why'd you have to say it so weird and stern-like?" Artimus contained her laughter this time, cupping one hand over her mouth as she leaned into Erin.

Erin smiled and pulled away to grab a small, dusty journal of potions from a shelf. The cover was blank—no image, title, or author name. It was so non-descript that Artimus wondered if the book's intent was to be lost. Erin got a cloth from Artimus's cart and gently wiped off the dust, then took a seat on the floor, leaning against the bookshelf.

"Sit with me." She motioned to Artimus. "I need to tell you a story about why we met, and why you may come to regret it."

There was no humor in Erin's demand, which caused Artimus to hesitate. "You're going to make a good day go rather bad, aren't you?"

"Quite possibly," she answered, waving at Artimus to sit down.

"But I've had so few of them," Artimus whined.

Taking a spot beside Erin, she inched closer until they were shoulder to shoulder, speaking in hushed tones like children avoiding their parents' attention. Erin opened the journal, letting its pages breathe the fresh air of the world around them, the musty smell of time and dust trapped within its bindings now free.

~ *The battle was won, but almost all was lost.* ~

They read the opening line on the first page. "Quite a skin-crawling introduction," Artimus sneered as she looked for the author's name or initials. "Who wrote this? Usually, the potion masters are more than happy to splatter their name across everything they've done."

"This journal wasn't undertaken for credit or glory but to save Ephorus from the world beyond." Erin's tone was muted, her playfulness gone.

"Oh, okay," Artimus said, pretending to understand. "Makes total sense now."

"You serve the Mast—"

Artimus cut her off with a line she had memorized: "Only by force for fear of reprisal to those I love."

It was a defensive statement she had shouted in her mind for years while working around Steinigen. Her voice was much louder than she intended, her tormented past present in the reverberations off the library walls.

"Sorry," Erin said, patting her knee in solace, placing the open journal in Artimus's lap as she went on. "This journal was written in a time of great trepidation. The

Jesting Master was quietly amassing enough power to hold sway over all of Ephorus. Unchallenged, he stayed in the confines of his fortress as he worked to bring an end to the separation of worlds and reign over them all."

"Separation of worlds?" Artimus whispered, looking quizzically at Erin. "What do you mean?"

"I mean there is more to existence than what you've seen; more to life than death; more to magic than potions; and more pain ever imagined if the wrong hand brings these worlds together."

"But this little journal stopped him from doing that?" Artimus's mind was racing to find the meaning behind Erin's words. In the past, she'd had scant time in life to ponder more than her immediate survival. "You do know he's still powerful, still menacing, and still intent on killing everyone one day?"

"Why, yes. Yes, we do, my dear little elf," a tired old voice called out from the pages in Erin's lap.

Confused, Artimus turned around but saw no one, her eyes peering through the shelves while she wondered if the voice was just in her head.

"Look here." Erin pointed down to the book. "It's the author's signature you were looking for."

Artimus had an ominous feeling as she looked down and saw an old man—a minuscule old man—moving about in the middle of the page and smiling at her.

"Is this...is he real?"

Before Erin could answer, the journal flew out of her hands and flipped over, suspended in mid-air. It began to shake violently, and they heard the gasps and howls of the old man as he came spilling out of the journal, growing in size until he stood a head's length above Artimus. Staring in disbelief, Artimus reached out to poke him, but Erin yanked her hand back.

"Let's find out where he's been these last few days before we start touching him."

"Who's 'him'?" Artimus asked.

"I, my dear little elf, am Paramel!" The old man spread his arms wide in preparation for her adulation. Then, with a slight sense of embarrassment and humility, he chuckled to himself, realizing she knew nothing of him or his name. "Oh, how the ages take away our relevance, Erin."

"Indeed," she replied, a longing for forgotten times shimmering in her eyes.

"I'm sorry," Artimus said, standing up, trying to get a better perspective on the situation. "But what in the world is going on? And why should I know who you are? And why am I the only one even a little freaked out about an old lecher dropping into the room from nowhere?" she asked, turning to Erin, who sat calmly on the floor.

The journal, still floating in the air, fell into Paramel's hands as he reached for it. "This little book requires a new owner, and I believe it should be you."

"That response only brings up more questions!" Artimus shouted while watching the old man dust off his work.

# Twenty-Five

Nance sat alone in the darkness of his chambers. With his shutters open, the nocturnal song of Steinigen crept into his mind as he focused on each creature's sound. A howling wolf, a cooing owl, the desperate screeches of prey when struck. It brought him a semblance of peace to hear the world as it had always been.

That was what he wanted. That was what Ephorus needed: a strong leader who could deliver them to their fate without fear. For far too long Ephorus had been allowed to survive in isolation, the Logi Mountains protecting it from the ravages of darkness the passage of time brought. He could feel time itself beckoning to have its rightful stewardship reinstated amongst the land he would claim as his own, its natural progression stymied by the First Walkers and the Vorkyre they left in their stead. He took from the mountains the ability to bring about destruction, to reinstate the true nature of life, but now his daughter was set to betray him.

His body began to ignite, steam creeping out of his nose, flames engulfing his legs and feet. He got up and made his way from his chambers to the library, a single thought occupying his mind: his daughter was betraying him. The halls were empty near his chambers, and he walked alone, his shadows making demonic shapes.

She's taken it, a voice hissed from within the fire, searing his ears. It had been years since he lacked the control to quell the inner voices that plagued his family.

"She knew nothing of it," he grimaced, cocking his head to the side, trying to absorb the pain.

"Nothing of what, sir?"

The voice startled Nance as it emerged from the shadows. Flames shot up his arms as he lunged forward and grabbed Phillip, whose eyes were full of fear. Nance looked down and saw his servant's clothes burning and released his grip.

"Why are you here?" Nance seethed, watching Phillip struggling to extinguish the flames before they burned his flesh.

"The Hearthwood, sir. We received word from an advance rider that it will be here before morning rises."

Nance scratched his forehead, inching closer to Phillip, forcing him against the wall. He drew the flames inward, reabsorbing them save for a small, orange flicker of light in his right palm.

"I find myself amongst those who wish to betray me quite often," Nance whispered to the flame as Phillip stared. "But you wouldn't lie to me, would you?"

"No, sir!" Phillip answered quickly.

He lies, the flame whispered to Nance.

A curious smile worked its way across Nance's face as he appraised his servant.

"I wasn't asking you," he said with a laugh, his hand clutching Phillip's throat as the smell of burnt flesh filled his nostrils. Nance leaned in to hear the whimpers of his servant, giggling at the young man's pain. "You should not speak unless spoken too," he sneered and released his grip, letting Phillip fall to the floor in a heap.

You let him live. How intriguing? the voice whispered once again before Nance tamped it down, the halls fading to darkness.

"If you live, see to it that Sever is roused early and begins to ready the warlocks. I will wait no longer to squash this land once I have the Hearthwood in my possession."

Phillip began to crawl away. Nance thought of freeing him from his misery. But there was work to be done, and he needn't bother himself with lowly prey that might still serve a purpose.

Leaving him behind, Nance went to his library, opening the door with pleasure as the smell of books hit him. The knowledge his family had accumulated over generations was tangible when he entered this room. The feel of the leather-bound covers, the rough-hewn pages, and the sweet aroma of age and wisdom emanated from every precious volume except for one.

"How could she have known," he said under his breath as he headed to the shelf on the far wall.

Nance cast his arms wide, releasing flames to all the candles in the room. With their light, he could see the many tomes and documents of his family's heritage, a testament to the greatness once bestowed upon them by their relation to the Logi. As he studied the tidy rows, he noticed a suspicious gap between two books and he heard the voice, Will you fail again?

The question scorched his ears while flames erupted around him. He heard his sister's laughter, a derisive screech tearing across his mind as if to violate his sanity, a daemon that he needed to overpower and silence.

# TWENTY-SIX

"I take it my family needs no introduction," Marian said softly.

Ian's voice was cold and blunt. "None at all. What we need is an explanation as to why we shouldn't toss you back to them and fortify our shop to keep them, or you, from getting in."

"I am not my father," she began slowly, subduing the flames on her fingers. She crossed her legs. "I risked my life to flee Steinigen to stop him. He's been mounting a secret campaign across Ephorus and—"

Ian cut her off. "The people are well aware of his plan." His fear and fascination were growing, his eyes fixed on the burned rope that moments ago had bound Marian's hands.

"You don't understand," she protested, unwilling to be silenced. "What you've seen is just his barbarism. That's where his cruelty toward the world begins, but if he succeeds, Ephorus will be a small penance, an offering for the power he needs to conquer something far greater."

She waited for Ian to grasp the significance of her

words. Benson gently reached over and touched Marian's hand with his paw to see how hot it was. She opened her palm and extended it, letting him feel her skin, which was cool and soft as usual. Benson smiled in approval.

"I need your help," Marian said, trying to let her vulnerability show as she smiled back at Benson.

"We know." Ian had little sympathy in his eyes, but his voice had lost most of its edge.

"What do you mean?"

"Whether or not you're a thief is still in question, but whether or not you're in danger isn't. And I'm fully convinced the same goes for us," he answered.

"I'm not a thief!" Marian shot back, unable to contain her frustration.

"We'll draw our conclusion on that one, but let's put that matter aside. The truth most likely is, if those three out there were with you, you wouldn't have needed to trek through the forest by yourself for protection. Just like you shouldn't have had such a hard journey from Redclave."

It's a start, she thought as she watched the two whispering back and forth. You've done well, the voice responded.

"Fine time for you to come back," she snapped at herself, before realizing she had spoken out loud. A sudden feeling of shame and embarrassment spread through her. Ian and Benson stared as she buried her face in her hands and grumbled, "Sorry."

"Okay, that wasn't abnormal at all," Ian answered, gazing at her bright red cheeks. "Before we decide our course of action, I would like at least some bit of truth to come from you that can be backed by evidence."

Marian was tired of holding back and answered immediately. "I received the mark in Redclave," she began, "but it wasn't because I was a thief! I had the money to pay for the food and supplies. The shopkeeper raised the price after I had paid, and, when I refused to pay extra, we argued, then fought, which led to me kicking him in the crotch." She sighed. "That earned me this hideous reminder of why some people deserve what's coming to them, but I'll still try and stop it."

Ian's eyes gave nothing away. His fingers tapped restlessly on the arm of his chair.

"You've explained the mark, but that does little to tell us why we can trust you," he answered.

Marian was at a breaking point. It had been a long time since she'd had a chance to rest or sleep without fear. There was a path of destruction already set in motion for the world, and she was still trying to figure out how to stop it. Let them see you for you, the voice said. She caught herself before responding to it, her teeth biting down hard on her lower lip.

"I can't make you trust me!" she yelled. "I made a mistake in trying to hide, but I haven't had much success, or experience, in interacting with people, so I took a chance. I made the wrong decision and I'm sorry, but I am trying to do what's right. I am trying to help people who would rather see me dead, or locked away. If they take me back to my father..." her words trailed off. "Those three out there are just the start.

More will be coming, and I won't be able to fend them off long enough to find out how to stop him."

Benson worked through the situation in his mind, trying to suppress his fidgetiness. He finally jumped up and hurried on all fours past Ian and Marian, down to the basement, growling in pleasure the whole way.

"What is he saying?" Marian asked.

Ian had a strange smile on his face and an eagerness in his eyes. "He said he's going to get the egg."

"What does that mean?" Marian was getting exhausted from the lack of clarity here.

"It means the three of us are going to go have a peaceful conversation somewhere more secluded, away from prying eyes."

"So you'll help me?" Marian asked hopefully.

Ian sighed. Marian's mouth opened slightly and her heart was beating hard as she waited for his answer.

"For now, yes. After tonight though, we'll discuss later."

Ian smiled when she ran over and hugged him.

"Thank you," she whispered in his ear, pulling him close before letting go. He stuttered a few unintelligible words, his cheeks flushed. His mouth was trying to figure out how to work again.

# Twenty-Seven

The sky appeared endless above Pight. Resting atop a large pine tree, she traced the stars with her finger, wishing she could see that world up close. It taunted her with its beauty far above, never to be within reach.

"What do you see tonight?" Inibri asked, her eyes on the trackers below.

They had been stalled atop the pine tree for some time now, waiting for the trackers' next move. It had been a struggle to slow them down, their leader refusing to take any of the bait they laid for misdirection, and now there was no room left for them to intervene.

"The Great Goblin has returned," Pight murmured as she found the mass of stars she had named a few years before.

"Has he caught the valiant young pixie yet?" Inibri asked, turning to face Pight, her colorful hair falling out from under the maple leaf she was using to hide it.

"As if he ever could," Pight answered with unabashed confidence. She opened her mouth to continue bashing the goblin in the sky but was cut off by noises from the men below.

Inibri began a fast descent down the tree with Pight in tow. They could hear the men's disgruntled banter.

"But it's right there," the rotund one named Ceril said, pointing across the field at a small shop. "Look at it. It has absolutely no defenses and is barely standing. A strong gust of wind could win this for us."

"He has a point," Pight whispered into Inibri's ear, staring across the field toward the little shop. Its moss-covered roof appeared to be sinking in various places, barely held up by the walls' bulging stones.

"Do not forget where we are, and who resides in these places," Inibri chided her. "The Aurian Hills is not to be taken at face value, nor anything within it."

Pight made to answer but bit her tongue. She was determined to be more vigilant after her near-disastrous mistake on the outskirts of Redclave. Placing her hand on Inibri's, Pight pulled herself closer as they listened to the plan being hatched beneath them; perhaps they would find a flaw they could exploit.

"Should we go warn them?" Pight asked.

"No," Inibri answered without hesitation. "Paramel was certain this was where she needed to come. We must trust his plan, or we risk placing it in peril."

Pight nodded, turning her attention back to the three men, who were arguing now, their voices loud enough to scatter the few birds that had been resting among the trees near them.

"If we continue to wait," Ceril snapped, "they'll have every advantage over us, and we'll just be sitting here waiting instead of celebrating at a tavern with a little mistress to enjoy the night with."

Pight watched as Lyco, the leader, unsheathed his sword and let the tip rest upon Ceril's throat.

"We will wait until I am convinced it is the opportune time. We do not have a force behind us, and we do not know the capabilities of those she has gone inside to meet."

"For all we know she could be dead in there," Ceril added, unperturbed by Lyco's sword, apparently an empty threat he had grown accustomed to.

"He has a point," the tall, quiet brother of Ceril offered while placing his fingertip on the top of the sword's blade to lower it from a deadly position on his brother's throat to a merely inconvenient location on his chest. "We do not know how long she has been in there, nor do we know what would've drawn her in there in the first place. Those are the Aurian Hills towering behind the shop in the darkness. Do we want to risk waiting to see if the creatures left among the hills will abide by the mandate to stay within their boundaries? The three of us would last seconds against an onslaught of river gnomes, or something far worse."

Pight's ears pricked up. "He must be the smart one," she whispered.

Inibri nodded, growing tense.

"We move at my pace, and the Master's daughter is to be kept alive at all costs," Lyco said, leading the men out from the tree line into the open field.

"Why is there a wheelbarrow out here?" Ceril demanded as he barged past it, ignoring Lyco's instruction to be stealthy.

"It's a good ques—" Pight began saying as the door

to the shop opened.

The silhouettes of a large bear and a scrawny human stood staring out into the darkness.

"Our sincerest regards to your Master," the man shouted while the bear lurched forward and hurled a projectile into the open field before them.

Breaking into a sprint, the trackers raced toward the shop. The man and bear vanished, and the door slammed shut. Pight lifted off the branch only to be stopped by Inibri's hands around her leg.

"Fly high and don't breathe in the smoke," Inibri said, pulling Pight close before letting her go. They both soared through the canopy toward the stars above.

# Twenty-Eight

Benson shut the door behind them, the sound of charging men silenced by the sanctuary of their shop. Marian sparked fresh flames on her hands, preparing for battle, her heart pounding in her chest.

"No!" Ian said sharply, swatting her arms. He gestured at the racks of potions around them: "Highly explosive."

"But they're charging!" Marian snapped back, her eyes darkening as the fire began to burn stronger within her.

"They're incapacitated by now," Ian scoffed, making his way to the door, opening it to let the sound of his and Benson's victory waft in.

"We're burning!" The shout shattered the night air, followed by another one, "Let us die in peace you beast!"

Ian stared out into the field, trying to catch a glimpse of the trackers. He saw three men writhing on the ground, fighting an invisible creature, each one of them screaming their acceptance of defeat and imminent death.

Scratching his head, Ian turned to Benson who had joined him at the door. "We might have overdone this one?"

Benson smiled and shook his head no, enjoying the extraordinary show.

Marian came to stare in fascination beside them. "What did you do?"

"We call it the Dragon Egg," Ian said, waving his hands for added flair.

"Okay, but what is it doing to them? And why do you call it the Dragon Egg?" she asked, imitating his dramatic gesture.

"Right now, it's just loosening them up to have a little fun. But in a minute the situation will take a turn toward the demonic."

"But they're already—"

Marian wanted to question what he meant until she heard new screams of terror.

"What is going on over there?" she asked, whether concerned or curious she couldn't decide. Definitely just curious, she assured herself.

Benson grumbled a bit and set to packing gear for their travel.

"He's right you know," Ian said.

"Right about what?"

"For someone we just met and helped get out of a jam, you sure are asking a lot of questions."

Marian's frustration was obvious on her face, her brow furrowing and her eyes glaring. Ian laughed and Benson threw his paws over his snout, pretending he was about to faint from fear. The two would have carried on, but they noticed the unmistakable glow of fire coming from Marian's fist.

"Don't worry," Ian said, grabbing her shoulders and moving her away from the door. "In a few minutes, the next phase will kick in and they will pass out. And when they wake up, they will be safe and sound." He paused momentarily. "Except maybe for some wet trousers. I can't speak on their behalf, but from the sound of their screams I would wager that at least one of them has soiled himself."

Benson couldn't contain his laughter and tumbled to the floor, pounding his paws against the wooden boards. Ian gave him a quick kick in his side to get him up, but neither was in much of a rush.

"So what now?" Marian asked.

"Now," Ian said, tossing her bag to her, "we head somewhere a little more private in the woods where we can talk without being tracked or threatened."

Clutching her bag, Marian felt for the journal.

"Don't worry," Ian scoffed. "We're not thieves, either."

Marian frowned, and Ian came over, placing a hand on top of hers.

"Just a short walk into the woods and then you can rest easy tonight. The world can wait to be saved until after we talk tomorrow."

Benson went and peered out the front door. The trackers were passed out on the ground. With a nod to Ian, he led them outside, heading toward the forest at the base of the Aurian Hills.

"Looks like you could make a friend or two tonight,

Marian," she whispered to herself. Looks like, the voice answered meaningfully.

Benson closed the door behind them, testing the knob to make sure it was locked. The three fell in line quickly, turning at the corner of the shop and moving straight toward the forest. When they reached the trees, Benson bumped into Marian, who had stopped still.

Hearing Benson's grumble, Ian turned around and stared at her. "Surely you can't be scared of walking in the woods?"

"It's...," she started, trailing off as she looked around. Focusing on Ian, she finished her thought, "It's these woods. I heard stories growing up of what happened here. What can happen here."

"I assure you, there is nothing in this forest more dangerous than your father. And those stories were only used by men like the Old King to build hatred and distrust amongst the commoners and peddlers of melancholic garbage to force their rivals into hiding. Everyone and everything in this forest is an outcast just like you."

Turning to the trees, Ian motioned for her to follow. Benson gave her a gentle nudge from behind, and the three disappeared into the forest.

-~-

Pight and Inibri hovered above the incapacitated trio sprawled in the open field.

"Do we help them?" Pight asked.

"No, we do not," Inibri answered. "They have help on the way, putting our charge at a disadvantage. They can suffer a little longer to help even out the fight."

Pight fluttered over to Inibri and kissed her cheek. "I love how your mind works," she said.

The two made their way to the potion shop, leaving the men immersed in delusions and hallucinations. The night was rather calm, but it was almost sunrise. The first glimmer of purple light had appeared on the horizon. Since the doors and windows were locked, the pixies flew up to the roof and decided to get in through the chimney.

"I hate ash," Pight moaned.

"You'll have time to clean yourself," Inibri said and, without hesitation, flew into the chimney, beckoning Pight to follow.

They landed in a fireplace on the lower level of the shop. The place was a mess. Inibri gingerly stepped into the room. Pight dusted ash off her tunic and fluttered over. She opened her mouth, preparing to let loose a tirade on the sloppy housekeeping until she saw the look on Inibri's face.

No words needed to be spoken to soothe the sadness engulfing her partner. Inibri's memories maintained a strong connection to her lost friend. Penelope had been an inspiration to Inibri, an invitation to a life outside the confines of the small world the Pixies had confined themselves to. Pight held her tight, resting her head on Inibri's shoulder.

# Twenty-Nine

The path was nearly indistinguishable from its sur-roundings. The dense trees confused Marian's sense of direction, and scarce light came down through the thick canopy from the moon. Marian pushed the fear from her mind and followed Ian and Benson. Benson's continuous humming made him easy to follow, and she found his childlike nature becoming more endear-ing.

Stumbling on a root, Marian looked down and caught a glimmer of soft, glowing light in the shrubs around her feet. Thinking she was hallucinating from exhaustion, or maybe she'd inhaled a touch of the Dragon Egg that had drifted their way, she tried to ignore it. But as they walked deeper into the forest, more lights began to appear on the path. Marian bent down and saw they were Harken Lilies, a breed exotic to her mind, too tempting not to pluck one from the ground. She cupped it in her palm and stared into the soft blue light shining from its petals. Bringing it closer to her face, she saw it moving, breathing, and whispering.

She lost all awareness of her surroundings, falling deep into the flower's trance.

Stay with us, the flower whispered into her thoughts as she held it close. Other flowers started calling out in unison for her to join them. Tell us of the fire from whence you came.

You are getting lost little one! the voice in her head cried out.

Her heart skipped a beat, and she dropped the flower, watching as its light dimmed and vanished, leaving her in the dark. She was alone.

"No," she pleaded. "Please tell me which way they went." She searched for Ian and Benson but couldn't find them. If she went the wrong way, she would either wander back toward the trackers or deeper into the forest. "They'll come back. Won't they?" she asked, hoping the voice would have an answer. "Now is not the time to ignore me," she whispered into the trees, her voice growing desperate.

"Who's ignoring you," Ian said, laying his hand on her shoulder. "Now, unless you and your thoughts would like to be left alone, I suggest you continue following me."

Marian grabbed his hand tightly to make sure he wouldn't walk off without her. "Company is requested and very much desired at this moment in time."

Ian caught a shimmer of light by the side of the path and realized what had distracted her. "Harken Lilies. You know, it's said that the dead can speak to us from the beyond through these. The only catch is that if you hear them speaking, you'll soon be near death yourself."

Marian laughed nervously. "I'd like to go from here now." She tightened her grip on his hand.

Ian blushed; thankful she couldn't see his face. "Yeah, of course. We're...," he pointed ahead, unable to find the rest of his sentence. "It's just a story, an old fable," he offered, hoping to calm the fear evident in her tight grip.

"An old fable," Marian repeated.

Ian nodded, pulling her close as he turned and made his way back up the trail, catching up to Benson.

"We have Harken Lilies at Steinigen, as well. But they don't glow like that," Marian said, squeezing his hand and closing her eyes, ignoring the faint glow that began to shine along the ground again, an image of her great fall from the walls of Steinigen replaying in her mind.

"A specialty of the Aurian Hills," Ian said. "Most people think the magic comes from the river that flows throughout the forest, emanating from Sorrow Falls. This was a really special place once."

"Is it true that pixies can communicate through them, as well?" she asked hesitantly, wondering if her tales from childhood would match reality.

"I haven't seen it firsthand, but I wouldn't be surprised if they could. Pixies are quite resourceful, but they abandoned much of civilization years ago. If you can find one that will talk to you, that's one hell of an achievement."

Marian's mind reached back, trying to recall Pight's jokes that she had become so enamored with. She giggled out loud as she remembered one punchline and walked right into Ian, who had stopped and turned to ask her something. Her forehead smacked painfully against his.

"You're not normal," Ian said, rubbing his forehead as he tried to dull the pain.

"And you are?" Marian chided, punching Ian in the arm for hurting her feelings.

"Ow!" Ian laughed through the pain. "It's a fair point, but you didn't have to hit me."

Marian was about to present a defense for her actions, but Benson growled at them to hurry up. The conversation faded, and Ian grabbed her hand once again, his touch gentle and warm against her skin. They made their way through the last of the trees and emerged in a clearing. There was a small log cabin resting in the center of it.

It's simple, she thought. And perfect, the voice answered back.

"Welcome to our home," Ian said, letting go of her hand as he walked toward the door.

"This is where you live?" Marian asked.

Benson had gone into the house to get a fire going and light a few candles while Ian and Marian waited outside to make certain no unwanted visitors had followed them.

"Sort of," Ian replied. "The potion shop is where we mainly stay now. My father built this years ago for when he wanted to get away from the world. Few people ever come this far into the forest. And not one of them could ever find this place if they tried," he said with a reassuring smile.

"Your father, he was a good man?" Marian asked timidly. Not knowing about his parents had already caused an awkward moment, and she didn't want to do that again.

"You've mentioned my father twice now," Ian said, his voice flat and tired. "I don't know why or how you heard of him, or your true purpose for coming to my shop."

"I—" Marian began to speak but was cut off.

"I don't want to look for answers now." Rubbing his eyes, Ian continued, "But in the morning I expect you to tell me the truth. Those men might do some damage to the potion shop, but nothing that can't be fixed. So if you wish for any more help from us, I'm going to need to hear the whole story. Not just what you want to tell us."

He gave her no chance to reply as he walked through the front door. The fireplace had been lit, and the warmth was spreading. There were no interior walls in the home; it was just a large open space with two beds—one large and one small—in a corner. Beautiful carvings and paintings lined the walls, almost completely obscuring the wood beneath. Many were of the forest and its inhabitants.

"Who painted these?" Marian asked in awe.

"My mother. She...," Ian paused, his words catching in his throat. "She was wonderful."

Marian watched his lip quiver before he turned his face from her. The candlelight made his eyes look wet with tears.

"She was just wonderful. My father as well. They were both just happy to exist, happy to live and be with us."

Marian wanted to say something sweet, something comforting, but she knew nothing of his mother or of what it was like to have one. "Would you like to tell me about them?" she asked, taking his hand in hers.

Ian shook off his sadness to give her a grand tour of their small home. He led her around the room, showing her each piece of art—and the minor imperfections he'd caused as a child when he'd bumped, grabbed, or pestered his mother while she was working.

Marian didn't hold back her laughter as he told her the kind of family stories she had always wanted to be a part of. The way his eyes lit up at those distant memories was enchanting to the child inside her who had longed for a family. She put her arm in his as they looked at the last few paintings.

Benson was rocking quietly in a chair, cradling a wood carving in his arms. Marian began walking toward him, but Ian grabbed her arm and motioned for her to stop.

"Not yet," he said softly.

"What's wrong?" she asked quietly, her smile fading.

Ian needed to take a few deep breaths before he could explain. "When my parents found Benson, he was just a cub. A normal cub, if you can believe it," he said with a smile. "For a bear and a human, we were practically the same age, and despite my parents' efforts to keep me safe, I couldn't resist going up to him to try and play. But he was so scared that he almost mauled me. My parents ran to protect me, ready to fight him back until they saw he wasn't angry but fearful."

"How could they tell?"

"It was easy to tell with the gaping wound in his side." Ian let the words sink in as Marian stared at Benson. "He and his family had been attacked by hunters looking to make some quick coin on their furs. My father cast a simple sleeping potion on Benson to calm him down, but it was my mother who saw the family he was still trying to protect until he joined them in death."

"What is the carving about?" Marian asked, thinking about the animal hides and displays in Redclave of the local hunters' trophies.

"It took some time for him to heal and become accustomed to our family. So to help him, my mother made him a carving of his family. She put an enchantment on it so that when he held it in his paws, the figures would move together in an embrace. She wanted to give him something to remember them by so that, even though he was with us, he would never forget his family. She wanted him to know their memory would always be safe with him and us."

They stood in silence for a few minutes. Then Ian motioned for her to follow him to the stove. Working out what provisions they had, he began to make a quick meal. There was no need to ask questions or pry for information. That would come soon enough in the morning. An aromatic smell began filling the cabin as Ian mixed the ingredients in a skillet on the stove, adding spices as they pricked his sense of smell.

Benson's demeanor had quickly perked up when his snout caught a waft of food, and he got up from his chair to join them. They ate quickly and hardly talked at all. The day had been long and wearisome.

Marian's worries seeped away for the moment. She felt more comfortable here than she had ever felt in her own home. Even if she only stayed one night, she knew she would go to sleep with a smile and hope for better times to come.

# Thirty

The subtle scent of lavender drifted through the room, filling Artimus's senses, relaxing the tension in her shoulders, and easing the pounding in her head. Her father had adored the practice of drinking tea at the end of a day to reward himself for still living, still trying. She remembered sitting at the edge of her seat as a child, moving her head closer and closer to his cup until there was no mistaking the wondrous odor that emanated from the tiny concoction. Some days it smelt of earthen tones, rich and dark, safe and strong. Other days it had the wispy and light sensation of a spring day, unconstrained and free, moving wherever the wind would take it. Artimus would close her eyes and feel safe beside her father, safe behind his shadow from the walls of Steinigen.

With a heavy sigh, Artimus forced the image of her father from her mind. She needed to focus.

"A cup for you," she said softly as she placed the tea before Erin, who smiled and mouthed the words Thank you. "And a cup for me," she added, pouring some hot brew for herself while staring at the old man, who was inhaling the scent of wildflower and licking his lips.

"It may not seem so, but I quite enjoy the delectable nature of a warm cup of tea as well," Paramel offered with a smile.

Artimus had not been impressed with the odd behavior of the old man since his sudden arrival from the pages of his journal, and she especially didn't appreciate his insistence that she join him on some sort of quest. Life was short enough, and she'd already lost many years to abuse and degradation. Artimus had no intention of running off to battle and dying without experiencing a full life, one that included moments that didn't cause her to cry or be filled with rage.

"There's more in the kettle if you would like to pour yourself a cup," she said as she took her place beside Erin, scooting her chair closer to her friend and farther away from the musky smell of the old man.

"I could use some stretching of my legs," Erin said to break the tension, giving her cup to Paramel as she stood up.

"You don't have legs," Artimus said, punching her in the thigh.

"Not all of us have features as accentuated as yours," Erin retorted with a smirk, running her finger along one of Artimus's ears.

Artimus's heart fluttered for a moment at the sensation, a confusing mixture of angry and passionate thoughts in her mind that left her staring blankly at the space Erin had left.

"She is quite the intoxicating mixture, isn't she,"

Paramel said, his eyes following Erin's path from the table to the kettle.

Artimus was taken aback, and the blood rushed to her cheeks as she stared into her cup. "Are you two...?" The question trailed off as she tried to find the words for something she could say aloud.

"No, my love is steadfast for another she merely reminds me of. My memories are more than enough to sustain that desire these days." Setting his cup down, Paramel leaned across the table, his eyes locking with Artimus's. "Sometimes the past is enough reason to fight for the future."

The pointed statement was a bit brash for Artimus's liking. She sharpened her glare at the old man as she put her cup down and leaned across the table too. "Sometimes avoiding the fight is the safest way to not die."

"This fight will not be avoided. You are its first soldier, leader of a reconnaissance mission, and an emissary to the forces who will soon come to destroy this place."

"I am not a soldier," Artimus warned, gripping her cup with both hands, trying not to shatter it.

"I agree that you do not want to be, but the choice has been made for you, I'm afraid. As it has also been made for these walls. Unwilling as they may be to endure a battle, it is coming for them no less. And should they fall, the Master will be one step closer to devouring Ephorus," Paramel sipped on the tea, his eyes slowly closing as he hummed in harmony with the gentle liquid replenishing his body.

"What would he have to gain by coming here?"

"Access," his voice grew curt, his eyes opening. "Something he lacked in his previous attempt. This place was built as a covenant between the people of this world and the Vorkyre; a place where we could meet, resolve disputes, and prosper amongst one another. It is where we bound the protective enchantments that keep Ephorus from falling into the darkness that has overcome so much of existence through time already. So long as these walls stand, the power of the Vorkyre will continue to protect the living. Hallenberry Halls was our final means to carry on the First Walkers' desire for their creation to continue in perpetuity. We failed in so many other areas they charged us with. I can only hope that my design will resolve previous failures."

"Oh, can it bring back the dead?" Artimus asked sarcastically, thinking of the culling of her people that had happened generations before her time. The few elves who managed to make it deep into the Aurian Hills were never seen again. Those who were less fortunate, like Artimus's parents, were sold into servitude. The Vorkyre had favored giving the brutish creatures more power and done little to protect the mystical species, hoping their connection to the land would be respected. The humans, goblins, dwarves, ogres, and their like may have agreed to not kill the elves, but they certainly would not consider them equal or respect them.

"Such lovely conversation," Erin chimed in as she took her seat. "Fill me in on who's dead and why."

Paramel chuckled as he leaned away from the table,

taking in the view of the library around them. Stacked high on countless shelves was knowledge gained from millennia of strife and struggle, persistence, and daring. But all of it lacked a single basic truth.

"This world is bound for destruction, my dear little elf," he began. "We fought to contain the destruction that continues to try and collapse this sliver of perceived prosperity, but the fight against reality is always lost."

"Then why fight it? Why not find someone to hide with and enjoy what you can before it's taken away again?" Artimus shouted, not realizing how loud she had gotten until her voice reverberated off the walls around them.

"Because we must," Erin said softly as she swirled the tea in her cup with her finger. "Because we have a chance to change the fate of life and death for the better. And because some things, and some people, are worth fighting and dying for."

It was a sweet sentiment, a kind idea that asked for more than Artimus was prepared to sacrifice. "But why me?"

"Because those who want to fight are often those who wish to do the harm we seek to stop. Our existence has one chance to continue, one path that leads away from destruction and chaos."

"This world is not chaos," Artimus scoffed, fighting back a slew of emotions. "I lived in squalor during my service to a mad man while others dined on fresh fruits and meats, their boots never so much as getting smeared with the dirt their horses galloped upon. I do not need a lecture in chaos, or death, or fear!" Slamming her hands on the table, Artimus watched as her tea spilled over the edge of her cup, pooling into a small well, worn into the wood by time.

Erin gently pulled Artimus close. They sat in silence, taking turns sipping what was left of their tea.

"A mistake was made in the beginning," Paramel began, breaking the silence. "An idea that flourished amongst the First Walkers was that to prevail over the impermanence of life, they needed to defeat death. They wanted eternity for all. They stripped the powers from the Pillars of time, and keep it for their creation, subduing the beasts in the process."

"What do you mean? What beasts?" Artimus asked incredulously, her interest piqued but her anger still near the surface.

"I mean the fabric of life is being torn apart by their ancient endeavor and because of it, the darkness is returning. There is but one way to repair this, and we need your help."

Artimus turned to Erin. "You knew he would ask this of me?"

"I knew he would," she replied. "And since meeting you, I knew he was right that there is no one else who can do what is needed."

There was too much roiling in Artimus's mind for her to focus on one thought or emotion. She struggled to understand as she blurted out, "So what am I to do now?"

"Now," Paramel began, his fingers lifting from the table, pulling the liquid from Artimus's cup into the air and letting it cascade back into place, "we begin your journey."

She stared at her tea as the ripples dissipated. "You just ruined my tea."

# THIRTY-ONE

The morning came too quickly. As the sun came through the windows of the small cabin, Marian woke up and fought off the urge to drift back under the covers and sleep. Ian and Benson were still fast asleep as she shrugged off the remnants of sleep. Her blouse was filthy, but then again so was she.

The sight in front of her was soothing. Ian's mouth hung ajar, his drool dripping profusely; Benson was at the center of a gathering of flies that had found their way into the cabin. She watched the bear haplessly swat at the flies gathering on his nose, missing all of them though managing to smack himself. He stirred, then settled back in his chair, unwilling to let an errant paw rouse him before necessary.

As she stood, Marian could feel the pressure and pain that had been building in her body since she jumped from the walls in Steinigen. The bed called to her, inviting her to lie down again and let her aches slip away in quiet slumber, but her mind would not slow down enough for her to enjoy such an endeavor.

Marian grabbed her bag and quietly pulled out the

journal and flipped through the pages. It had seemed as though the journal had spoken to her from its dusty place on her father's shelf. It knew it didn't belong there, just like her. But she had yet to find any meaning within the words written on its pages; its enchantments and poetry did nothing to ease her mind or provide a path to follow. She put it on the bed beside her and pushed her hair off her shoulders and neck so they were exposed to the sunlight. Her skin loved the heat.

She closed her eyes and focused only on the warmth. "Maybe I'm just crazy," she whispered to herself.

"A little, yes. But so was I," the voice whispered aloud. The pages of the journal fluttered to life as it started spinning, rising from the quilt and into the air

Marian fell off the bed and landed on the floor with a thud. She wasted no time as she scurried across the room, pressing her back against a wall, shivering while a chill ran up and down her spine. The journal had stopped moving, its pages open, resting quietly on top of the bed. She breathed in deep, hoping to calm her nerves, and checked to see if either Ian or Benson had roused. Neither had moved, their mouths still agape while they slept through her nervous breakdown.

"Okay, so we both know you're crazy, Marian, no need to prove it," she whispered to herself. She dug her nails into the wood behind her, trying to get a grip on reality when the voice called out to her again.

"Dance with me."

"Who are you?" Marian spoke softly, afraid to wake Ian or Benson for fear of them thinking her mad.

She felt the sudden warmth of a hand on one of

her shoulders; when she turned, she saw a woman in a flowered dress standing beside her, smiling and offering her other hand to dance. Marian let the woman take her hand and spin her around to the joyful sound of laughter. They swirled gracefully, spiraling toward and away from each other, their hair streaming with the rhythm of their feet.

It was wonderful until the voice called out from behind her.

"Please don't be this crazy just as I'm waking up. Give me at least some time to have a meal and a smoke before I have to deal with..." Ian waved his hand at her, "you."

Finding herself dancing alone, Marian blushed, her pale skin turning blood red. "She was here," she whispered, her eyes landing on a painting of a woman—the woman—who was dancing in a meadow of tall grass, a waterfall behind her.

"I'm sure she was," Ian said, riffling through his bag until he produced a pipe and a small bag of tobacco. He made quick work of lighting the moistened leaves and let a few puffs of smoke roll from the bowl, slowly making his way to Marian's side.

Marian desperately wanted to pull her eyes away from the woman, but she found herself walking toward the painting. She inched as close as she dared, staring at the woman. It was all she had wanted since she was a child, to be happy and free, and this woman was offering it.

She raised her hand to the painting, and the woman reached out to help her climb in. Marian's fingers touched the canvas, and the grooves in the paint appeared to give way to her hand. The woman was pleading with her to come join her, both arms waving for her to hurry. But the painting refused her entry, pushing back against her hand until she could feel its cold and callous surface. Her fingers could not push into the enchanted world any more than they could push through the wooden walls holding the painting up.

The lady of the waterfall backed away, a sullen look in her eyes. No longer dancing or laughing, she slowly walked out of sight.

"Please," Marian whispered. "Come back."

Tears began to fall down her cheeks as she hoped her words would convince the beautiful woman to return, but she was gone.

"These paintings can be cruel," Ian said rather somberly, the sweet and fruity scent from his tobacco cutting through her sadness.

A wave of embarrassment swept over Marian. She avoided his gaze and went toward the beds, only to find herself swaddled in a massive bear hug.

"Don't be ashamed. I swear I've heard her calling for me from these paintings before, too. Never can seem to find her, though." Ian's words were laced with disappointment as he made his way to the door.

Benson grumbled something under his breath and gave Ian a gentle shove.

"I cook dinner, you cook breakfast. That's the deal," Ian grumbled in return while stepping into the fresh air and sunshine outside their cabin. "You can join me if you'd like," he called out to Marian.

Marian smiled at Benson when he nodded for her to follow Ian. He seemed content to be alone with the food, and she could certainly use something bright in her life at this moment.

# Thirty-Two

Nance and his warlocks rode on the back of cloaked horses, the blazing emblem of Steinigen on their helmets. The small flames licked at the low hanging leaves as they rode past, casting a sinister glow that had earned them the name Muspelheim, the walking fire, ages before during the reign of his ancestors – a time when Steinigen would not be content to simply survive. Muspelheim rode in the darkness by the dozens; small in numbers, but with a fury of power to unleash at will.

Having set his mind on Crescent City, Nance was traveling south, following the minor villages and hovels that littered the banks of the Gallen River. As they advanced into a small settlement, startling those gathered for a meal under the stars, the people began to cry and run from the ghastly apparitions coming toward them. Nance smiled, gripping the reins of his horse, aching to use the Hearthwood that was fitted to his hand like a glove.

It was time to proclaim his dominance, time to invite the people of Ephorus to bow before him. In generations past, Ephorus had been ruled by kings, who presided over circumscribed territories, his ancestors being granted Steinigen in a costly deal with the Vorkyre. Greed and lust had brought many to their knees without intervention, but Nance had exploited the few that remained when he convinced his father to let him lead the charge to take control. Inviting the most wretched of the last Kings to join in his service, Nance convinced Tomas McCordian, the dying King of Crescent City, that he could reign undisputed over his peers if he waged war on them with Nance. With McCordian's men marching north from Crescent City, and Nance maneuvering south from Steinigen, they forced their prey to fight or surrender.

Months of blood lust followed, destroying much of Ephorus in Nance's first campaign to seize power. But the fighting taxed his abilities and shrank Steinigen's forces. After the war, Nance heeded the advice of his sister Maven and seated McCordian on the throne as the single King of Ephorus while he rested. The two manipulated McCordian into obedience to a single authority, the Master of Steinigen. They had intended to depose their father and split the Kingdom between them, but Nance couldn't resist the craving of power – couldn't resist betraying those who secured his reign. He could never, and would never, share with another. Ephorus belonged to Nance now, and it was time the people bent their knees.

Nance dismounted at the front of his horde, his eyes lit by the flame burning within him, searching for a potential victim. He would not be able to rest his feet upon the charred ground of Crescent City for a few more days, but he would make sure they knew he was coming.

"We offer no ill will!" a man shouted, standing tall among a cowering group of people. "Please take what you need and be on your way."

He stood before Muspelheim and the Master, meager but steadfast. The dirt and sunburnt skin gave easy hints to the time he must spend working the fields surrounding their village. Life had given him and his people little, and would offer no more.

An empathetic man may have summoned pity for the frightened people surrounding him, but Nance saw only prey. Of all the villagers cowering before them, Nance estimated that only four wouldn't run immediately if he were to attack. He felt some semblance of respect for the ones who recognized death when it walked toward them and desired to fight back.

"I commend you," he said, his voice was raspy as flames flickered from his mouth. "Not many would stand in our way." With a wicked smile, Nance walked over to the man. The flames in his eyes turned bright blue. Nance offered him a hand to shake, chuckling as three of the men behind him scattered, only to find they were surrounded by Sever and his warlocks. "Shake my hand," Nance said as a flame sparked in his palm and stretched to his elbow.

Beneath the flame, the man could see a crude wooden construction that fit the Master's hand and fingers like a glove. Voices called out from it, hissing through flames, begging him to join them. He saw no means of escape. Villagers cried in the distance as fires erupted in their homes. The warlocks had set to their task and were leveling the village and its inhabitants according to their command: no mercy, no one spared, and leave the mark of Steinigen on all of the bodies.

"Will you spare me and mine?" the man asked as he watched the warlocks moving toward his home, the shouts of his wife and children piercing the night air.

He's weak, the voice hissed in Nance's thoughts. Let us devour him.

Nance's lips curled with delight. "We did not stop here for a drink and a bed. I need soldiers," he said. "My war has just begun and my army awaits at Crescent City. Lay waste to as many villages and their inhabitants as possible before I return, and I will grant you and yours their safety."

His neighbors were dying. His wife and child were being dragged from their home. "Agreed," he shouted, reaching for Nance's hand, gripping it tight.

The man's face contorted instantly from the searing pain. Underneath the skin of his arm, the veins were bubbling and engorged. A black line shot up his arm, cracking through his skin, and clawing through his chest and neck until it reached his head. The man's eyes went black as his body convulsed and the echo of his screams howled from his flame-filled mouth.

You belong to us now! the voices shouted in his mind, dark ooze trickling from his lower lip to the ground below.

Nance watched the ooze smother the grass. "The world shall be covered in the death that it deserves," he mused, his cackle breaking free from his chest and spreading over the sound of flames and devastation. He released the man's hands and turned to Sever who stood patiently waiting with his sword drawn.

"Slow and painful for the cowards," Nance said with a wave of his hand. Sever smiled as he grabbed the closest man and dragged him past the burning embers and into a line alongside the others. "Now," Nance turned his attention back to the man before him, "which of these men are you willing to sacrifice to prove your loyalty?" Taking the sword from his sheath, Nance held it out, his laughter gone and his eyes burning red with bloodlust.

The world turned quiet around them as Nance lifted his right hand high in a fist, a signal to his horde to hold. He stared eagerly into the man's eyes. It took so little to turn a good man into a murderer, and Nance relished the moment. The man looked at the sword in Nance's hand. Sever was knocking villagers to their knees, ignoring their pleas for mercy, readying them for the slaughter.

"All of them," the man replied without emotion.

"Good answer," Nance laughed as he clasped his hands, causing a massive spark. "Finish them. I want you to be my calling card. I want all the people of Ephorus to know that we will be coming, and you, our messenger, shall be the sight they see. Find your neighbors and poison the souls of the strong so they shall be ripe for my return. Let the rest find death to be an ungraceful release from their daily struggles."

"I will bend the kne—," said a villager, standing up,

hoping his life would be spared, but the Master's newly appointed messenger quickly ran his sword through him.

"It will be done," the messenger said, pushing his former neighbor's quivering body off the blade of his sword before bending a knee to the Master.

The voices hissed from the Hearthwood, pleading for more souls to harvest. Nance turned and called out for Sever.

"Yes, sir," Sever sprang to his side.

Nance lifted his hand, staring at the Hearthwood glove as he stretched out his fingers then balled them into a fist, determined to fulfill the voices' request. "Let us not hesitate and waste time amongst the damned. Ready Muspelheim, and let's be on our way. I wish to continue spreading darkness and fire across the world."

# Thirty-Three

Ian took his first long drag of the day from his pipe, relishing the tobacco's aroma while he watched the woods of the Aurian Hills come to life with the morning light. Inside the cabin, Benson was diligently collecting whatever edible morsels he could scrape together to feed three hungry mouths. Mostly his own, but he wanted to have something for Ian and Marian as well.

"Don't get your hopes up," Ian snickered as he caught Marian looking in on Benson. "He's a horrible cook, but it keeps him occupied and lets me ease into the morning."

Marian was sitting quietly on the porch beside Ian, her mind preoccupied while her eyes continued to glance around. Ian imagined she was thinking about the woman in the painting. He mused on life's wondrous ability to bring pain from beauty, taking another drag from his pipe, watching the smoke slowly disappear from existence as he exhaled.

"There was a voice inside my head," Marian whispered, glancing at him then turning her eyes away. "She... It guided me at times."

"You mean your conscience?" Ian said. "That's not abnormal. I find myself in conversation with my mind quite often."

Marian laughed. Ian saw her mouth contort as if her words were arguing among themselves to decide which ones would come out.

"Maybe I'm crazy," she said sadly, her shoulders slumping.

"That's a definite," Ian chimed in with a smile. "But I'm not one to cast shame over such a mental state, seeing as my best friend is a bear that only I seem to be able to speak with."

Marian smiled. She listened to Benson grumbling away in the cabin. Ian watched her closely.

"I don't think you're a bad person," he said after taking a drag from his pipe. "I'm not keen on the way you introduced yourself to us, but I don't feel like you're someone I can't trust."

"Thank you." Marian's voice was hardly more than a whisper as she watched a cloud roll in over the trees, blocking the light of the sun.

"What is it you wanted from my shop?" he asked.

"I'd rather not say," she answered.

"I'd rather not ask, but you brought this situation to me. I didn't bring it to you." He wasn't scolding her, exactly, but he wasn't giving in.

"No."

Caught off-guard, Ian took a moment to prepare his response.

"That wasn't really a yes or no kind of a question. I was hoping for an explanation. Not necessarily an entire life story, but maybe a synopsis. Kind of like—"

Marian interrupted him. "No, as in, no, I did not know your parents. I didn't even know about your shop until a few days ago when I was being accosted in Redclave. Before I was taken to jail—"

Benson growled and Ian laughed. Marian was confused. "What did the bear say?"

"He called you a jailbird and said that breakfast will be ready soon. But please go on."

Marian shot an angry glance at the bear, but Benson didn't notice. "Before I was wrongfully taken to jail," she said, loud enough for the bear to hear, "I had a brief interlude with a rather strange dwarf. She told me she knew who I was and what I was planning, and that, if I had any wish of succeeding, I would need to find Ori and Penelope's potion shop. And, the thing is...," she hesitated, searching for words that did not make her appear insane, "this wasn't the first time this happened. I had a voice, and even pixies, guiding me even before I ran into the dwarf who sent me here."

Maybe she is crazy, Ian thought. "Did you ask why?" he said.

"Ask who?" Marian looked confused.

"Any of them. If they were all guiding you, did you happen to ask them why?"

"Well, no. I didn't... I just..." Her words trailed off. "I don't know why I didn't." Marian's voice was soft. "For years now, there's been a voice helping me, and I've always trusted her, so when she told me to..."

"Told you to what?" Ian asked, leaning forward in his chair.

"She told me to 'jump little darling, and'—"

"Don't be afraid to fly," Ian whispered.

They stared at each other.

"What's in that journal on the bed?" Ian asked.

"A lot," Marian muttered. "It's a mixture of spells, poetry, drawings, and enchantments."

"I'd like to see it if you don't mind?" Ian asked, but he wasn't planning to take no for an answer. He was just hoping it wouldn't come to that.

Marian stared at him. Her lips moved as she debated how much she trusted him.

"Yeah, sure," she finally answered as she got up to fetch it from the bed.

"No need to get up," Ian said as Benson leaned through the doorway and handed him the journal.

"At least you feigned an attempt to be civil," Marian said.

Benson growled at her, and she retorted, "I am not a jailbird!"

"Did you steal this?" Ian said sharply, interrupting their bickering.

"No!" she said. "Well, maybe. I don't know. Possibly." Marian began to lose confidence in her initial response. "It was hidden in my father's study, covered in dust on one of the shelves. Where he got it from, I'm not sure. You need to believe that something or someone spoke to me through this journal and told me to leave, to trust that help would come to guide me on my quest."

The shape of the letters, the complex ideas, the poetic language: Ian had immediately recognized them.

"The purpose of the journal, I'm not entirely sure of," he said. "But the who—that I know for certain. It's my mother's."

Marian's heart raced as she leaped from her chair and grabbed Ian's arm. He blushed at the warmth of her touch.

Benson suddenly appeared and grabbed the journal from Ian's hand. "I believe it's time to carry on this conversation over some food." He headed back inside.

Ian got up and said, "I'll tell you more about my parent's work while we eat, and what I've learned from my father's journal." He reached for her hand and pulled her toward the door.

"Do you have it?" Marian asked, her hand gripping his.

"Of course," he said, thinking about the sensation of holding her hand. "And there's a third journal as well, but I don't have that one."

"Let's see your father's journal!" Marian exclaimed.

"Definitely. But there's just one tiny problem we may have in doing that."

Benson roared impatiently and slammed his spoon on the table. Ian motioned for him to go ahead and start eating, and the bear began devouring his food.

The joy vanished from Marian's eyes as she realized what Ian meant. "It's back at the potion shop, isn't it?"

"Food first," Ian answered.

"We have to go back, don't we?"

Ian smiled. "But first we'll eat," he said.

# THIRTY-FOUR

"Try again!" Paramel shouted at Artimus. "There is very little time left, and you must be ready!"

"Ready for what?" she shouted back, getting angry glances from the nearby scribes.

The Elders had been obliged by their relationship with the Vorkyre to allow Paramel to take Artimus under his tutelage. It was considered payment for the protection he had provided for their travels over the years, though those days had ended a long time ago. His constant disruptions, however, frustrated them, and they took it out on Artimus.

"You'll get nowhere shouting at each other," Erin said, perched atop the bookcase, stretching out her wings. It was exhausting to watch them bicker for hours.

"Owls aren't always so wise, you know," Paramel said teasingly. "I've known quite a few in my day to be imbeciles."

"Coming from the man who's managed to forget more in his life than he possibly could have learned," she hooted, flying to the floor and shifting into her human form. "What's wrong?" she asked Artimus.

"Other than his ceaseless nagging?" Artimus said, shooting him a dirty look. "I just don't...I don't understand any of this. The script in this journal is nearly illegible, yet I'm supposed to somehow repeat it while meditating as this crass imbecile shouts at me."

"But it is within you, my dear," Paramel interrupted. "I can see it as clear as I can see the sun! The script is part of your existence. You can control the power wrested away from time."

"It's been raining for days, it's well after midnight, and what you just said makes no sense!" Artimus shouted as she stomped away with Erin in tow.

"Actually, it's morning again," Erin said with a smile.

"I can see the sun shining behind the clouds as I can see your abilities shining through your fog of doubt," Paramel's voice rang out.

"You are the embodiment of idiocy!" Artimus's voice echoed off the walls around them, her fists balled in rage.

Dropping to the floor, Artimus stared at the ceiling of the library. The wooden beams appeared to stretch on forever. She was still responsible for cleaning all the chandeliers and replacing all the candles as needed, and she could see several wicks burning out. Evidently, in addition to her new, dramatic responsibilities, the world still expected her to tend to its tedious tasks.

"I thought I'd have a chance to be normal," Artimus said to Erin, who was always ready to offer comfort. "I do not understand why this is happening and why I'm supposed to be a part of it. If existence is crumbling at the seams, what am I going to be able to do to stop it?"

Erin knelt beside her. "Is he an old and crazy man? Without a doubt," she said. "But I believe him. And no matter what we want, the world is in motion and will not stop for us."

"Why, though?" Artimus snapped. "It doesn't sound real. It doesn't make sense."

"And it never will, that's why the First Walkers couldn't accept the boundaries of creation. Life is tenuous and death is inevitable: that's what they sought to change, and it's cost us all a chance at peace. Paramel's the last of the Vorkyre, and the knowledge he holds within that senile brain is still more than what's in every journal and scroll in this library. So when he speaks of your potential, when he speaks of the impending darkness, I have to believe him."

"But how does that make any of this acceptable or believable? How am I supposed to help simply because he's," she stopped and looked around, "because he's old and dying?"

"I am not dying yet," Paramel said, appearing above them. "And I'm not training you to help me, little elf. I'm training you to replace me. I just need you to light the fire that I cannot reach. And the way to do so is by embracing what you are to become."

"Privacy, please!" Erin shooed him away. "Artimus, if you were an incompetent, idiotic, incapable dunce, I would not have befriended you."

"You make me feel ever so special, Erin."

"It's just my natural charm," she said, fluttering her

eyes.

"If this is so important, then why don't you do it? You're a shape-shifter. You have more power than I do."

"I can change myself, yes. But you," she grabbed Artimus and pulled her to her feet. "The fates chose you to change the world, to set right the errors of the First Walkers' creation. I think that's worth training for."

Artimus stared at Erin and crossed her arms.

"Was that a little too much?"

"I almost vomited."

"Me too," Erin said with a laugh. She pulled Artimus behind a bookcase. "Things are going to get much worse soon. The venom of time, in its natural progression, goes unnoticed amongst the aging of the living things around us, aiding in the decay of the past." Erin let the fingers of her hand shift to her darkened state, resting above Artimus's skin. "When the First Walkers chose to defy time, to destroy the distinctions between the realms, the venom leaked through the cracks they could not fill."

Gently swaying her outstretched arm, the shadowy fingers burned and scraped Artimus's skin, causing her to flinch.

"What did you do?" Artimus demanded, looking at her arm, expecting to see her skin peeled away, but thankful it was unscathed.

"I showed you what I'm made of; what the world beyond the Logi Mountains has become. I learned to subdue the venom's call to darkness, but this fight is against those who will struggle to unleash the venom, letting it consume all of life."

"I've been struggling since I was a child," Artimus said, watching as Erin shifted her hand back to the beautiful pale skin she had become accustomed to gazing at.

"Which is why you're invaluable. Whatever it is he sees in you, it is needed and will be tested. Many people are going to die in Ephorus before this is completed. Some things are already set in motion that cannot be stopped, but they can be mitigated. We can make life worth living here so that the fear of what comes next can slowly slip away. The First Walkers were scared of the darkness beyond life, scared of not being able to carry on thinking and existing and it has cost us all dearly, and not just those who are living. Existence is beautiful, but only when it's left to achieve its natural progression."

"Am I going to die?" Artimus asked, her voice trembling.

"Yes. If you choose not to help, certainly it will come quicker. If you stand and fight with us, we may live to see many more years together."

"Such a stark and amazing difference between the two options."

Erin laughed as she hugged Artimus. "We need you, Artimus. Death is inevitable, even for Paramel and me, but that's worth fighting for as well."

"But what's going to happen?" Artimus asked. Right then, Paramel stepped through the bookcase and stepped through Artimus.

"That was so gross and so completely unnecessary!" Artimus screamed, her body shivering.

"My apologies," the old man answered. "But we have little time left to prepare, and I need to know if you'll be joining our quaint little adventure to save this side of existence."

Artimus took a deep breath and trudged back to the table where the journal was lying open, its near-impenetrable scrawl mocking her. It was just too much to take in at once.

"If we're going to do this, can we at least do it in a way that I feel I can learn?"

"She's got a point, Paramel," Erin added. "If the spark is in there, she'll have to light it."

"Then we shall send her into the darkness so she can find her light," he said, his mischievous smile scaring them.

"What does that mean?" Artimus asked with dread.

Paramel closed his eyes and sucked in the air around him. The pages of the journal began to flap back and forth as it danced atop the table.

"What did you just do?" Artimus shouted as she tried to pin the journal down, the floor shaking beneath her.

"Do you think maybe this is a bit too much?" Erin snapped at Paramel, grabbing Artimus's hand.

Artimus gripped Erin's outstretched hand and tried to say something, but her words were caught in her throat, trapped by a powerful force within that was sucking her into another reality. Her grip loosened and she could feel the cold air swirling around her.

-~-

The smell roused Artimus, the pungent stench of sulfur. She wanted to scream, but nothing would come out of her mouth. Defenseless and exposed, she could feel countless eyes watching her, hating her. She crawled on the ground, her knees scraping against the pebbles and sand beneath her while her eyes fought to adjust to the soft green light. There was something behind her.

She began to shiver when she saw the faces, their features covered in shadows. They were screaming for relief, pleading for mercy, and asking her to sacrifice herself so they could be spared. Their screams made her feel insane. The stones beneath her feet shifted and slid while she fought to keep her balance. Tears flooded her eyes. She tried to wipe them away but found herself in severe pain. The tears ripped open her skin on contact, penetrating her flesh and entering her bloodstream. It was all too much, and she felt herself letting go of everything.

Artimus opened her eyes and found herself bathed in the soft green light. The voices and screams were far behind her, locked in darkness. "What did he do to me?" she asked as she sat up in a pool of water.

"I don't know, but you shouldn't be here in this form."

Artimus tried to find where the voice was coming from, but the green light consumed her, and the world around her vanished once again.

# Thirty-Five

Benson's extended protest against returning to the shop before the trackers had left lost them the remaining cool hours of the morning, and the sun had gotten high enough above them to cast its heat on every acre of woods they would need to trudge through. The thought of armed conflict made Benson want to curl up in his chair and sleep. Ian could understand the sentiment; a full stomach, an increasingly warm day, and a group of henchmen threatening to murder you was a great reason to stay inside. But seeing his mother's journal had sparked a vague memory in Ian. He needed to see his parent's journals together, to see if any answers came from joining what had been separated. His father loved codes and secret messages, filling pages of his journal with incomplete ideas that made no sense on their own. But with Marian's—or more precisely, his mother's—journal, he might be able to find out what had truly happened to them before they vanished.

Making sure to arm themselves with whatever potions and supplies they had, the three steeled their courage and started on their way, exiting the cabin and entering the heat of the late morning air. Benson's unease was somewhat satiated by the copious amounts of snacks Ian encouraged him to bring.

"Are you familiar with using potions to fight?" Ian asked Marian, who was cinching her uncomfortably heavy bag, stuffed with provisions.

"I can if needed," Marian answered as she snapped her fingers, sparking flames in her hands. "But I prefer to play with fire."

Benson pushed Ian out of the way so he could stare at Marian's flaming fingers.

"It's not that impressive," Ian said, trying not to show his fascination.

They had gotten a glimpse of her abilities when she burned through the ropes, but this display was much more powerful.

Marian clasped her hands and held them to her mouth. She took a deep inhalation, opened her hands to show the flames were gone, then exhaled a torrent of fire into the sky. Benson charged her, pawing at her mouth, trying to see where the fire came from.

"Benson!" Ian shouted.

The bear turned around, wondering if Ian was going to tell him how the trick worked.

"It's not a trick, buddy. She's just that powerful." He smiled at Marian. She returned the favor, and he wasn't sure if she was blushing or if her cheeks were hot from the fire. He motioned for them to follow him.

"Didn't we just come from there?" Marian asked, pointing to some small trees she recognized from the night before.

Ian kept going. "Walk the same trail over and over and it becomes recognizable to all who pass by."

Benson grumbled his approval as he nudged Marian to stay in line, making sure she didn't stray from their sight. Marian spotted a patch of Harken Lilies as they entered the thick green forest, but she averted her eyes. She wasn't going to make the same mistake twice.

-~-

Marian could barely feel the warmth of the sun slipping through the gaps in the trees. Her fear of the forest still made her jump whenever she heard the sound of a stray limb cracking. Maybe they were all just stories, she thought, recalling the creatures she had read about as a child. Or maybe you're the monster creeping 'round that everyone fears, a voice hissed in her mind. The cruel words caught her off-guard, but the bear growled something over her shoulder, and Ian responded.

"No, but that would be very helpful if it did."

"Huh?" Marian said, trying to focus on the moment.

"He asked if I had thought the dragon was real this time and ate the three trackers outside the shop."

"Oh," Marian mused. "That would have been very helpful."

The three carried on in silence until they heard the distant sound of rushing water. With the adrenaline coursing through her body the night before, Marian hadn't noticed any signs of water, and she was curious about it.

"It's a wide creek that flows from Sorrow Falls," Ian said. "It is a beautiful place, the creek and the falls, but we don't go there unless we have to."

"Why?" she asked.

Benson grumbled his disapproval from the rear, and Ian shook his head in agreement. Marian cleared her throat loudly to remind Ian that a translation was required.

"Long story. Old acquaintances turned new rivals from a harmless prank they took too seriously."

Marian's pale skin turned even paler at the thought of more enemies. "Who's 'they,' and will we need to fight them too?" A small spark lifted from the index finger of her right hand.

"Put your fire away before you burn the world down," Ian said, smacking her hand. "It was just some river gnomes, and they've probably forgotten all about it by now. So let's leave the more murdery aspects of your nature on the inside and save them for when they might be useful."

Marian fought the urge to strike her irritating accomplice. She took a deep breath and let the air tame the fire inside her, exhaling a long, mesmerizing trail of smoke. Her eyes fixated on the smoke, her thoughts departing from reality as she stumbled over them, unable to keep track of where they led her. Time disappeared into the haze.

She drifted into a different realm, surrounded by the swirling smoke and the sound of rushing water. Her words stuck in her throat as the smoke dissipated, revealing a drastically different landscape than the one she had anticipated. She was in the company of another woman, who was sitting with her beside a waterfall. There was an odd familiarity with the woman, but all Marian could focus on at the moment was that Ian and Benson had disappeared.

Marian looked up at the water pouring down. She was sitting on a pile of rocks, yards away from the shore somehow. She tried to stand up, but a crushing weight held her down.

"Do not fear," the woman whispered to Marian as she tried to move.

"Now is not the time to go crazy, Marian," she yelled at herself, her voice fighting its way through the fear. She couldn't get up from the rocks. Her mind was beginning to crack from the pressure until a hand came down on her head, caressing her hair.

"You are all right here, child," she spoke again, her voice calm and caring.

In an instant, the pressure was relieved. She could still see the waterfall, but she couldn't hear it. Marian caught a glimpse of the woman's floral dress, recognizing her instantly.

"How?" was all she could manage to say. "Why do you talk to me?"

The woman knelt beside her and wrapped Marian in her arms. "All in time. We will meet soon, but for now, take caution and safeguard your spirit. I did not bring you here. There is another lurking, and I cannot control what she is about to do."

"What do you—" Marian's question was cut short when the woman disappeared.

The sound of the water came back, but now it was only a slow drip. The beautiful water had turned into a bubbling black ooze. The world had turned gray; the flowers, the grass, the trees were all slowly dying.

"How lovely to see you again," a voice hissed with a trail of laughter.

"Maven," Marian whispered in fear.

She turned around and saw Aunt Maven peering into her eyes as she reached for Marian's shoulders, her nails piercing Marian's skin. Looking down, Marian could feel her veins boiling throughout her body. She tried to scream, but her throat was full of black ooze that dripped out of her mouth. Her eyes shut tight as the pain became unbearable.

"Do not disappoint me, my child," Maven hissed, releasing her grip and disappearing. "I would hate to have to destroy my creation."

Marian forced her eyes open to find Benson and Ian were pulling her into an upright position.

"Let's try not to get lost in any more daydreams when we're on our way to face off against a bunch of bad guys, okay?" Ian said.

Marian looked around to see if they were even close to a waterfall, but she saw only some Harken Lilies among the trees.

"Yeah, okay," she said as she grabbed Ian's hand. She was desperate to tell him what she had just experienced, but she didn't know how to say it. After a short silence, she told him to lead the way as she held tight to his hand.

# THIRTY-SIX

"I'm not sure I've ever woken up in so much filth before," Pight complained, trying to remove the dust and muck from her wings.

The two had been roused minutes before by a growing clamor outside the shop. The trackers' reinforcements had arrived.

"You could see if one of those fine creatures would allow you to sleep in their hovel for the night," Inibri said, her mood boosted by the thought of gaining some much-needed rest.

"I would rather die," Pight said. She grimaced as she watched an ogre relieve himself of his bodily waste without so much as turning away from the group. "Their existence does not seem necessary!" she said, trying not to scream.

"Pace yourself, my dear. It's going to be a long day."

Unable to watch the horde any longer, Pight fluttered off. Inibri sighed, listening to the lead tracker's instructions. Only a small group was to be sent into the woods to try and find the path the criminals had taken through the forest; the rest would remain on guard.

Why don't you all just leave? Inibri thought.

The horde formed a perimeter around the shop as if they knew the trio would be returning shortly and they were preparing for a confrontation.

"I do not understand why humans build their little hovels to avoid sleeping in the dirt and yet they let so much of it come in," Pight said as Inibri fluttered down in a panic, grabbing her arm and dragging her across the floor. "Wha—" Pight's question was cut off when Inibri planted her hand firmly across her mouth.

Inibri pulled Pight under the desk, and the door burst open.

"Ceril. Arman," a man said. "Check for traps and hidden exits. When they return, I want no chance of escape."

"And how are we supposed to find their traps without suffering permanent or irreversible damage, Lyco?" Ceril asked from the doorway, gingerly peering in.

"I do not care, but get it done," Lyco grumbled.

Pight found a small crack in the desk and motioned for Inibri to join her.

"In that case," Arman spoke up, walking past Ceril with a minuscule goblin in each hand.

Pight and Inibri watched as Arman slowly made his way down the aisles, the squirming, unhappy goblins his protection if something were to happen. When Arman got to the stairwell, he hurled one of the goblins down it to see if it triggered any traps.

"I think we're secure," he said with a smile, still gripping the second goblin in his hand.

"Well, what are you gonna do with that one then?"

Ceril asked.

Arman shrugged, then tossed the goblin after its counterpart. They waited briefly for the impact, but then panicked and ran for the exit.

"Trap triggered!" they shouted, bursting into the open air.

Pight saw a puff of blue smoke in the air by the stairwell and turned to Inibri. Her partner's gaze was firmly planted on Lyco, who stood just outside the door, letting the smoke trail past him.

"What's wrong?" Pight whispered in her ear.

"I've seen a look like that before," she answered. "His heart is poisoned, and his quest for destruction is absolute."

"Then we will stop him." Pight placed her hand on Inibri's shoulder for reassurance.

"No," Inibri said, pulling away from her touch. "We will leave."

"What?" Pight snapped. "What is any of this for if we abandon her?"

"It is not our job to fight her battles, just to guide her. There are no words that will stop this clash today, so we must move on to our next task."

"We're not even going to try and trick them?"

Inibri cautioned herself, feeling a rumbling of anger within her. Pight's questions were valid, but she was too inexperienced to know her own flaws. "There is nothing in the Aurian Hills for them. She must come out and it is far safer for them to remain on the outskirts and hunt her down here. They will not be baited out of this situation."

"And if they die?"

"We will all die someday," Inibri said softly as she headed for the chimney. "Our best purpose until then is to find Paramel and inform him that Marian met with the son of Ori and Penelope as planned."

# Thirty-Seven

The day was trailing away from them, and Marian could see the sun cresting in the sky for the day. They had hoped to be back at the shop by now but every noise had sent them plunging into the nearby bushes. The constant stress left Marian questioning their ability to succeed at such a daunting task. Her negative thoughts started to eke their way out as she mumbled her doubts aloud.

"Would you like some company in your conversation, or are you and your thoughts okay on your own?" Ian asked.

Marian blushed, realizing she had been talking to herself in front of them.

"It's a condition, shut up! And sorry," she said, trying to hide the embarrassment burning on her face. "Never got used to having company for more than a few minutes at a time, so I made my own."

"No worries," Ian said, hoping his doubts were hidden. "Well, I do have some, to be honest, we just don't have time to address them right now. So, care to let us know what you're thinking about?"

Benson began giggling behind her, further adding to her embarrassment.

"I'm trying to figure out what the hell any of this is going to lead to and what comes next," she said, letting her frustrations show. "It's like I've lost my guiding voice, and now I'm just wandering around the woods hoping to find the right thing to do."

"It feels like that because it is that," Ian said. "We have a vague plan based around the certainty that your father has a very specific and insidious plan."

"Where does your certainty come from?"

"We haven't lived with certainty for years. No reason to start now."

Benson smirked, mumbling something to Ian, who shouted back to him, "I know, right? Just assume there's no plan. As if we're just a couple of traipsing idiots." They were moving quickly, and Marian had to speed up to stay with them.

"So, what is your vague plan?"

Benson grumbled his disapproval at Ian.

"If only, buddy," he laughed out.

Marian grabbed Benson and spun him around to face her. Her eyes went dark as flames leaped out from them, smoke creeping out of her open mouth. Benson howled in fear and fell over backward. He got up and began scrambling away to hide behind the nearest tree.

Erupting in laughter, Marian was ecstatic not to be on the receiving end of their ridicule, but then she began snorting. She had never heard herself snort so loudly before, and she didn't like it. She looked at Ian, her eyes still glowing with fire, and insisted, "That never happened."

"Fix the bear you just broke, and my memory goes blank on your snorting," he offered with a smile as he pointed to his cowering cohort.

Marian walked over to Benson, who was shaking vigorously behind a young evergreen that was barely tall enough to hide a raccoon. She let the flames die out, her eyes returning to normal, the last puff of smoke curling from her lips toward the treetops. She wrapped her arms tightly around the bear, nearly getting her fingertips to touch.

Benson stayed rigid in her arms until his desire for affection took over. His body softened, and he dared to check her eyes for flames, pawing at her face until he was content that she wasn't hiding them anywhere. Satisfied, he wrapped his arms around her and squeezed while he licked her face adoringly.

"I believe you are forgiven," Ian laughed.

Trapped in his embrace, Marian relented. "Anyway, shall we return to the vague plan?"

"You know, considering I've only had about half a day to wrap my brain around all this, you should speak of the vagueness with much more respect and gratitude. And I don't want to point fingers here," he paused, waiting for Benson to release his grip so both of them could point at her, "but some people have had more time than others to make plans."

"Sorry about that. Again."

"As you should be," he said. "However, we shall graciously forgive you. And after we recover my father's journal, we shall make our way to the third."

"Wait," Marian's hands raised, her eyes wide as she remembered the third journal. "What's the third? Whose is the third? And where is the third?"

"Wow. Your conversational skills are not on par with being a savior of our humble world," Ian laughed.

"Yeah, I suck at talking to people. Back to the topic," Marian scoffed.

"It's the journal of an old crackpot who used to get me in a lot of trouble with my parents when I was a kid. He was always writing in his book when he wasn't teaching me new tricks, or convincing my parents to follow him into the woods for days on end."

"You think he still has it?"

"I can't be sure, but it's the best path we have to take," Ian said with a sigh. "He seemed to forget we existed after my parent's disappeared, so we haven't seen him in years."

Marian began to ask a question, but Benson placed his paw over her mouth. She spun around, annoyed, but before she could say anything, he pointed past Ian. A group of men was creeping toward them through the trees. Benson had to yank her into the bushes to keep them from being seen.

The group was comprised of three men, armed like typical ruffians with swords, daggers, and hunting bows. They appeared to have an awful sense of hygiene, as well. The leader looked fierce, but the other two must have been random mercenaries for hire—they were only in it for the coin. They traveled past without noticing them as Benson began whispering to Ian.

"Speak for yourself, buddy. You're not that much

better."

"What's wrong?" Marian asked.

"He thinks your stench might give us away. Apparently, your hair smells like a rotting toadstool."

Marian shot a deadly stare at both of them, and Benson averted his eyes, following the flight path of a blue and gold butterfly dancing along with the breeze.

"A rotting toadstool," Marian said slowly and menacingly.

"His words, not mine." Ian held up his hands in surrender, watching a flame lap along the edges of her fists and contemplating who was most likely to kill him today – Marian or the Master's henchman.

In what he felt was an attempt to apologize, Benson growled from a cowering position. Ian did not translate.

"What did the bear say?"

"I don't want to repeat it. We've kind of got some issues to deal wi—"

"I don't care! What did the bear say?" the flames erupted in her palms as she reached out to him.

Resigned to an already stressful day becoming even more so, Ian gave in. "He still thinks you're pretty. It's just you stink worse than a dwarf working in a gold mine on a midsummer's day who hasn't bathed all year."

Ian braced for whatever onslaught Marian might unleash on Benson, only to see her breathe deep and extinguish the flames. She ran her hands through her hair and straightened her clothes, taking time to knock off a little bit of mud that was caked on her boots.

"Well," she said. "I'll just save my response for a more appropriate time. After all, I am a lady."

Ian and Benson stared at each other, amazed at her self-restraint, and they could not decide if they should be happy or very, very scared.

"So," Ian said tentatively, trying to gauge her mood. "With these trails being watched, it's only reasonable to assume your trackers are awake and now have the reinforcements on patrol around the shop. So let's also assume we're not getting out of this without a fight. We've got a secret entrance that will lead us into the basement of the shop, but there's little room for error. If we go in that way, we may not be able to leave from it. So stay close, stay quiet, and let's try not to die or get horribly disfigured."

"Agreed," Marian nodded.

Benson grumbled but nodded in agreement.

Ian motioned for Marian to follow as Benson held the rear, maintaining a safe distance from Marian in case she decided to seek revenge for his comments. They walked quietly through the woods until Ian put his hand up for them to stop. He knelt and began removing foliage from a large boulder, revealing a small hatch carved into the rock. It was a secret tunnel to the shop that his parents had created.

"What's wrong?" Marian asked as Ian paused.

"Oh, the new normal, I suppose," he muttered as Benson jumped to his side and the two began pounding on the hatch to pull it open.

"Normal being..."

"Several deviants running from multiple directions

right at us to, one must assume, cause us great bodily harm!"

# THIRTY-EIGHT

The burning sensation never left Phillip's throat, and the pain never eased. It was near impossible for him to even speak, though he managed when needed after the Master decided to relieve his aggression on him. During his ride ahead of Muspelheim he felt closer to death than he ever had before. But his journey alone on his horse allowed him time for peaceful contemplation.

Villagers and travelers alike let him be as he made his way south. No one knew he was merely a servant to a tyrant. In their minds, he could be just as dangerous and maniacal as the Master. And his taste of power had opened a window through which madness could creep. He'd even imagined himself as the Master of Steinigen, pulling strings and controlling the world around him, bending it to his will. But those fantasies dissipated when he saw the broken and destitute common folk. The squalor in which so many were forced to live without any chance of reprieve softened his heart. He'd known about the poor souls living in the Morkere that his Master had crushed, but now he saw that degradation was widespread among the villages south of Steinigen leading toward the Crescent City. All of Ephorus appeared on the path of ruin, save for those wealthy enough to buy a brief reprieve from the Old King.

It had occurred to him to stop and veer from his path, to disappear into the world around him and help those he came across, but he knew what was coming. No one was going to be safe, and no one would be able to hide. He would most likely die in the coming days, and he'd rather do so somewhat peacefully rather than being tortured beforehand. Maybe it was cowardice, but he'd rather work for the devourer of life than be its victim. He had seen the powers the Master's daughter brought with her from within the mountains when she arrived, and he knew the horrors that would be wrought against Ephorus when his Master took them from her.

Lost in his thoughts, Phillip rode on through the night and early morning hours until his senses became aware of a lovely scent drifting around him. Leaning his head back, he breathed in the air and felt his throat burn. He coughed furiously for a moment while scolding himself for trying to relish a moment of joy when in service to the Master. Kicking his heels into his horse's side, he rode down to the merchant's alley at the edge of Crescent City.

Crescent City was the only town outside of Redclave whose citizens had enough money to live comfortably. The Master made sure his puppet, Tomas McCordian, stayed in power, and to do so required the Old King to not be challenged by the people surrounding him. By keeping those closest to the King the most prosperous, the Master had erected a wall of defense should the destitute outside the city dare to rise against the Old King's, and the Master's, rule.

The fear that Phillip had seen grip other townsfolk when he rode through was now replaced with indifference and disdain by merchants and citizens who were accustomed to prosperous fishing grounds and the light-handed touch of the Master. He wondered which was more dangerous, an ever-present fear or a nonexistent one.

He would find his answer soon enough.

# Thirty-Nine

Benson shoved Ian and Marian through the hatch in the boulder so he could follow suit. He was complaining again as he struggled his way through the small entrance.

"This is neither the time nor the place, Benson!" Ian yelled, struggling to light the closest torch.

Marian pushed him aside and snapped her fingers, sparking a cavalcade of light down the tunnel as the flame bounced from one torch to the next, illuminating a path through the earth that was supported by thick wooden beams. She let out a sigh: it was well lit, but there was no place to hide should the mercenaries follow them.

Benson's displeasure with their situation became clear as his grumbling grew louder behind her.

"What's wrong with him now?" Marian said, her words echoing in the tunnel.

"He wants to discuss the possibility of your stench having led them to us."

"What?" Marian shouted, turning on her heels, swinging wildly.

Ian, who was following her closely, ducked her right hook and hoisted her over his shoulder. "Like I said, not the time. Feel free to beat him later, but we might need him conscious for the moment."

Benson was trailing behind, having barred the tunnel's entrance with a piece of wood to try and slow their attackers. He began running to catch up as the noise of shouting increased overhead.

"What did that fat fur ball of a bear say?" Marian shouted, trying to get off Ian's shoulder.

"He just wants you to know how much he appreciates your company and how glorious our time has been since we met you." Ian dropped Marian without warning as they all turned to look back at the entrance.

"Give me your bags," he said to both of them. "We're going to have to improvise a little to buy us some cover. It's just..." His attention became focused on the vials in his hands.

"It's just what?" Marian asked impatiently.

"It means we only have one way left to leave, and that'll be through the front door of the shop."

He let the words sink in. Trading glances, they all smiled nervously, fighting back their fear.

"Fine by me," Marian quipped, hoping her confidence wasn't disproportionate to the moment. "How many do you think will be there waiting for us?"

"Hopefully, no more than we can handle. When we go in, you both need to follow my lead and engage only if you have to. We aren't mercenaries or warriors, so we have to fight smart."

"Maybe a little extra power will help," Marian said

as she ran her hand across some roots that were sticking out of the earthen wall. A loud crack echoed through the tunnel as the piece of wood began to give way at the tunnel entrance. She broke two large sticks off the roots and began reciting an incantation over them. When she was done, she handed one to Ian and the other to Benson.

"And what's the stick going to do? And, secondary question, quite possibly more relevant than the first but which can wait until later, when were you going to inform us of your ability to use incantations and enchantments?"

"First, they're not just sticks anymore, and second, I've never really met anybody that wants to know me so I don't talk about myself very much! My sincerest apologies for not meeting your standards of personal disclosure," she snapped, her ears fixed on the piece of wood as it splintered, nearing its breaking point.

"Apology accepted," Ian mocked, watching Benson give his newly minted armament an in-depth inspection before holding it up. "A stick," Ian muttered. "We're going to fight them with a stick."

"A weapon!" she shot back. "This is basic magic through projectiles. How could you not have learned this already?"

"Projectile dysfunction is a completely understandable issue in potion mastery, so don't be judgmental. And calling them weapons just seems overly confident about something that gets broken by the wind! Completely impractical."

A final crack rang through the tunnel as the wood

gave way and sunlight poured in through the entrance.

"Fine! What would you two like to call them so we could get on with the not-dying part?"

Benson's eyes lit up, and he whispered in Ian's ear. The sound of heavy boots filled the tunnel.

"That's not bad," Ian said. "I think we can work with that."

"Work with what?" Marian shouted. There was no need for a measured tone as the mercenaries were creeping into their attack positions, checking for traps before they charged forward.

"Twigs of death," Ian said happily.

"I hate you right now. I absolutely hate you," she paused as she fought back the desire to strike him, igniting flames in her palms. "Focus your mind and energy on a target, and it will follow your command."

Ian set his bag on the ground, motioning for Benson to follow suit to prevent any errant discharges or explosions. Following Marian's command, they both pointed their twigs down the tunnel, letting out roars as they focused their minds on their assailants. Ian's body vibrated with energy, a throbbing sensation that started deep in his cells and finally burst forth from the stick in his hand. The trio watched a streak of light hurtle through the tunnel and connect vigorously with the lead attacker.

"Oh, this could be fun," Ian giggled as the man's scream echoed off the tunnel walls.

As the other mercenaries began to charge, Benson roared again and sent a spark of fiery light careening down the tunnel. The haggard man in front threw himself against the wall to avoid the blast but left a pair of goblins without cover or time to react. The orange light flashed across their pale green skin as they shrieked, crashing backward and halting the charge of the others.

"Don't you need one?" Ian asked while Marian stepped forward to attack.

Snapping her fingers and sparking a fire in her palms that leaped up her arms, Ian watched silently as her eyes went dark, a faint orange glow replacing her irises. "I am one," she whispered, smoke seeping from her lips.

Ian was a little embarrassed to realize he was completely outmatched by her power. "So do you want to keep fighting in here, or would you rather go fight inside the shop?"

Benson squealed when he turned to see Marian nearly covered in flames. He motioned for Marian to help him with his next attack. Yes, she nodded, and when he sent off his next projectile, she released an enormous flame from her palm that followed it. Benson's aim was off, however, and it hit a wooden beam instead of the attackers.

Ian watched helplessly as Marian's flame barreled after it. When it landed, the beam lit up and ignited, creating a wall of fire that reached from the ceiling to the floor.

Benson smiled, watching the mercenaries turn and run away until he turned and saw Ian glaring at him. Marian, realizing the magnitude of their error, slowly backed down the tunnel, toward the underground entrance to the shop, her flames dying out as her eyes widened and she realized what was to come. The sound of the wooden beam cracking filled the tunnel.

"You better hope that doesn't—" Ian was cut off as a mountain of dirt whooshed into the tunnel not far from where they were standing. The section quickly caved in and the catastrophe was moments away from consuming them all.

The flames refused to be extinguished as they leaped down the tunnel toward them. Ian watched as the wooden beams that had fortified his parents' secret tunnel for years without warp or damage began to splinter and break apart.

He heard Benson behind him and then felt a mighty paw yank him into action. A terrible boom ricocheted through the tunnel, and his parents' work was destroyed, the beams unable to withstand the flames any longer.

Unwilling to meet the same fate, Ian led them to the shop's door. Raising his twig of death, Ian nodded for Benson to open it, and he stepped through with Marian and Benson following close behind him. The burning world vanished and gave way to darkness when Benson shut the door.

# Forty

Hellebores, Artimus thought, chasing a smell from home before her eyes opened. "It smells of hellebores flowers," she said out loud, hoping to rouse her captor's attention.

"That's a new one," her captor said, pulling a small journal from under her seat and writing down the remark.

Artimus was far out to sea, with no sign of land in sight and just faint hints of green light on the horizon. The light pulsated as if it were a cognizant entity, communicating with the world around it. Highlighted by the faint glow, Artimus's captor was youthful but her hair was nearly as white as her skin. She had a green glimmer in her eyes that sparkled when it caught the light.

She had no markings on her clothes: a simple tunic draped down over her shoulders, leaving her arms free to row. And of her pants, there was nothing beyond the knee. Her bare feet rested in the open air.

"But why?" Artimus asked her. "Why does it smell of hellebores?"

"I don't know you, and you're not supposed to be here," the woman answered, placing her journal back under the seat and gripping the oar beside her. "I have no answers for how your mind is interacting with this world."

Her tone was neither cold nor careless, but she conveyed no signs of emotion. Artimus watched as the woman set the oar in the black water, a faint glow emanating from the wood as it breached the surface of the sea.

"Where are we?" Artimus asked, her mind fascinated and horrified by the possibility that she was somehow in another world.

"Nowhere," the woman said, standing as the small boat came to a halt in the water.

"Do you, or nowhere, have a name?" Artimus's voice raised an octave, her concern growing.

"My name is Cataren, and this is the place where existence comes to die." Cataren grabbed her oar and leaped into the water, leaving Artimus alone.

The ripples from her splash lapped against the wooden boat. Artimus couldn't see any hint of her beneath the water.

"If this is where existence comes to die," she paused, her words momentarily stuck by fear, "am I dead?"

She stood, wobbling with the boat, and made her way across its length in search of any sign of what to do. Her anxiety cut deep inside her, gripping her heart and lungs as she fought to maintain control and calm herself from a swelling fear of the dark. The dim green light was setting in the distance, and the little she could see was fading into the darkness.

"Erin," she cried out in fear. "Erin, please!" she shouted, her eyes welling with tears until they began to drip down her cheeks. With the last of the light fading, and her sanity slipping away with it, Artimus began to hear cries of pain and fury all around her.

She tried to shout but nothing came out; her voice was muffled by the cries that were crawling on top of her and inserting themselves within her. She was being eaten by the darkness, and she couldn't fight it off.

Her thoughts drifted to Erin again as her sense of self dissolved.

In a dream, she saw wildflowers blossoming under the warmth of sunlight. She was peaceful. Then the grass began to glow fluorescent green, rising around her and repelling the darkness from her body.

"Erin," she whispered, her voice barely audible as her eyes opened again.

The white hair of Cataren came into view as she pulled herself into the boat, slipping into a seated position beside Artimus. Her hair was wet, but the rest of her body was dry.

"Why...," Artimus coughed, spitting droplets of black ooze into the boat. "Why does it hurt so much?"

Cataren stared at her with no apparent concern.

"Existence comes at a cost that must be paid." Standing upright, Cataren lifted Artimus to her knees and showed her the water. A whirlpool had formed to their starboard side, glowing green deep within, rotating endlessly into an abyss. "You can pay me later, and go home now if you desire. You do not belong here yet."

Words refused to form for Artimus, but Cataren understood the look in her eyes and, with a powerful shove, she cast Artimus out of the boat and into the whirlpool. Artimus closed her eyes and thought of Erin again, sinking into a dream she hoped was real while the water crashed in around her.

# Forty-One

The dirt was following them up the steps from the tunnel. It was seeping through the cracks in and around the door and covering their feet and ankles. They turned and saw that the door was bulging from the pressure of the collapsing tunnel. They felt an ominous ripple beneath their feet as the earth groaned and the shop above them shook violently, threatening to give way, but finally, the earth righted itself, and the flow of dirt subsided.

"So only one way out then," Ian joked, turning to face his companions.

Neither cared to return his inappropriate humor. The thought of them being trapped and suffocated still rested heavily on their minds.

Marian became alarmed when she saw Ian staring past her, his eyes growing wide. "What's wrong?"

"Everything!" he shouted as he pointed behind her at three dripping Traskins creeping toward them.

Traskins were in essence the scum of Ephorus. They'd evolved over generations from a band of power-hungry river gnomes who made a depraved pact with a wicked, fallen Vorkyre. The gnomes got part of what they wanted—they grew in size and vanquished their brethren—but every bit of land they stole turned from muck to swamp, to wasteland. Over generations, the Traskins began to resemble their land: their faces warped from the moisture, their skin covered in thick green slime.

"I may vomit," Marian said.

"Don't go weak on me now," Ian said frantically as his hands patted fervently down his sides. "Not good."

"What's not—" Marian was cut off by projectile vomit emanating from the bear behind her, splashing over her boots. Choking back the desire to reciprocate, Marian forced her gaze back to Ian. "What's not good?"

Ian's eyes were locked on the bile covering her boots, his stomach twisting. The hissing sound of the Traskins helped him focus. "I lost my twig in the collapse. My twig of death has died."

There was no time for Marian to reply. The Traskins charged simultaneously, three wretched swamp monsters blocking any escape. Slinging her bag toward Benson before returning their guttural hiss with a scream of her own, she lit her palms and let the blaze climb up her arms as she ran forward to meet them. Fire poured out from her eyes as she lost control of the fury that had been building inside her. A flame shot from her arm as she swung at the first Traskin. Its hiss turned to a screech when the flame ripped through its leathery, slime-covered skin.

Before she could remove her arm from the chest

of her fist attacker, she caught the glimmer of the second Traskin's sword swinging down toward her. She sidestepped, breathing in deep to retract her chest, and the blade sliced down tugging the frayed fringes of her blouse, nearly leaving her bloodied and defenseless. When it connected with the stone floor, she raised her leg and stomped on the hilt, crushing the Traskin's fingers against the blade and forcing it to release its grip. As the sword clattered to the ground, she pounced in fury, placing her hands on either side of the Traskin's head until her flames pierced it, destroying all that remained of the life within.

A grim look soured the third Traskin's expression. Raising its sword, it let out a deep, gut-wrenching howl. Marian harnessed her power and screamed, the orange flames coursing through and over her body erupting in a furious blue blaze. It charged, raising its sword and pointing the blade at her heart. There was little room but Marian swiveled and the sword smashed into the stone behind her. She raised her boot and kicked the Traskin with all the might she could muster, sending it flying. She began to lunge after it, but the Traskin disappeared. Benson roared past her and caught it, slamming it into the ground and pounding on its head until the hissing stopped.

Ian walked up to Marian and watched her breathe deep, absorbing the fire back into her body. Flecks of slime now covered her clothes. "Next time I forget that you can kill me in an instant, and I make jokes at your expense, please show mercy."

Marian stared at Ian, the flames slowly fading from

her eyes. She smiled and raised her hand to show him a solitary flame burning on her finger; she moved it close to his chin. "With just one finger, I could end you," she said softly, leaning in just enough for the flame to singe a single stray hair.

Ian blushed, realizing he was unable to tell the difference between fear and attraction. He reminded himself to keep the hair on his face as short as possible while around her and turned his attention to the commotion above. They needed a hiding place. The screeching of the Traskins had given them away.

"Just after the next two doors on the left..." Ian said, stopping when he noticed a pile of boxes in front of his study where his father's journal was. "Should I have expected anything less?" he muttered to himself, turning to confront Benson.

"Could you have possibly picked a worse time to stack boxes of empty bottles and vials in front of my study?"

Benson growled at Ian, unwilling to accept the blame.

"Okay, okay," Ian said, stooping to move the boxes. "I'm sorry."

Benson's tirade continued as he flung bits of Traskin off his paws.

"Of course I forgot I did it," Ian said, "but that's really no excuse to use such foul language or to not accept my apology like a gentleman. And it would be a kind gesture of your undying friendship if you would help me move these boxes. I would greatly appreciate your kind and courteous nature in this, my dire moment of need!"

The commotion grew louder as they heard the mercenaries upstairs calling out to the Traskins they'd posted as guards. Ian knocked over the last few boxes and swung the door open. The men were charging down the stairwell with a scream and there was no need to be quiet now. Benson shoved himself past Marian and Ian and almost closed the door on them as they struggled to get in.

Safely behind the door, Marian's small sense of relief faded. "I hate you two," she muttered.

"We know," Ian said as Benson grumbled his agreement. "But our mutual levels of affection can bask in their similarities at another point in time."

Marian took in the floor littered with papers and the shelves stacked to the ceiling with journals and scrolls, and her shoulders sank. Nothing would be easily found in this room.

Benson growled, planting his feet firmly on the floor as he leaned his entire weight against the door behind him so Ian could move freely.

"Exactly," Ian said. "We may be childish, but we're not morons." Ian walked over to his chair, covered in clutter, and grabbed a vial he kept stored under the cushion for such emergencies.

He dropped it to the floor and Marian recoiled momentarily in fear, covering her face with her hands. She peered through her fingers and was pleasantly surprised when she saw that the room was sorting itself in a hurry, journals and scrolls scattering to their proper places on the shelves. As the last few scrolls took their proper position, Ian went to his immaculate desk, which had a single journal sitting on top.

"Outward appearances aren't everything. I would think you of all people would know that," he said.

Marian was amazed at the ingenuity. Everything was in place—except for one book that was following Benson. The bear had gotten in its way and slapped it down as it returned to its proper home, and it was nursing a grudge.

"We don't have time for this, Benson," Ian said as he handed the journal to Marian.

She grabbed it, flipping quickly through its pages. Benson placed her bag on the desk so she could compare her journal with this one. Seeing the two journals together felt like an accomplishment, small perhaps but significant, in the dreadful series of events that she had experienced since leaving Steinigen.

"You still with us?" Ian asked Marian.

Marian laughed off the question, her eyes connecting with his, a sense of fearlessness breaking through as she smiled. "Never left," she answered, slinging the bag over her shoulder and tying the strap tight against her body for the battle to come.

She walked over to him, letting her hand rest on his shoulder for a moment, as they both tried to laugh.

"So we can't go back. And we can only go up," Marian said.

"What are we talking about?" Ian asked, confusion furrowing his brow as he backed away to join Benson at the door.

"The one exit with all the bad guys waiting around

for us to show up is the only place we have left to go!" Marian snapped.

Ian slumped at her words. "Oh yeah," he said. "Forgot about them for a second."

"How is that even possible?" Marian groaned, exhausted by the swing of his and Benson's attention spans.

"Never mind that for now," Ian said, brushing off her question. "What we need is a plan." He and Benson leaned heavily against the door, stroking their chins as they pondered the options.

"Well, just idly standing by will get us nowhere!"

"Hey, if anyone's standing idly by, it's you," Ian shot back.

"How is that a justifiable response?"

"Because Benson and I are the only things keeping this door from being busted down by a bunch of angry mercenaries. Haven't had time to strike up a conversation with them, but I don't think they're willing to settle things amicably."

Marian stared at them, wondering if he was telling the truth. There was no noise to be heard, but she could see the door pulsating as if it were being pounded on.

"But I can't hear anything."

"Yeah, that's just the spell on the room, but that doesn't make what's going on outside any less real. So, new plan."

"Yes, I agree. New plan," Marian nodded.

Benson grumbled beside Ian.

"Love the idea, but I don't think now is the time."

"The time for what?"

"For you to take a shower. The stench of a Traskin only gets worse if it settles into your clothes."

Marian's eyes lit with fire, a flame sparked on her finger, and she sent a projectile directly at Benson's head. Ian, playing the odds, had assumed her reaction would be slightly violent and shoved Benson out of the way, letting the door swing open. The fireball burst through the crowd of mercenaries at the door, scattering them across the hallway floor.

"Like I said," Marian held up her hand, "one finger."

# Forty-Two

Paramel rested in the top of a tree, hidden from view by a maze of leaves and the haze of smoke from smoldering homes.

"It has begun," he whispered to himself.

He watched quietly as the people turned on one another, offering closed fists instead of open hands to those weakened by the attack.

"It's almost as if we were still asleep, trapped in a nightmare," a voice said from behind him.

Paramel turned to see Inibri fluttering toward him before landing on his shoulder. Pight was following behind but chose a lower branch to get a better view of the villagers. The look in her eyes was not welcoming so he let her pass, offering only a brief but warm smile.

"It could hardly be a nightmare with you here." He gently leaned his head against Inibri's tiny body, feeling her lean against him as well. "I take it our young maiden has made it to her next destination."

"She has, but trouble followed. We could not stay to protect her."

Paramel let out a low and mournful sigh. "There is

much we cannot protect anyone from now," he said, "and she must be prepared to fight when the time comes. You did well, my friend."

"I hope we did." Inibri was unwilling to accept his praise in light of the devastation below.

"How many villages have you seen like this on your way here?" Paramel asked.

"Two others to the east just outside of Cosen." Inibri sounded defeated. "There's a darkness to the people after the Master's messenger leaves them."

"What do you mean?" he asked.

"It's in their eyes," Pight said as she flew up to join them.

Paramel smiled. He found her endearing. He remembered when Inibri had told him she had found her partner and introduced them. Inibri had been so alone after Penelope's passing, but she became warm and joyful when Pight came into her life.

"Please explain," he said to Pight, closing his hands over some leaves and blowing on them. He wiggled his fingers, letting a plume of smoke escape, then opened his hands and pulled out a lily. He offered the purple flower to Pight, watching her eyes widen as her hands grasped the delicate petals. If he could make her smile, he thought, there's still joy left within her.

Pight dipped her face into the flower, taking it in all at once. The sweet smell set her wings abuzz, and she giggled. She slowly pulled her head out, a layer of pollen covering her cheeks. It was a brief respite.

"The one who leads them, the one the Master sent, his eyes go dark as the night. I hear the people saying those he infects are not the same person, that they've gone crazy with a lust for violence," Pight said as she toyed with the petals of her flower. "They turn to demons."

"It's true," Inibri added, fluttering toward her companion.

"The Master has more power than before," Paramel said, watching a group of men below, fighting over armor and weapons. The ones who refused to take up arms scattered to the trees. "Do all the people fighting have darkness in their eyes?"

"No, at least not yet. For some, it creeps up their arms like black veins. And some people don't have it at all; they're fighting just so they can kill. The power for it to spread seems to weaken the further away from the source it becomes," Inibri's eyes locked on Paramel's. "The ones who do not join them either flee, leaving their families behind, or stand their ground, so their families can run. But death now follows them all."

Beneath them the men began shouting, pointing toward the running villagers who refused to fight. Hoots and hollers rang out as they shouted the names of those they once called neighbors but now saw as prey. Their leader stood quietly as the other men roared around him, waiting for permission to be set loose.

"This is but the beginning, my dears," Paramel said. "We will lose many more in this world than we care to count. The Master was brash and impatient in his first attempt. But he is not anymore." Paramel walked to the edge of the branch, his footsteps light, the branch barely noticing his presence. "In time, it will even take the lives of ones we know, and we must be ready to say goodbye. Ready yourselves, and remember our place in this world should never be permanent."

He did not wait for a response but stepped off the branch and rapidly descended, landing with a thud among the group of men thirsting for the chance to attack those they once called friends.

Pight and Inibri rushed to the edge of the branch to see him standing tall, the men shouting in fear and wonder around him, confused and scared by his sudden appearance. The Master's messenger barked out orders and they lifted their weapons. Pight tried to rush to him, but Inibri grabbed her arm and held her tight, not letting her leave.

"He needs us!" Pight shouted at her.

"No," Inibri said calmly, "he doesn't."

She pointed at the growing heap of bodies on the ground. Paramel was a Vorkyre, and the Vorkyre were protectors, borne from the very light of the First Walkers to guard over the rest of their creation. They were powerful, they were fighters, but the people left in Ephorus had forgotten they were not just a fable.

Without pause, he battered the armed men and women who charged toward him, their hatred poisoning them. One by one, Paramel laid waste their souls, smashing them against the rocks and trees that had stood on the ground they soiled with their blood for ages before these people even walked.

"Look," Inibri whispered to Pight, pointing at the leader, who was retreating, letting his men be dismantled and overpowered.

"What do we do?" Pight asked.

"All that we can." Inibri took flight, careening through the canopy, tracking the man with venom in his eyes.

# FORTY-THREE

Artimus awoke from a dreamless sleep and found herself tucked into her bed as though it were a normal morning and nothing had happened. The small window in her room let in the dull light of an overcast day. Rain will be coming soon, she thought to herself, her mind drifting to the mundane to avoid thinking about her recent experience.

She would need to take the initiative to remove herself from beneath the comfort of a warm sheet on a cool day, but the nagging conception of pointlessness anchored her desires. Melancholic and unmotivated, she sat there, unaware and unconcerned for time, waiting for existence to prove its necessity to her once more.

A knock gently broke the silence. She was going to answer the door, but she merely stared at it, waiting to see what would happen. After a moment, the latch creaked and the door groaned, and with a rush of joy, she saw Erin's hand pushing the door open, her hesitant smile following closely behind.

"You're awake," Erin said, a hint of surprise in her voice. "I did knock." She stood in the doorway. "Can

I come in?"

Artimus nodded, adding "Yes," as she watched her friend close the door behind her.

"You've been out for a while now." Erin took a seat on Artimus's bed.

"Where did I go?" Artimus asked.

"What do you remember?" Erin was avoiding her gaze.

"I remember death and darkness. I remember being ripped apart from the inside out. I remember screaming in agony." The words hung there, the tension building while Artimus waited for Erin to look at her. "And I remember crying out for you to help, but you never came."

"I couldn't." Erin's expression turning somber. "I promise I would have been with you if I could have, but there are things I cannot do."

Artimus watched her lips quiver as the world rolled out across them and into the air. She believed her, but it brought no comfort. "Where did the two of you send me?"

"It's hard to explain," Erin started, her eyes drifting toward the window.

"Try harder." Artimus was intent on getting an answer.

"Death is natural," Erin began, getting off the bed and beginning to pace, "but an extension of consciousness is not. This life is unique in having the ability to allow multiple beings the chance to experience it in a variety of ways, one of which is consciousness."

"But...," Artimus inserted herself into Erin's train of

thought to move her along.

"But consciousness does not extend past the notion of the self. It ends with life. It ends in darkness."

"Then what was that place you sent me to, and where is that wretch of a man you convinced me to trust?"

Erin evaded the first question while she focused on the issue at hand. "Paramel had to leave; the Master's plan is advancing and he needed to move to his next position. It's just you and me now."

"Then I leave it to you to explain why I should not be angry," Artimus's voice rose sharply. "I leave it to you to let me know why I was trapped in the darkness. And I shall leave it to you to tell me why I should care to help either of you if that hell is what awaits me if I die."

Artimus realized her anger had carried her out of bed, her feet planted firmly on the rug beneath her though she didn't remember standing.

"Your anger is justified and you have every right to it, but it is neither Paramel nor myself who set life in that direction. We're trying to alter its course so that it can't happen to others. So that no one has to suffer such torrential pain and agony. He sent you there so that you would see it for yourself and know that what we need to ask of you is justified. He sent you there so that when the time comes, you will know that the pain you may cause in this world is far less than the terror that awaits in the next."

"You make no sense!" Artimus shouted. "I cannot stop death, and I don't even know what it was that I saw in that world."

"But you felt it," Erin said flatly, raising her hand and pointing at Artimus's eye. "Turn to the mirror and remember."

Anger boiled inside Artimus. She grabbed the small mirror resting on the nightstand beside her bed and raised it, glancing at her reflection. She almost didn't notice at first. Something was different. Something wasn't right.

"What's in my eye?" she asked, a sense of apprehension beginning to grip her as she stared at her left eye. It was glowing and green lines were coming out from her pupil and spreading out over her eyelid. "And why has my hair gone white?"

"There is a cost that comes with life. A cost that must be paid so that when creation ends it can begin again in another form in another world."

"Erin, what's in my eye?"

"Long before we existed, the First Walkers sought to end this notion of death, thinking that their creation could inhabit existence permanently and never rescind their power. They sought immortality, placing the conviction in the hearts and minds of their creations that it was not just achievable but inherent. They convinced all they brought to life, including the Vorkyre, that what they had done was just."

"I can feel it," Artimus whispered, running her finger over her eyelid. "It burns."

"Their ambition, their presumption turned into a venomous mistake. Life was not meant to continuously persist, and consciousness has no place in eternity.

What the First Walkers did caused a collapse of the natural progression of life and existence, causing countless beings to suffer needlessly."

"Why does it burn?" Artimus snapped, but Erin didn't answer. She turned away from the mirror to face Erin, who had shifted to her shadow form.

As Artimus looked at her friend's shifting, swaying shadow, she realized she could see her emotions and thoughts, all of the lovable qualities that she had grown fond of. Erin's beautiful, she thought.

"It burns because it sees the damage done to this world and the realm beyond and it wants to do something about it. Our allotted time for existence ended ages ago, but the spells cast by the First Walkers on this land have disrupted the normal course of nature. The world you went to is where former life is recast, its energy used for other purposes. But now all the lives that have ended are trapped there, locked in the anguish of conscious thought."

"That wretched place?" Artimus recoiled.

"That place is only wretched because of the disruption that has occurred. Pain is not natural there. Darkness is not natural there. When we die, our consciousness is supposed to come to an end, but the First Walkers refused to accept that. They insisted that consciousness be eternal, though they didn't expect it to become a prison. We have to eliminate consciousness from that realm and end the First Walkers' mistake."

"Why is it inside me? What does it want from me?" Artimus asked, staring at the beauty within the darkness of Erin.

Erin shifted back to her human form and took her friend's hands. Artimus was shaking, unnerved and distraught by her appearance and the sensation in her eye.

"It wants to stop the venom. To each form of life, there is a counterpart. What lays restless and burning within you is the only thing that can save us from it."

# FORTY-FOUR

Marian grabbed the strap of her bag and yanked it over her head. She tied a quick knot to keep everything secure then slid it underneath the table.

"What are you doing?" Ian asked.

"We can't risk me burning the journals, or having them taken back to my father. We have to protect them."

"And if we need to make a run for it?" Ian said.

Marian could tell conflict was not his specialty, nor was it hers, but there was no other option. The sound of many footsteps had begun charging toward their door. Benson roared, and the feet changed direction and ran off. But they'd be back. The time for discussion was over.

"There is no running. We win, or we die." Marian spoke softly as she walked into the hallway, stepping over the bodies sprawled on the floor. "Will you stand with me?"

"I feel like we're not allowing ourselves to relax anymore."

"Ian!" Marian snapped. "They have no intention of

letting either of you live. You need to be prepared for what we have to do."

She offered her hand and he reached out for it. He nodded at Benson to fall behind them, and the bear let out another roar. Marian was filled with adrenaline and fear, along with a dash of unexpected desire caused by the touch of his hand. She had pulled Ian closer than she had planned, his chest nearly touching hers, and Benson tapped them on the shoulder, pointing up the stairwell at the soon-to-be-arriving mercenaries with the better position.

"Thank you, Benson," they said in unison as a mass of wretched men came storming toward them.

Marian let go of Ian's hand and took her place in front of Benson, who bared his teeth and claws, letting out another massive roar that shook the walls of the shop. The mercenaries paused, giving Marian ample time to ignite. Her eyes went dark and smoke drifted out of her nostrils, small flames coming out of her mouth along with the faint sound of laughter.

She could see the filth before her, their weapons drawn and aching for the reward. "Ephorus knows to fear my father," she spoke, exhaling a stream of smoke that meandered toward their attackers. "Let me show you why you should fear me."

Marian raised her hand to her mouth and snapped her finger while charging toward the mercenaries. She let the small flame dance from her fingertips to her tongue, before violently exhaling the breath from her lungs. A bolt of fire flashed through the air and tore through the two decrepit-looking men leading the charge. Their cries echoed off the walls as they collapsed on the stairs. Marian stopped at the bottom step, ignoring their cries, ignoring their burned flesh, and stared up at the other attackers, waiting to see who else would challenge her.

"And to think," Ian said from behind her, "we tried to tie you up with rope."

Marian turned to look at him, flames in her eyes, smoke seeping from her lips, and smiled. "That was rather cute of you two."

Ian smiled at her before turning his attention to the incapacitated mass of life around him. He wrenched a breastplate off one man and grabbed a sword as he made his way to Benson.

"I think we should continue to let the lady lead, Benson," he said.

Benson roared his approval, the two taking their positions behind Marian on her sides. They were outnumbered and at a tactical disadvantage but charged up the stairs nonetheless.

Two Traskins hissed and groaned while a smattering of small goblins inched back to avoid the dragon's breath that had taken down the front line. Unwilling to be bait, the Traskins began snatching up goblins and tossing them down the stairwell. The goblins squealed and screamed as they bounced on the stairs, their bones breaking and heads cracking from the impact before they even met their opponent. The stairwell was now cluttered with bodies, preventing any hasty charge upward. The Traskins, feeling they'd revived their advantage, charged down the steps to meet them, using the goblins still standing at their side as shields.

Marian dropped quickly to a knee and planted her right fist on the bottom step, screaming while pushing down with all her might against the wood, sending a scorching flame up toward the Traskins' legs, burning through the goblins along the way. The Traskins managed to jump, but only at the expense of their shields, which were weighing them down. The goblins screamed in pain as they were dropped into the fire.

Marian grabbed the two squirming goblins they had dropped and hurled them up the stairwell, the flames still burning bright upon their clothes. The Traskins managed to avoid the burning specters, but the upstairs shop was not so lucky as their limp bodies crashed into a shelf of potions. A raucous sound of breaking glass erupted from the shop floor where the various concoctions were now haphazardly blending.

"There might be a problem," Marian shouted.

"Benson and I love consistency so, you know, no worries," Ian answered as some of the unconscious bodies beside the study door began crawling with life.

Benson turned toward the dregs pulling themselves up from the floor and roared. For a moment, they looked prepared to run away and abandon the fight, but the only way out was up the stairwell. They raised their weapons.

"Take them!" a man's voice called out from the top of the stairs.

Marian met the call with a spark of fire and charged up the stairwell. She swung her arm and a flare leaped out, slashing the closest attacker across the chest.

"Spear!" she shouted as a metal arrow flew toward her. She ducked and turned to see it just miss Ian's face and land in one of his attackers.

"Who fights with spears inside?" he shouted, watching blood drip from the attacker's wounds as his comrades pushed past him, leaving him to bleed out alone.

Benson snarled in agreement, lifting a Traskin and slamming it against the wall. He started swinging the unconscious, slimy mass into everyone who came toward him.

Ian chuckled at the sight, paying for it with a blow to the chest. Marian tried to fend off the next two attackers with a quick volley from her hands, but they managed to duck her fire, rising to take some quick shots. Ian felt his breath leave him as he doubled over, coming eye to eye with what he assumed was the hairiest human he had ever seen.

Ian raised his sword instinctively, parrying a thrust from the man's blade and countering with his own. His adrenaline took over and gave him unexpected strength as he pierced the man's chest and watched in momentary shock while the life drained from his face. He had seen death, but he had never been its cause before. The thought scared him. He watched the man go limp, slowly slipping down from his blade to the floor, his hands trembling beyond his control.

Marian's flame swept by his face, rousing his attention to the present danger as it struck a goblin aiming for Ian's chest with his dagger. He smelled its burning flesh. Benson was roaring behind him, covered in slime from the Traskin he'd been swinging like a battle axe.

There was a growing heap of bodies on the steps, and as they continued their advance, the mercenaries retreated up the stairwell into the open room of the potion shop.

"Benson!" Marian shouted as she turned to see a Traskin dangling from his paws, slime covering the walls, and men on the floor around him. "Time to leave. Grab my bag and meet us up top."

Benson bared his teeth, lifting the unconscious Traskin above his head and hurling the heap of slime at the one remaining fighter. The man was briefly pinned to the wall by the flying Traskin before being knocked unconscious by the bear.

Marian saw Ian watching Benson, his mouth smiling while tears rolled from his eyes. Only one of those two emotions would be helpful in the next few minutes, so Marian played to his strengths.

"I thought Benson didn't like to fight," she said with a smile, the blue returning to the iris of her eyes, the flames dying out across her body.

"He just doesn't like it when people hit him," Ian laughed.

The two stood in silence for a moment, an odd interlude given their current situation. They watched Benson enter the study to get the bag before turning back up the stairs, a faint hissing sound of mixing potions warning them of imminent danger.

"Didn't seem like we'd have time to come back down and get it," she said, her voice shaky.

"Yeah, our chances of dying are definitely higher than we imagined if we try to come back down and not escape the first chance we get." The eyes of the dead man at his feet were still open, but his breath was completely gone.

"Are you with me?" Marian reached for Ian's hand, gripping it tightly.

"Ladies first," Ian said, gripping her hand and swallowing his fear.

"Aw," she said, igniting the flames on her arms and stepping forward, "you still think I'm a lady." She moved slowly up the wooden stairs, scorching the wood with every step.

Reaching the top of the stairwell, she saw the Master's head tracker, Lyco, who snarled at the sight of her. Marian knew he must have paid out of his own pocket for the extra men, only to see them cower and fall before her, or run away in fear.

"A retreat, of some sort, may be in order here," Lyco's rotund companion said as he began to back away.

"Agreed," said Lyco's other companion, who also took a step backward.

"Leave this place, now!" Marian shouted, raising her arms.

"We have every intention of leaving," Lyco snarled, "we just need your heads at a minimum to come with us." Lyco grabbed his companions by their necks and pulled them close. "Arman, Ceril, take out her accomplice. I'll take care of this petulant child myself."

"This is a great example of why people hate Steinigen," Ian said. "Not one of you is polite enough to enter someone else's home with permission." He tried to laugh but his hand was shaking violently on the sword while the two men moved toward him. "Now would be a good time to make it up the stairs, Benson!" he shouted.

"Don't worry, little man," Arman said. "Death only takes a minute before eternity takes over."

"You don't have the power to stop us now," Marian snapped, but the three men continued to creep forward.

"Alive or dead, I will see you bend the knee again to your Master," Lyco spat.

"Only a wretched beast would have my father as a master!" she shouted, her rage taking hold as she stepped forward.

Ian saw a flash and he stepped back just in time as the floor lit up with poisonous green flames. Marian's fiery goblins had ignited the soupy mixture of potions leaking from all the broken vials. Arman and Ceril appeared unfazed, stepping between the flames while drawing their swords. Somehow, to Ian, the confines of the stairwell and the downstairs hallway had made the fighting seem easier. He hadn't even contemplated his demise down there, but now his heart raced, hoping to get in as many beats as it could before being forced to submit to fate.

"Benson!" Ian shouted, his voice cracking. "A little help needed on the shop floor!"

It was hard to interpret the mumbled roar that came in response, but Ian heard something, or someone, being smashed against a wall. He turned to Marian, whose eyes were focused intently on Lyco.

"New plan!" Ian cried out, backing away from Ceril and Arman, sword raised. Marian lunged through the flames and headed right for them.

"You said you had this one," Ceril said to Lyco, raising his sword to fend her off.

Marian grabbed their swords. Her palms erupted in a white blaze; her mouth shut tight as she clenched her teeth. Ian saw that the drops of blood falling from her hands to the floor sparked small eruptions from the spilled potions.

When Marian let go of the swords, the blades were dull. What was left of them sagged and cracked. One strike, even a poor one from Ian, would shatter them.

"Now you," Marian commanded, returning her attention to Lyco.

"You betray your people, your ancestry, by using your powers against us," he spat.

"My people and my ancestors deserve to be betrayed!" she shouted.

He lunged forward and tackled her. Ian tried to rush forward but was knocked in the head by a flying sword. The hilt cracked his temple and he heard voices shouting, "Just beat him to death!"

His knees buckled and he fell to one knee, catching a glimpse of a boot before it collided painfully with his head. He plunged backward. Staring up at the ceiling, his mind drifted to memories of playing on the shop floor while his parents puttered around him.

"Benson!" Ian shouted with his remaining breath while another boot landed on his stomach.

He could see Marian trying to free herself from her

attacker. Her head smacked on the wood floor, and her fire sputtered and dimmed as Lyco continued to punch her, his armor holding strong against the flames she tried to ignite. Ian felt his ribs give way to another blow. The two men were toying with their prey. At this rate, he thought, we'll be dead in minutes.

Marian cried out, still trying to break free. "Marian!" he shouted. His fingers managed to grab hers. With the little strength he had left, he tried to pull her away from Lyco, but a red haze burst out from beneath her as a potion ignited, knocking everyone, their attackers included, to the floor.

"Is this what death looks like?" he said, staring into the hot red haze.

Benson roared.

"Here. I'm over here, buddy!" Ian called.

Draped across Benson was Marian's bag, covered in slime. Ian tried not to cry out when Benson pulled him up from the floor. Something's definitely broken, he thought.

"Find Marian," Ian said. "We need to go!"

Benson disappeared into the fog as he searched for Marian. Ian heard their attackers waking up.

"Running out of time, Benson," Ian yelled, heading for the front door. He stepped on the sword he had dropped and bent down to grab it. More pain. He inched forward, Benson way ahead of him.

"Stop!" a voice called out behind him. It was Lyco, lying on the floor. His armor was cracked and broken. "Leave the girl," he shouted, "and the two of you can walk away."

Ian could see Marian and Benson outside the shop door; Benson was holding her up, and her face was covered in blood and bruises. Ian was growing angry from the pain and frustration. His shop was a loss, and his life had been upended. He saw the two men get off the floor and hobble toward him.

"Leave the girl," Lyco snarled again.

Ian didn't care to talk. He lifted his sword and ran it through the largest crack in Lyco's armor, piercing his chest. The man gasped, defeated, his life beginning to end. Blood poured from his lips while he gagged and choked on his final breaths. His body writhed and gave up. Ian pulled the sword from Lyco's corpse and pointed it at the two men. He was struggling to maintain his balance but refused to reveal any sign of hesitation.

"Leave us be, or you will die as well."

Ian's words were backed up by Benson's roar. Arman and Ceril stopped and stepped back while Ian staggered toward the light filling the doorway. Stepping into the daylight, the air entered his lungs with a painful effort he had never known. He could feel a trickle of blood running down his nose and over his lip. Wiping it away with the sleeve of his shirt, he looked down to see it blend in perfectly with the rest of his bloodstains. He approached Benson and Marian, but her eyes were dim and her body was limp. Benson was supporting all of her weight now. A rattling sound intensified in the shop behind him as the red haze began to mix violently with the scattered potions. Ian thought he could hear thousands of fragile vials quivering as the potions bubbled up. He motioned for Benson to run away as fast as he could manage. The concoctions were extremely sensitive to heat; the volatile mix Marian ignited was surely wreaking havoc as well. Finally, the toxic brew burst and the explosion was filled with the screams of the Master's men, those who had survived the fight but would now die in agony.

Ian stared at Marian, the shadows on her pale, freckled face, the tangles in her long auburn hair. He had never imagined he would take the life away from another, but it was worth it to see her safe. It was worth it to hear her mumble incoherently. It was worth it to be with her.

# Forty-Five

The foul stench of a sun-drenched day hung in the air, and the cool breeze of night slowly moved in from the sea. An orange and purple tapestry colored the sky over Crescent City as the sun began to dip beneath the horizon. It was a peaceful sight for Nance. He had grown to loathe daylight, finding the darkness more welcoming of his powers.

He lit a spark on his fingertip as he held his bare hand out before him. The small flame gently swayed with the breeze. The world wanted to put him out. Steinigen had always been feared for its connection to fire: a living embodiment of destruction and chaos.

Nance let the flame grow stronger. It danced before his eyes, and he felt its warmth spread over him. He was at peace in the fire. His fortress walls protected him, but they were not his home. Nance held up his right hand so the Hearthwood could get warm in the light of the flame. He had traveled down the Galen River, destroying everything, and was now at Crescent City.

Are you too weak? an eerily familiar voice called out, cackling with laughter.

"I was strong enough to defeat you once," he seethed under his breath. The voice was getting bolder, more persistent, and, to his dismay, more familiar. The fire had always spoken to him since he was a child, but the voice had been subservient in the past, begging for his permission to act. That voice was gone, now, supplanted by wicked denunciations that cut to his core.

The fire surged up his left arm, his entire body quickly igniting with flames as his eyes went black and he yielded to its searing embrace. The Hearthwood had pierced his skin beneath the glove, dripping its venom into him, letting the madness creep into his body. Now it was trying to take control of him.

He let the fire burn bright over his body, breathing in deep as the flames reached his neck. The fire chased away the venom and gave him control of the madness.

Parlor tricks and childish games, the voice called out above the roar of the flames. You have no clue of the true power we hold; the power I still hold.

Stretching his arms, Nance grabbed hold of a tree branch, his fingers digging into the bark until he heard it ignite, drowning out the laughter echoing in his ears. Maven wanted to return; she wanted control over him as she had before. He was unsure how she had infected his mind, but he would not bend to her will. Nance screamed, smoke billowing from his mouth while the rest of the tree caught fire. It had been some time since the last rainfall in Crescent City, and the fire quickly scattered across the canopy that stretched to the city's border.

"We await your orders, sir," Sever called out.

Turning, he could see his warlocks sitting patiently on top of their horses. Their helmets reflected the fire as the emblem on their cloaks glowed in the night. They were death incarnate. They'd torn through villages on their march south; they'd lit the night on fire with the homes and lives of the people of Ephorus, fully earning their Muspelheim name. Nance smiled.

"If Phillip has done his job, the Trofasthet will have prepared the city for us, so keep the men reined in," Nance answered. "I want to see if the Trofasthet have broken the people's spirit and readied me an army."

"And if not?" Sever asked.

"Then I shall let you experiment with as many tortures and terrors upon the people as you wish."

The fire began to rage around them, the forest screaming with the cracks and groans of wood succumbing to an onslaught. Limbs then whole trees started to fall.

Watching the destruction with delight, Nance turned to his warlocks. "We are the fire, the onset of the darkness to come. Let us claim what is ours!"

Nance dismounted, marching forward on foot, letting the fire within scorch the ground he walked on. Riding just behind the Master, Sever led the Muspelheim, backlit by the burning forest, the hooves of his horse shaking the ground beneath it. The beast had been crafted to carry the weight of his stone figure with ease, its strength unmatched by any other of its kind. Together, the two were a formidable and horrific sight.

Cries from people in the outskirts of the city could

be heard as the fire took hold. Those cries increased when the source of the flames marched toward them. Nance was pleased to see two quiet figures, Phillip and Sir Garrin, approach and kneel before him, unconcerned with the chaos, standing only when Nance permitted them.

"On second thought," Nance mused, motioning Sever to come forward. "Let us make sure the people know they belong to us."

Sever smiled and raised his sword, signaling attack, and the warlocks broke formation, rearing on their horses and charging into the ramshackle homes around them. Sever dismounted amidst the shrieks of the villagers, the hefty stones of his feet splitting the ground beneath him. He joined the three men, taking his place by Nance's side as they followed Phillip and Sir Garrin toward the Old King's Tower on the shoreline.

"It's a sweet melody," Nance said, taking in the horrible screams around them.

"It is quite peaceful, sir," Sever answered.

"One day, my dear Sever. One day Ephorus will be aflame and screaming for our pleasure."

Sever nodded, holding his tongue to focus on the city guardsmen riding fast down the cobbled street, armed and ready for battle. Drawing his sword, Sever stepped ahead of Nance, unwilling to let his Master take the lead during an assault. Nance reached and motioned for Sever to sheath his sword, pointing at Sir Garrin and Phillip as they strode forward.

"Let us see if Sir Garrin was worth the effort put in." He watched Sir Garrin closely as the city guards in their blue and gold cloaks circled them, weapons drawn, eyes fixed on the Master. A few hapless villagers came forward to assist them in dispatching Nance and the evil he had brought with him. The right flank of the guard turned and dispatched the citizens with ease, running their swords through them and then pulling them out, the blades soaked in blood and shining in the light of the fire.

Nance nodded at the guardsmen and turned to Sever. "Round up the warlocks and meet us at the Old King's Tower. I wish to reign over my dominion now."

# FORTY-SIX

Ian stumbled through the woods, glancing at the stars to check his heading every few minutes, desperate to keep them moving in the right direction. They were bruised and bedraggled, and their desire to return to the cabin was overwhelming. If he let his mind wander from the pain, he could lose track of their direction and lead them deep into a long night of discomfort and pain in the woods. Their wounds and morale needed time to heal and a place to rest easy before they could make their way to the third journal. They would be worthless in another round with the Master's men.

Unlike them, the forest was tranquil. Dense evergreens and blooming wildflowers surrounded them. Benson was the most unscathed, so he carried Marian's bag while helping her walk. Marian stumbled forward with her eyes nearly shut, blood caked around her lips and eyebrows, her face swollen and covered in bruises.

Ian had to look away from her to stay focused. He was filled with anger, and he kept picturing the dead men and the sword he carried dripping with their blood. I killed two people, he thought, trying to steady his emotions. I killed two people, and the fight has just started.

He bit his lower lip, and a small trail of blood flowed down his chin. The pain helped him get his emotions under control. He would have to confront his sorrow of ending another life later. The woods stretching out from the Aurian Hills were not to be ignored, or taken lightly. His father had spent many nights teaching him the history of this forest, and how to be wary of the power trapped within it.

The earliest potion masters called this forest their home after the people of Ephorus started treating their work as dark magic. The potion masters had intended to help those around them improve their lives, but as the commoners' fear of them grew, they became unwelcome in the villages of Ephorus and had to search for a new home. Pixies would often find these lost wanderers and guide them here to the Aurian Hills, where the dense canopy supported a plethora of powerful flora and fungi that could transform their potions.

With guidance from the pixies and river gnomes, the potion masters soon began to travel to the tops of the hills, searching for better and even more powerful ingredients. They found themselves at the feet of the Vorkyre. It was said to be the first time a human interacted with a Vorkyre. There was one Vorkyre in particular who had taken a keen interest in the potion masters settling in the woods stretching out from the Aurian Hills, and his name still burned in Ian's memory: Paramel.

Ian's foot got snared in a fallen branch while he pictured the old kook in his mind. He almost lost his balance, and he put his hand out to steady himself on the trunk of a tree. Benson let Marian slide to the ground and rushed straight to Ian.

"I just needed—" Ian started, but Benson wouldn't let him finish, growling and pointing at the tree. Ian looked closely at the tree. "A Hearthwood," he muttered.

Benson urged Ian to keep moving. They were only a few hundred yards from the cabin, and there was work to be done when they arrived. Ian backed away from the tree, which was an ancient trap set by the Vorkyre during the struggle to save Ephorus. Taking no chances, he turned away and moved on, hearing Marian groan as Benson hoisted her into his arms. He would carry her the last stretch. They needed to rest, or death would find them long before they confronted her father.

Trudging forward, Ian kept his eyes on the path, refusing to slow down. They finally broke into the clearing, the cabin a welcome sight in the fading sunlight. Benson shoved past Ian, Marian's swinging legs kicking him in the head as they passed, and set her down in one of the chairs outside the door.

Ian was about to gripe and needle his friend, but he didn't have enough energy, mental or physical, to make it worth the effort. Instead, he took a seat beside Marian. Benson was unusually obliging: he retrieved Ian's pipe and even went so far as to fill the bowl and set it alight for him before heading out into the woods again. Ian took a grateful puff and laughed despite the pain gripping his chest.

Looking at Marian, he saw her eyes begin to open. "How are you feeling?"

"Like I should be dead," she answered. She started to laugh but grimaced instead.

Ian gave her his hand to grip while she fought off the pain. "Maybe we should avoid laughter for now."

"But you two are such buffoons. It can be quite funny sometimes." Marian smiled.

"You know, you should get beaten up more often," he added, taking another puff from his pipe.

"That's a novel thought. And why would you say that?"

"Your blood matches your hair well. It has quite a stunning effect."

Marian wasn't quick enough to stifle the laugh and she gripped Ian's hand tight as she fought off a surge of pain in her side. "Not funny," she mumbled, her eyes shut tight until the pain lessened.

"I hope you know you're not a good liar." Ian reluctantly let go of her hand and pushed himself up, grunting through his aches and pains. "Benson's grabbing some wood and will be back to get a fire going."

"And you?" she asked, watching him stagger a few steps.

"I need to find more water. We've got to get ourselves cleaned up and make sure we're not getting infected. Plus, I've got a few nifty potions to help the pain, but they'll need an activating agent."

Marian nodded, pulling her legs in as close as

her broken body would allow. "You'll be back soon, though?" she asked.

"Benson before me, but I'll be back soon. There's a stream not too far from here."

He saw fear in her eyes, but he couldn't stay with her. It was already hard enough for him to walk and gather what he needed as the sun set. Reaching into her bag, he pulled out his father's journal. He knelt beside Marian and thumbed through the pages, smiling when he found what he was looking for.

"It took me a while to rummage through my parent's things after they died. I didn't know how to handle it, or, really, anything at that moment. Me and Benson were pretty lost for a time," he paused, his emotions running high. "But," he placed the book in Marian's lap, "I stumbled across this journal one day, and it was bookmarked on this page."

"What is it?" Marian asked as she stared at a page filled with incomprehensible letters.

"It's an old trick used by potion masters back when they were being hunted and jailed. Anyone who harnesses the power of Ephorus, through enchantments, potions, or, in your case, fire, can run their finger across the page to read the message. Just don't set it on fire," Ian warned. "I've noticed you tend to destroy the things you touch," he added with a wry smile, gripping his pipe between his teeth.

"Jackass," Marian mumbled, staring at him before she gave in and tested the page. Gently pressing her finger on it, she channeled the fire into her hand, letting it warm her finger, and the letters on the page began to shine as they changed form, revealing a new passage.

"Amazing." She started reading quickly.

"By the time you're done, Benson should be back," Ian said. "Me too, if you're really slow."

He offered one last smile, but Marian couldn't stop herself from glaring at him.

# Forty-Seven

The large hearths of the Old King's throne room were toiling away to fight the cold nights, their light casting a faint glow around Nance. His mood was sour, and his presence reeked of disdain and contempt. Word had been waiting for him of his trackers' failure to retain his daughter, and her presence near the Aurian Hills was troubling him. She had known nothing of how he was defeated years before, but his insecurities were nagging at him, gnawing away at his comfort; a weakness within him was being unleashed. He needed to take the power the Trofasthet had harnessed through the years and make it his own to stop the spread.

The Trofasthet had managed to harvest the power of Ond, a fallen Vorkyre who had succumbed to the venom during a battle beyond the Logi Mountains generations before. Breaking from his brethren, Ond had declared himself the sole possessor of the First Walker's intent. Forced into exile, he built a temple to himself on the rocky grounds of Trension and began siphoning away lost souls to follow in his teachings as he fought to regain his place above all creation.

With a growing army of worshipers, the Vorkyre were left with no choice but to depose him of his throne. Those who remained in the wake of his death formed the Trofasthet, passing down the teachings Ond had managed to pass on.

Tucked away in the manuscripts penned by their ancestors were enchantments to control the world and all that live in it if someone were powerful enough to harness them. These ancient writings and the Trofasthet had become invaluable to Nance, and he was beginning to see how much they understood that. After delaying the completion of the Hearthwood, Sir Garrin now dared to make him wait. He was going to have to reassert his dominance before they crept too far from his control.

His eyes wandered down to the chest at his feet containing the Hearthwood, aching for a chance to cause terror and fire once more. Nance thought to give them a demonstration of what could be done with such a force, but the voices in the Hearthwood needed to be tamed first.

"Am I to sit here all day with just my thoughts to keep me company, or are these people ever going to show up?" he asked Sever, growing more impatient by the second.

"I believe their worship ceremonies are almost over, sir. If you wish, I can go pound on the door of their chapel and tell them to hurry it up."

Nance considered the proposition but declined. He wanted any show of force to come from him. "No, no," he said, waving his hand, turning to a portrait the

Old King had commissioned of himself with Sir Garrin and his Council. The image was indulgent drivel, but the brushwork was impeccable. The king stood out in his gilded white linens and jewelry, a pathetic attempt by a meager mind to prove his worth and power. The Trofasthet behind him were clad in black robes. No insignia, no markings, nothing of this world beyond the necessary. They understood power, and it made Nance uneasy.

"No need to get their robes in a bunch," Nance scoffed. "Speaking of which, who wears a black robe all day? I mean, take my outfit for example: dark, yes," he stood to show off his outfit, "but look at these accents I had them put in. You've got some nice purples, a little dark maroon, and," he pulled his vest forward, showing off the buttons, "amber buttons to symbolize the fire that grows restless inside. Elegant, yes. Indulgent, no. The perfect accoutrement to power that so many overlook."

"Fully agree, sir," Sever said. "Never could find it in me to trust a man who hid behind a black cloak, whether literal or metaphorical."

Taken aback by the insight, Nance stared at him. "I didn't realize you could be so eloquent, Sever. That was quite a poignant statement."

"Thank you, sir," he said with a smile. "I felt the moment may have called for a bit of brevity."

"Too true, too true. I always find that—" he stopped at the sound of boots in the hallway. The lighthearted banter ceased, and Nance made a low, guttural growl as he awaited his chance to prove there was no one above him.

Your fear amuses me, Maven's voice cackled loudly in his thoughts, breaking his concentration. He immediately looked around the room for his sister. She was not there, but his skin still crawled as if she were running her sharp nails down his back. Why must my family always disappoint me? her voice rang out again.

The doors to the throne room swung open, and the Trofasthet entered, forming a line around the throne, their backs to the wall and their heads bowed to the floor. The Old King walked into the room with Sir Garrin, visibly perturbed with Nance's presence in his throne. He said nothing to them. The doors swung shut with a loud clang, and the three men waited for the reverberation to end before speaking.

"I am glad to see that you are comfortable." The Old King's voice was curt and tinged with displeasure.

"Oh, quite so. Thank you." Nance smiled, showing no sign of moving from his seat.

"You remember Sir Garrin, the high priest of the Trofasthet," the Old King said.

"But of course, we've kept in touch quite often," Nance answered, glancing down at the Hearthwood chest. "And now that we are all here, let us bring to the table the matter of recapturing my daughter and bringing her companions in for some new and marvelous kind of torture." He paused and looked at Sir Garrin, trying to see his face under the shroud of darkness his hood provided. "I say new because I assume with all your free time and pent-up frustrations, you must have come up with some remarkable ways to make people scream."

"We do what is necessary." Sir Garrin's voice lacked any shred of humor.

In generations past the Trofasthet had used the destructive power granted by Ond as their inquisitions tore through Ephorus, torturing and killing those who would not convert. Were it not for the few remaining good Vorkyre who stopped them, the Trofasthet would have taken over Ephorus. Beaten, but not destroyed, the founders of the Trofasthet took the dead bodies to Trension and buried them outside Ond's Temple in the restless volcanic soil, worshipping the Hearthwoods that grew from their graves—the same Hearthwoods that gave their power to Nance's endeavor.

Nance knew the Trofasthets' faith was powerful. They were unshakeable in their devotion to and pursuit of restoring the name of Ond as the true ruler of creation, and their desire for the destruction of anyone who opposed them brought out the anger and darkness in the hearts of all beings. Their willingness to die for their beliefs had taken all but one of the Vorkyre to their graves. The Trofasthet wanted to bring death to Ephorus, to wipe clean the pox that was civilization, and allow the venom to restore it to its purest form: a dark and fiery hellscape. Theirs was a bleak and dismal desire, but it afforded Nance an ally to help him break the last links of protection the Vorkyre had placed at Hallenberry Halls.

"As for you," Nance turned slowly to the Old King. "What need do I have of you to live? If I call on you to be ready, and you cannot provide such a simple service, should you even be allowed to live?"

"Service," the Old King spat back, insulted. The curly, white whiskers stretching from his chin to his chest bobbed with his head. "What 'service' do I have to provide for you? I am the king of this realm, and I intend to stay on my throne. From the shores of our city to the Logi Mountains that sit behind your walled-off little fortress, this land belongs to me and its people." His eyes locked on Nance's. "All of its people are my subjects."

Resistance was to be expected, and it was quite enjoyable to see. So few people sought to stand up to Nance, especially those with no ability to defend their positions of power. The petulant man had been given the title of Old King after Nance helped him take back the power he had bestowed on his son. Wasting away in irrelevance, watching his heir ignore his desires, the Old King sought to regain his pitiful reign in Crescent City, and Nance had obliged him. Many thought it was Nance who sank the blade into the heart of the Old King's son, but he had merely watched.

Bathed in the blood of his son, Nance enlisted the Trofasthet to use the power of their enchantments to grant him strength and life, washing away the decrepit nature of aging. The Old King took solace in the teachings of the Trofasthet, aligning the murder of his only son will the will of Ond, and was eager for Nance to bring their presence back to the mainland. Nance bartered with the King and ended up with an army that could vanquish any uprisings. But, to his surprise, few people revolted under the heavy-handed rule that fell upon them from the influence of the Trofasthet. The cities and villages of Ephorus submitted to the rule of the Old King and the Trofasthet, and in a matter of years, the world had devolved, wallowing in the muck and depravity of its evangelical followers, bringing itself closer toward the wickedness Nance knew rested at its heart.

"No one is subject to you." Nance smiled as he spoke, his eyes flaring red and his hands sparking flames. He towered over the Old King, and the man began to crumble at his knees; the weight of years he was never meant to have dragged him down. The Old King had let the spoils Nance had rewarded him with inflate his sense of worth, forgetful of what it took to gain back a life that was draining away.

"I am Tomas McCordian!" the Old King called out, summoning the scattered remains of his courage. "Ruler of Crescent City and protector of its great Tower. King of all Ephorus and protector of its mighty shores. All who stood in my way were laid to rest as I ascended to the throne! You are to bow in the presence of your king." His voice grew weak as he carried on, his threat hollow and pathetic.

Nance stopped inches from the Old King, letting his flames lick at the man's clothes. The fine garments would ignite quickly. Smiling, Nance let the flames settle in his eyes so he could take in the trembling man before him without distortion.

"Your kingdom, this realm, this world," he began, his malice building deep within, "has always, and will forever, belong to me. Not even death will be able to hold me back from my reign."

"I am king," the old man protested. "We agreed that I would rule, that I would command Ephorus!"

"And so you did, for as long as I deemed necessary."

"But the people!" he shouted. "The people will revolt. They will not bow to the likes of you and your kin." The Old King spat at Nance's feet, inciting a wave of maniacal laughter from him.

"My dear Old King," Nance said through his laughter as he gripped the man's clothes and ignited them, "you underestimate the desire in our world for darkness and death."

Nance roared with laughter as he listened to the Old King scream with pain. The fire scoured the man's body, ripping through the spell cast upon him years ago that kept him strong despite his age. Within a few moments, Nance held in his hands a frail old man, weakened by life and failure and begging for mercy. Letting him drop to the floor, Nance turned to Sir Garrin, indicating that he should have his men remove the shriveled mess on the stone floor.

"This world will not fall to you or darkness," the Old King whimpered as he was hoisted to his feet.

"Interesting notion. Please give it some more thought as you fall from your precious tower to the street below."

Sir Garrin nodded toward his men holding up the Old King, and the doors flung open as they dragged him away, ignoring his cries.

"Phillip!" Nance shouted, catching a glimpse of his

servant waiting patiently outside the throne room.

"Yes, sir," the young servant spoke, his voice barely audible from the damage caused at Nance's hand.

"Escort the Hearthwood down to Sir Garrin's workroom." He looked at the leader of the Trofasthet and said, "You know the power that I seek from my sister."

"We have been unsuccess—" Sir Garrin was cut off by the raised hand of Nance.

"Spare no fiber of her being. Bind it to the Hearthwood and my will. I demand her obedience."

Nance's words echoed off the walls as the men around him fell silent. There was panic behind the fire in the Master's eyes, but his voice did not show it.

"It will be done, sir."

Sir Garrin motioned for his followers to file out, taking his place at the rear while Phillip and Sever joined him with the Hearthwood chest.

Alone with his thoughts, Nance tried to trace the nagging feeling he'd had since receiving word of his daughter's location. He closed his eyes, and when he opened them, he was in his study at Steinigen. His eyes roamed around the room, examining its contents. He stared at a row of books that had been left askew.

How is it that you've forgotten already? Maven whispered; her voice far too close for comfort.

Nance's eyes darted from the shelf to a chair in the corner on which sat a decrepit-looking figure.

Creeping around in my thoughts, dear sister, how pedantic of you. Nance masked his surprise and fear. He kept his eyes on her while trying to move, but his body would not oblige.

Maven's fingernails pierced the wooden arms of the chair as she pushed herself up, a familiar scent of brimstone filling the room when she began to laugh. Moving across the floor, her feet appeared to hover as her black robes dragged behind her. She stopped beside the shelf that he had been looking at and began riffling through the books.

My dear brother, I told you to keep control of your mind, or you would lose it.

"I have lost nothing," Nance seethed, desperately trying to raise his fists and light the fire within him.

That's not what the enchantress says, Maven cackled, watching Nance sort through his thoughts.

A small, leather-bound journal appeared in his hands, and he had a heavy feeling of defeat.

"Old enchantments mean nothing to the power I now control, and you are far too dead for me to continue dealing with your annoyance." Nance shut his eyes, seeking to return to Crescent City and escape the inner realms of thought, but a searing pain ripped through his body.

His eyes opened to see his sister's frail body standing before him, black ooze dripping out of her hollow eyes and trailing down her cheeks, searing the gray, leathery skin that struggled to hold her bones in place.

We had an arrangement, Maven hissed, her nails digging into Nance's side, her venom pouring into him. You disappointed me.

Yes, but you're still dead. Nance felt powerless against her.

Death is but one means of existence. When you fail at the hands of my creation, I will show you what your disappointment will cost.

Nance's eyes opened, his body bursting into a furious rage, fire consuming the throne he sat on as he fought the pain gripping his body. His daughter's motive was clear. He strode toward the doors, scorching the stone beneath his feet, flinging them open as the wood cracked and groaned from the heat.

"Sever!" Nance shouted.

Sever's stone feet clashed with the floor as he sprinted toward his Master's call. Nance's rage set fire to each gaudy painting the Old King had commissioned of himself hanging gaudily on the walls around him.

"Yes, sir!" Sever shouted, turning the corner to see Nance striding toward him, the hall aflame behind him.

"Send word to our forces at Steinigen that I want them to bombard Hallenberry Halls. Tell them to gather what mercenaries they need and leave no one left alive who does not bow at their request. I want Hallenberry Halls burned to the ground. No excuses. No failures. When the job is done, they are to raze every speck of land between Hallenberry Halls and Crescent City. My daughter does not live past the day she steps foot in that place. It's time for Steinigen to serve its purpose and sever the covenant set at that hideous place. No more waiting."

"Yes, sir," Sever answered sharply, before turning to leave again.

"Wait!" Nance shouted, stopping the stone behemoth in his tracks. "Make sure we collect the body of the Old King. I just had an awful idea spring to mind."

"Right, sir." Sever turned and hurried away. At any moment the Old King would be pitched from the top of the Tower and though it would take a few minutes for Sever to get to the street below, the old man's body would reach it in seconds.

# Forty-Eight

Fear gripped Inibri's thoughts. She had seen the power wielded by the Master a long time ago at Sorrow Falls and it haunted her dreams. Now she watched Nance's handiwork in the woods beneath her—the tall man who had become the Master's first victim and messenger. They followed him in hopes Paramel would track them and dispatch the wicked creature from existence. But the man raged forward relentlessly, from village to village, poisoned and driven by the darkness that flowed within him until his body finally collapsed beside a stream.

Pight leaned down from the branch they rested upon, hoping to hear the man as he argued with himself. Distraught sobs mingled with ruthless cries for more blood.

"What do you think he's waiting for?" She fought to control her rage.

The man sat beside a river, cursing his reflection and clawing at his face, dispatching the discolored blood from beneath his skin.

"I don't know." Inibri grabbed Pight's shoulder to

stop her instinct to charge forward.

"We can get closer. We're too high up for him to even see us."

"We've seen what he's capable of," Inibri said. "Our purpose is best-served to—" Inibri clapped her hands over her mouth as Pight leaped from the branch and flew toward the evil resting by the river, retching black bile into the water.

She tried to follow Pight's path with her eyes, but she was gone, disappearing into the foliage and weaving through the branches with ease.

"No!" Inibri shouted, unable to contain her fear as she dived through the canopy, her eyes catching Pight creeping up to the man writhing in agony beside the creek. Inibri's heart fluttered and her wings froze when the man shouted, and she descended in a heap upon the ground.

"I know you're there!" His voice was a mixture of pain and joy; tears mixed with laughter. "You don't have to hide from me."

The man turned to face Pight, causing her to cry out as she stumbled away from him. He leaped toward her in bounds, slamming his hand on top of her before Inibri could fly over and protect her.

Pight stared at the man. There was black liquid dripping from his eyes as he cried above her, the stench of brimstone engulfing the air when it landed on the ground.

"She did this to me," the man said through clenched teeth. Clawing at his skin, he tore chunks of flesh from his body, fighting the venom.

"Please," Inibri shouted, edging closer, landing just out of his reach. "She's innocent. There is no need for this."

The man's face burned bright red. "For what cause do I deserve to suffer!" His hand tightened around Pight, and she gagged, her breath forced from her lungs.

"We know someone who can help," Inibri pleaded, desperate to find a way to free Pight. "We know someone who can destroy the wickedness inside you."

"No," a screeching voice hissed from within him, venom dripping from his rotting teeth. "There is nothing that can help him now."

Before Inibri could speak the man began convulsing violently, the black liquid pouring out from his mouth, soaking the ground beneath him. Pight screamed as his grip loosened and the ooze covered her body. The man shriveled up on the ground beside her, the ooze flowing toward the river with Pight in its grasp.

"Help me!" she screamed, caught in the thick liquid.

Inibri flew to her but had to fall back as the liquid reached up to capture her as well. No matter where she flew, its grasp followed.

"Pleas—" Pight was cut short by the liquid seeping into her mouth.

Planting herself beside the river, Inibri sank her palms into the soil and, with every ounce of power she had, called a swath of mushrooms to the earth's surface. They glowed brightly in hues of varying shades, rising above her head. The mushrooms shook and shriveled, turning grey and withering as they became engulfed by the liquid. Inibri fought with the soil beneath her to call forth more, desperate to stop Pight's body from being washed away.

With one last effort, Inibri screamed, giving every ounce of energy she had to the earth, intent on surrounding Pight with a plethora of fungi. The ground beneath her shivered, rumbling as they shot up, their light too bright for Inibri to look at. She could see Pight's body stuck precariously between two withering mushrooms soon to lose their grip on the soil.

"Pight!" she screamed, lunging for her, ready to die alongside her rather than watch her be carried away. Grasping what felt like a hand, Inibri pulled as hard she could. As the light from the fungi faded, Pight was lying beside her, choking on the liquid coursing through her lungs and throat.

Turning her over, Inibri pounded her back and squeezed her stomach until her friend stopped retching, ignoring her cries of pain until the last of it was out.

"Inibri," Pight whispered, her voice weak.

"It's okay now," she replied. "We're okay now."

"No," Pight answered as her voice broke and she began to cry.

Inibri looked up to see traces of the liquid coursing underneath Pight's skin as she writhed on the ground. The black ooze was crawling through her veins and working its way to her eye, where it seared black streaks on her sclera, reaching into her pupil.

"I don't want to die," Pight cried as Inibri lifted herself up, kneeling over her friend.

The world around them lost its life, turning gray from the venom, leaving Inibri and Pight in near darkness. The sun was setting behind the trees, taking what little hope Inibri had left with it.

The black venom was flowing upstream toward the Aurian Hills. Inibri pulled Pight into her arms and chanted softly into her ears. They were alone, and no help was coming.

# FORTY-NINE

From the outside, the Tower of Crescent City was one of the magnificent structural achievements of Ephorus. It stood over ten stories high, making it visible from every corner of the city. On a clear day, fishermen could see its parapet from miles out at sea as it beckoned them back toward the prosperous shores. Before being routed out by the Trofasthet in their first attempt to assert the will of Ond, potion masters and enchanters used to gather at night to perform light shows for the people, channeling dragons and bears, falling stars and exploding suns, entertaining everyone for the sake of goodwill.

The parapets stayed dark at night now; pious idolatry had done its damage. Now, anyone other than the Trofasthet caught using potions or enchantments near the Old King was apprehended and given a chance to convert or die. The people of Crescent City no longer looked at the Tower with wonder and awe. They stayed quiet, their eyes forward. Content with their safety and wealth they were granted, they didn't dare challenge their place.

Phillip had seen many wretched sights, but even he was cautious walking behind the Trofasthet as they made their way to the depths of the Tower. The light of the outside world ceased to exist, the walls were chilled from soil and rock that had never felt the touch of the sun. Fire lit their way, bouncing on torches and swaying with their movements, but they did little to add warmth in this dark and desolate space. Phillip tracked the number of steps he had taken, memorizing a map of twists and turns as they passed cells filled with bedraggled men and beasts resting between punishments. The smell of rotting flesh caused his eyes to water. Death lingered everywhere.

As they went farther down, the smell diminished and the chill increased. Even Phillip's heavy cloak was useless against the cold. He grabbed a torch from the wall, hoping it would provide some warmth, and its light fell into one of the cells beside him.

Phillip saw stacked bodies. None were moving. None were alive. A thick black liquid covered each of them.

"We do not waste experimental material here," Sir Garrin whispered in Phillip's ear.

Startled by the man's presence, Phillip swallowed the bile that fought to free itself from the confines of his stomach. "Is death not the end of your experiments?"

"Not anymore," Sir Garrin answered, his eyes fixed on Phillip's face.

Their shadows danced along the walls. Phillip could see his breath lingering in the air but not Sir Garrin's.

"Shall we carry on? I can show you what we are working on for your master with the Hearthwood," Sir Garrin said.

"Yes." Phillip wanted to say more, but the words stuck in his throat.

He watched Sir Garrin slip back into the procession, taking the lead as they moved forward again, his followers two by two behind him. Letting out a deep breath, Phillip joined the end of the line and stiffened his resolve, cautioning himself against distraction while around the Trofasthet. But before long, somehow, he found himself at the front alongside their leader.

Sorcery, he thought to himself, searching for an answer. He walked cautiously, listening for every sound, realizing he had nowhere to hide. At Steinigen he had grown arrogant in his stealth. Now, on floors far below the light of day, he was a loud and obvious target for a group that was devoted to torturing and destroying everything they saw as impure.

Phillip continued counting his steps as he moved alongside Sir Garrin at an agonizing pace. There had been many moments in his life when he thought he would surely die, but he had never felt more fear than now. What little sanctuary he may have had in the presence of the Master slipped away with every step.

He dared not look into the cells anymore. He knew what was in them, and he could not afford to lose concentration again. The men came to a halt, Phillip realizing he was now meters behind them all. When they parted, Phillip saw Sir Garrin facing him far away at the front of the line. Phillip's breath became short, his mind struggling to understand how he had slipped behind everyone again. Sir Garrin's lips formed a wretched smile. Phillip's breath became short, his chest visibly beating beneath his cloak. The Hearthwood case was open in the arms of a man beside him. A faint glow beckoned to him from it.

Phillip reached into the box, his fingers gingerly sliding across the rugged bark of the Hearthwood. Feeling a sharp prick, Phillip could sense a drop of blood forming at the tip of his finger. The Hearthwood seemed to groan with pleasure, its edges warping and creating an undulating opening for Phillip's hand to slide into. It yearned for him, but its light grew dim as a hissing sound of laughter echoed in the darkness around him.

Looking up, Phillip found himself beside Sir Garrin, a cell door open in front of them. He tried to take a step back, but the force pushing him forward was too strong.

"Do not fear," Sir Garrin's words rang in his ear. Phillip turned around but found himself alone, locked in the cell, the Hearthwood in his hands. "This cell already has an honored guest who will be helping us complete the process your Master so desperately seeks to control with the Hearthwood." Sir Garrin's voice rang out before silence gripped the darkness around him. Even the Hearthwood's light bowed to its power.

Phillip peered into the darkness, aching for sanity to return, his mind crumbling as he began to mumble uncontrollably. Light burst forth, illuminating the walls of the cell, casting a green glow on all it touched.

As his eyes adjusted to the light, Phillip saw the Plaga, the bringer of sorrows, the Master's sister, lying on a stone slab. She was motionless with her arms crossed on her chest, a peaceful look on her face. Phillip had not yet been born when she was sent away, but she had been his father's last sight and the one who sent for his mother.

"You have a connection," Sir Garrin whispered as he crept over to Phillip, his form distorted by the light.

"There is no connection with the dead," Phillip muttered, turning his eyes from the body before him so he could try to focus on the malleable figure dancing around him in the light.

You disappoint me, child.

Her voice rang through his head, breaking what little grip on sanity Phillip had left. He turned to see her hollowed eyes staring at him, her fingernails gripping the stone as she lifted herself off the slab.

Wake up, and know that your nightmares are real, she hissed, her hand lunging forward, her nails digging into his chest, making their way to his heart.

Phillip screamed, falling to his knees in agony. His skin was boiling, his flesh burning from within. He yearned to see the light one last time before the darkness gripped him for eternity.

Maven, the Plaga, was gone with the darkness, and the sun shone upon Phillip. Screams surrounded him, drowning out his own as he peered over the parapet and saw a crowd of people gathered on the street beneath the Tower, the limp remains of the Old King crumpled on the earth before them. Phillip was standing among the Master's warlocks, who were content with their work, content with their fledgling sense of power.

# Fifty

"No, sir, I haven't," Artimus said through her teeth, her hair covering her eyes.

Elder Rollins, one of the three chief scribes at Hallenberry Halls, had increasingly seemed to find pleasure in her misery. When drunk, bored, or lazy, he made her his whipping post until his desired level of amusement was reached. Artimus had dealt with the horrors of being a slave in Steinigen, so having a cranky old man act like a child outside her living quarters at night was merely annoying rather than frightening.

"Well, have you at least organized the scrolls from yesterday's studies?" the rotund Elder Rollins asked.

"No, sir. Once again, I have not."

"Would you care to tell me why?" His bark was far worse than his bite considering the foul odor that was his breath coming out in waves when he yelled. Somewhere in that bulbous open mouth were rotting teeth and the flesh from a previous meal he was too lazy to address and remove.

Through the haze of her half-opened eyes, Artimus could make out his flapping jowls as he moaned in disbelief, a flush of anger spreading across his pockmarked face. She lacked any desire to deal with his intoxicated rampage any longer as he began to try and push his way past her and into her quarters. No matter her place in these Halls, she would not be pushed around or sacrifice what little sanctuary she had. Artimus shoved his engorged figure back into the hallway, his head cracking against the stone wall.

Time had not been kind to her mood, or her body after she returned from the depths Paramel had sent her to. The burning sensation in her left eye had dissipated, but the green had begun to reach past her eye, streaking across her face and down her neck. The jagged green marks were stark against her pale blue skin and had become a source of disgust and fear for everyone around her, except for Erin, who had been avoiding her and her questions.

"And where do you think you're going? I am an Elder and you will show me respect!" he shouted, his bulbous body staggering from his impact with the wall. "Would you like me to have your privileges taken from you again?" He spat more than spoke, his senses dimming further as the alcohol coursed through his blood.

Artimus turned on her heels, the green in her eye flaring as anger surged toward her fingertips. Her hand reached out, her fingers spread wide, and the shadows surrounding the bulbous man before her whipped him back into the stone wall.

Elder Rollins dropped to the floor, his eyes glazing over quickly as he lost his grip on consciousness. The loud thud his head had made gave her a moment of worry until she heard his irritating chuckle and then a steady snore.

Turning toward her room, Artimus managed to muster a "Goodnight, Elder Rollins," refraining from the desire to kick loose the rotting teeth in his mouth as the light in her eye dimmed.

Pushing past her door, she lumbered toward her bed, her legs feeling heavier with every step as the sweet release of sleep came closer, the warmth and safety of her bed giving her refuge from the looming disaster that awaited her thoughts every morning.

"I see the old drunk is at it again," a voice rang out from behind her.

Startled, Artimus leaped into her bed and yanked the covers over her head. "Who's there? And go away, I want to sleep!"

"It's just me, you weird little elf," Erin said as Artimus slowly lowered the sheets to see her walking out of the shadows of the night.

"Fine, but get under the covers because I need to sleep."

"Sorry my dear, but—"

"But nothing, he abandoned me in that wretched place and you stopped answering my questions. I'm not dealing with this tired, so you can join me in bed or leave."

Artimus pulled the covers over herself, holding them tight against her skin, the soft fabric bringing a small moment of joy as it caressed her body.

Erin walked to the nightstand, lighting the candle

there before using its flame to bring life to the wicks on the other candles around the room. Artimus relinquished her desire for a peaceful night of sleep. She pulled the covers off her body and pressed her feet on the cold stone floor to help her wake up.

"And why have you decided that, at the very moment when I feel comfortable closing my eyes again, you should come to disturb me?"

"It's not me that comes calling on you at this hour, but your former Master. A carrier pigeon arrived with this minutes ago." Erin offered a sealed letter to Artimus. Erin's unease at the previous question showed in her eagerness to avoid Artimus's eyes. Erin pulled away as Artimus snatched the note from her and walked over to the small window slit, barely big enough to catch a glimpse of the moon.

Sealed with an emblem of Steinigen and seared at its edges, there was no mistaking the letter's origins. Artimus grabbed a small knife she kept with her things, letting the blade make quick work of the seal, carefully opening the folded parchment to read her instructions; a garrison of soldiers was on their way to destroy her new home, and she was to ready the Elders for death or obedience. After she finished, she dipped the edge of the parchment into the candle by her bed and let the flame consume it. A sickening howl was released as the ink, the blood of an unfortunate victim, burned up. A green glow began to emanate from Artimus's eye, the marks on her cheek and neck following. She was tired. The cadre of anger, sadness, and confusion was breaking the fortitude she had spent years building.

"I hate being alone," Artimus whispered into the air.

"What?"

"I said I hate being alone!"

The shadows cast by the candles all around the room seemed to fill with Artimus's mood. They swelled with indignation and turned to Erin, trying to grab hold of her. Erin instantly shifted into her shadow form and hid in the dark under Artimus's bed.

"Artimus, you are not alone! I was with you all day and evening. We parted ways just minutes before you came to lie down."

Ridiculous, Artimus thought, her mind plagued by the pang of solitude. She began to retrace her steps that day hoping to prove her anger valid only to realize that she had seen Erin's smiling face at almost every turn. Her chest began to tighten, fear gripping her heart. "Why does it feel like I've been alone for days?" The green glow in her eye and on her face died out, and the angry shadows subsided.

"This light, this power you have," Erin said softly, slipping out from under the bed and moving toward her, "it traps you in time, so you experience hours in a single moment." Shifting into her human form, she raised her hand to caress the mark on Artimus's cheek. "If you focus on pain or sorrow or abandonment, you will feel every moment you've ever had through time. It will distort all your memories and compress them into one if you let it."

"Get it out of me," Artimus begged, grabbing Erin's hand and pressing it against her heart. "Please."

"There is no other way." Erin choked back the desire

to give in and save her friend from the madness. "But I can help you control it. I can help you use it to save yourself."

"If you can help me control it, then why haven't you yet?"

"I've tried. You've just forgotten."

Scattered memories of desperate attempts to maintain control tumbled through her thoughts. In each one was the journal... The journal, she thought to herself, her hands digging frantically around her bed until they stumbled across its gentle leather surface. It was Paramel's journal, but now hers. As she flipped through the first few pages, she found copious notes in her handwriting scribbled in the margins. As she read about her struggles of the last few weeks, her mind reached back and recreated those lost moments vividly. She had been working near nonstop, furiously fighting the passage of time and the breaking of her mind.

"You must keep this journal with you. You must fight against the darkness creeping into your mind or you will be consumed by fear and doubt, and it will all too easily continue to warp your thoughts." Erin pressed the journal to Artimus's chest before pulling her in tightly, wrapping her arms around her body.

"They're coming to destroy this place," Artimus whispered.

"They're coming to destroy our world," Erin added, pulling away. "If Hallenberry Halls is destroyed, the last line of protection the Vorkyre gave to humanity will fail, and the Master will be one step closer to controlling life in this world and death in the other."

"Will Paramel know?"

"He knows. And we won't see him here again."

"So we're alone," Artimus's voice began to shake as she held the journal tight.

"No, not at all," Erin smiled, leaning in to kiss her forehead.

# FIFTY-ONE

Inibri sat in silence, her mind racing through the possible levels of torment she would endure were she to lose Pight. None were appealing. Inibri had built her life around their bond. Pight was the only one ever brave enough to venture out with her; the only one to continue to acknowledge she existed and deserved love amongst their people.

A new round of gagging broke Inibri's thoughts. She turned to see Pight struggling, her chest heaving while the black liquid dripped down her chin. Inibri had done the best she could to get Pight to safety, but her strength had been expelled during the fight for Pight's life, and she was passing her breaking point. Tears streamed down her cheeks while she wondered if she was watching her friend slowly die. Inibri couldn't hold her feelings in anymore, and she released a scream to the world around her.

There was no reaction from her surroundings; Inibri's scream barely registered with the birds and other creatures as they went about their lives. The cries of pixies had been ignored by this world for generations.

"We're alone." Her voice was hollow. "But we will not stop. I will not stop."

Her legs were weak and her body ached, but Inibri intended to carry on, for better or worse. She did her best to lift Pight into her arms and trudge with her through the forest. There was a hidden pixie village to the east, toward the Gallen River. It would take them days to reach it at this speed, but it was their only option. There was nowhere else they could go.

She had never been grounded in such a way, weighed down by Pight's limp figure. Inibri had always seen the world from above, and, even in dark times, she could find hope while flying. That was much harder now as she felt every sharp pebble under her feet. The ground was hard and unforgiving compared to the air, and while trying to carry Pight over a large, exposed root, Inibri tripped and tumbled, her head slamming against it. The ringing from the impact was loud and ceaseless, and it took her a few moments to realize she wasn't the only one in pain.

"I'm sorry!" she shouted, pushing herself up and stumbling back to Pight, who lay on the ground, writhing in pain, black droplets dripping from her eyes as she cried out. Inibri rushed to her side to try and soothe her. "I'm here."

Pight continued squirming, her arms and legs lashing out uncontrollably, unaware of what they struck. When Inibri tried to wipe away the ooze that had congealed around her eyes, she felt a sharp sting on her fingers, as if a knife tore into her skin, and she recoiled. Pight opened her eyes and Inibri nearly screamed: the whites of Pight's eyes were covered with strange black lines, like spiderwebs spiraling out from her pupils. Her eyes became fixated on the lines as they slowly spread, reaching out from her eye and grabbing hold of Pight's skin.

Inibri rocked back in fear but moved closer when Pight began to mumble under her breath. She was desperate to hear Pight's voice, but it wasn't Pight speaking. Her arms latched around Inibri and dragged her down so that her body was pressed close to Pight's. The black liquid crept from Pight's skin toward Inibri's.

"I'm coming," a voice hissed from within Pight. "I'm coming."

"What are you?" Inibri cried.

"Death," the voice howled as she felt the ground shake beneath them.

Laughter erupted from within Pight, her body twisting along the ground until the laughter faded into gagging. Inibri turned her onto her side and watched the black liquid pour out from her pores, seeping into the ground, destroying everything it touched.

The root they rested beside began to crack from the poison, releasing its centuries-long grip on the ground. The cracking quickly got louder, drowning out the world around them. Inibri looked up and saw the tree withering, turning gray as the venom worked through its system. With a loud boom, the tree started to topple to the ground.

Inibri dragged Pight to safety, ignoring her screams, and the tree crashed into the woods beside them, sending up an immense cloud of dirt and debris and knocking Inibri off her feet. When the cloud settled, the venom's power was revealed: the land around them had turned gray, all life it touched gave way to death.

"This place looks horrible," Pight muttered, sitting up beside Inibri, taking in the destruction that lay before them. "What did you do?"

# FIFTY-TWO

Benson's whimper grew into a full-blown tantrum after several minutes of failure: the firewood refused to bow to his command and ignite. He had returned somewhat victoriously to find Marian asleep in her chair, the journal earmarked and resting in her lap. With concern for her comfort, he had hoisted her up and set her down gently in his large padded chair inside. Through all of that, Benson had managed not to wake her, but as the wood continued to defy him, his groans became a wake-up call for Marian.

Marian stared at him for a few moments, letting her body adjust to the pain she'd be carrying for the next few days; even though she'd be strong enough to heal herself by morning, the pain would linger. It always loved to linger. She took a moment to adjust her body in the chair, its comfortable embrace beckoning her to close her eyes and drift off again, but the sun was fading quickly and the stars were starting to shine. They needed to get the fire going to keep the chill from settling down in the cabin.

"I can help if you'd like," Marian offered with a

smile, snapping her fingers, a tiny flame jumping from the tip of her fingernail.

Benson's eyes lit up as he leaped over, pulling her up out of the chair and wrapping his giant paws around her.

"Still in pain. Still in pain," Marian squeaked as Benson squeezed.

He loosened his grip, but he wouldn't let go until she confirmed he hadn't done any permanent damage, nuzzling her face to make sure she knew he was sorry.

"It's okay, you big oaf." Marian laughed through the pain, hoping her legs wouldn't give out on her when he let go.

The first few steps were the worst, her coordination challenged to maintain the course while her legs begged to buckle. She managed to keep herself upright long enough to get to the fireplace. She reached in and spread out the damp firewood and then cupped her hands around her mouth, slowly breathing in and out, pulling forth the heat from within her. Then she closed her eyes and let the fire flow out.

She watched the flames surround the wood and infiltrate its cellular structure, the complex layers of life that the tree had accrued over decades if not centuries. It was a necessary destruction. Through the death of one life, another could continue.

Benson grumbled quietly behind her, breaking her concentration on the flames. Turning, she saw he had brought his chair for her to rest in again by the warmth of the fire. She wanted to refuse the offer and let him rest in the comfort he had grown accustomed to, but her body couldn't resist its soft cocoon, its gentle embrace giving her the ability to rest and heal herself properly for the remainder of their journey.

"Thank you," she said with a kiss to his cheek as Benson helped hoist her up from the ground, placing her carefully onto the seat. "How much longer do you think until Ian returns?"

"I don't know," a withered voice said from a dark corner of the cabin behind Ian's bed. "But I am starting to get a little worried."

Benson roared into the shadows of the room, the paintings on the walls rattling as a faint light poured out from above the headboard. Marian's eyes focused, trying to find the intruder but seeing no one. She wrested herself from the chair, gripping it for balance while spinning around, trying to help Benson find the owner of the voice.

Marian's heart began to race, and her mind offered up an image of Lyco's fists pounding on her body. Fighting the pain, she ignited her palms and let the flames crawl up to her elbows, walking toward the shadow, casting enough light to scare the darkness away from the cabin. Her rage caused the flames inside the fireplace to surge up the brick chimney.

"Rather impressive," an old man sitting in Benson's chair in front of the fire said with a smile. "But also quite unnecessary. I am not here to harm. I am here to guide." With a wave of his hand, the fire settled down, and he continued to make himself more comfortable, stretching his bare toes out to feel the warmth.

"Thanks for the help!" Marian snarled through

clenched teeth as Benson scurried toward the bed, trying to get under it for protection. "And what do you mean by guide?" Marian didn't feel a sense of immediate danger from the old man, but she would not let her guard down, keeping the flames burning on her fingertips.

"I will answer that question in due time. But it is your first question we must find an answer to. It is getting dark, and I fear the boy may have fallen prey to some unsavory characters growing restless in these woods."

"Ian!" Marian called out loudly, surprising herself.

"That is his name, but I don't believe he's close enough to hear you," the old man said, spreading his toes wide, loosening the dampened moss that had grown between them.

Marian stepped beside the old man, a flame in her palm stretching toward him. "Where is he?"

A pitiful smile crossed the man's face as he grabbed Marian's hand and pulled himself up from the chair. The flame extinguished on contact, and he groaned his way to a standing position.

"My dear, let us not begin to threaten friends and allies. It is a sure way to defeat."

Benson growled from beneath the bed, baring his teeth but holding fast to his position. He would have looked rather intimidating had he not been cowering in fear.

"Come now, Mr. Benson. Would Penelope care to hear you speak in such a manner?"

Benson went quiet, his ears perking up and his eyes

softening.

"How do you know that name?" Marian asked.

"My name is Paramel, and I am a very old friend of the family," he said with a snicker before carrying on. "Let us take a walk to save your friend, and I shall tell you a story."

"No need," a strange voice moaned from the doorway. "I've come to you."

The three turned to see a grotesque figure glowing in the light of the fire, its exposed limbs covered in tree bark and adorned with Ian's clothes as if trying to appear human. It leaked water from every crack and crevasse in its cobbled-together body as it walked. But it was the deformed human features painted on the bark where its face should be that made Marian and Benson gasp.

"It's been some time since I've seen the boy. Is that what he looks like now?" Paramel asked.

Benson roared, shaking the walls around them while he crept behind Marian for cover.

"Seriously?" she snapped at Benson. Taking her cue to protect the massive beast cowering behind her, Marian ignited her palms and limped toward the creature posing as Ian. "Where is he?"

"I am he, now. The other no longer exists," the voice creaked through the cracking bark of the tree.

"Isn't that convenient? My dear bear, have you and the human boy not made peace with the river gnomes to disperse the traps in these woods?"

Benson grumbled sheepishly, avoiding eye contact, creeping forward behind Marian like she was his shield.

"What kind of a trap is this?" Marian's energy was fading quickly, but she refused to show an ounce of vulnerability in front of this new threat. Ian needed her help, and she would rather die of exhaustion than back down.

"It appears he may have stumbled into a Hearth-wood."

Paramel scratched at the hairs on his chin, slowly stroking them as they lengthened into a full beard replete with glorious colors from sprouting wildflowers. He shook his head and the bright hues of the beard faded to gray to match his hair, the petals withering and falling to the floor at his feet.

"Can we go rescue him now, or do you need to trim your hair or change your clothes before we leave to save our friend from death?"

Marian's impatience amused Paramel. He reached up and cinched his fingers before the imposter as its bark cracked from the pressure.

"Take us to the boy," he demanded.

# Fifty-Three

The sulfrite burned the back of Nance's throat as he paced around the throne room, contemplating his next move. The Hearthwood had been harder to handle than he anticipated. It had taken years to have the materials painstakingly harvested on the island of Trension and formed into a weapon. At first, the Trofasthet had been unwilling to sacrifice the Hearthwood trees that had taken root where Ond and his first acolytes had been laid to rest, but they acquiesced when given the chance to reinstate their religion and regain the power they once had.

He stared down at Sir Garrin's addition to his Hearthwood glove: a rib from his sister was bound amongst the strands of wood; it was the closest he had been to her since his betrayal. When they began assembling the weapon, the Trofasthet realized they needed a powerful source of energy to give the Hearthwood life, to give it the awareness necessary to respond to Nance's commands. Maven had appeared to be the ideal candidate for sacrifice. However, her continued insistence on forcing her way into his mind was proving to be problematic.

Those who drew their powers from the Logi Mountains shared a bond through the fire inside them, and it was a weakness his sister was now manipulating with the Hearthwood. Her sorcery endangered his power, and Nance wanted her close, close enough to feel that she was dead. He stared down at the black lines that spread across her bone like a spider's web. They seared his arm wherever they touched, the black liquid tearing into his skin, digging into his bloodstream. Nance resented his sister's persistence in spoiling his conquests, but he also felt an odd sense of loss. Memories of his sister took hold as he closed his eyes. He could see her beauty shining in the dying light of the sun, her auburn hair stretching down to her legs as she glided across the grass outside the fortress. He could even feel her breath blowing on the back of his neck.

*I'm coming for you, brother,* her voice hissed in his thoughts.

The woman he once knew, the sister he had betrayed, dissolved, and the Plaga emerged. Her skin was cracked and leathery and her hair was black as night. A black substance dripped from her eyes and mouth as she held out her arms to welcome him in an embrace.

Nance stiffened as he felt the venomous substance crawling painfully up his forearm toward his chest. He forced his eyes open and saw the venom coursing through his body, trying to claim victory over his life. Nance gripped his wrist tightly, refusing to give in to its power.

"Not today, dear sister," he said through his teeth,

letting the fire within him surge through his veins.

His body began to glow orange, his skin bubbling from the fire burning beneath as he let it rip through his system, clearing out the venom that was intent on tearing down his mind. As it dissipated and the pain vanished, Nance felt his sense of control returning. He exhaled a plume of smoke, letting the fire within die out. The power her life had given to this weapon was immense, but her desire to control it was becoming troubling.

"A fierce weapon, sir," Phillip said softly, his throat burning from the memory of being on the receiving end of his Master's fire. His eyes remained locked on Maven's rib, the bone he had seen pushing against the withered skin of the dead body in the dungeon.

Nance peered through the smoke to see his servant staring at him with a look of horror not-quite hidden behind his reserved features.

"One in which I shall bring life and death to their knees before me." Nance turned from Phillip and made his way to the throne. He sat down enthusiastically to let his body rest. "Now, what is it you've come to bother me with?"

"Sir Garrin has informed me that the Old King is in a more understanding state of mind if you wish to speak with him again."

Even with the fear of his sister's power growing, Nance was intrigued at the chance to see just how powerful his grip over the Hearthwood had become.

"Yes, haul him up. Let's see how amenable he's become to my authority." A wicked strain of thought crept through his mind while he gazed down at his hands. "And," Nance paused, moving his fingers back and forth as the bone scraped against his skin. "Inform Sir Garrin to burn my sister's corpse. We no longer require her presence in this life, and I do not intend to have his allegiance split between myself and her corpse."

A sharp pain gripped his hand after he spoke; splinters broke off the bone and tried to stab through his skin. His fingers curled as a searing pain shot up his arm. Bracing himself against the throne, Nance wrenched the Hearthwood from his hand, setting it quickly in its case, his bloodied hand resting on top of the lid. Both Nance and Phillip sat quietly as creaks and groans emanated from the case and reverberated throughout the room. Maven's cackle bounced off the walls around them.

"Were he to refuse, sir?" Phillip asked, breaking the silence, his eyes still fixed on the case.

Nance stiffened at such a question. His mind turned quickly from the Hearthwood to the potential disobedience, but Phillip's eyes were filled with fear, not defiance. None of his trepidation appeared to be for Nance, though.

"Why would you ask?" Nance asked, unsettled by his servant's concern.

Phillip quivered, sensing a trap, and his gaze broke away from the Hearthwood. "Just being thorough, Master."

"Inform Sir Garrin I wish to see her corpse aflame in the center street where I can view it from the tower.

Should there be any refusal, Phillip, I expect to be informed immediately." Nance let his words hang there as the two men stared at each other.

Nance needed Maven's existence annihilated. Even in death, she was using her powers to claw away at his. This world had been his birthright as the male heir to Steinigen. He had once thought they could rule together, a notion Maven had even been quite keen on, but his father had decided to give it all to her. Because of his father's mistake, Nance would make the world burn.

# Fifty-Four

The nocturnal creatures of the forest were not pleased with the new arrivals. Marian's nerves were on edge with the screeches and howls that circled them and faded away into the darkness of the Aurian Hills. Benson hung close to her side as they followed Paramel's lead, watching him bicker with the tree-bark version of Ian from a safe distance. She let a flame dance atop her fingertips, its soft orange glow lighting the rough path beneath their feet.

"Where do we go from here, Marian?" she asked herself, the words slipping into the air before she could stop herself from speaking.

Benson grumbled beside her before patting her on the head.

"Sorry, I do that sometimes."

"As do I," Paramel called out cheerfully.

Marian let her question go unanswered, turning her focus to the chunk of tree leading them farther into the darkness. "Are we certain this thing can be trusted?"

"To take us to Ian, yes. To not try and trick us into being absorbed by another Hearthwood when we arrive, no."

"What do you mean?" Marian picked up her pace. She didn't want to be too far from Paramel should a threat arrive.

"This is a beast-of-burden trap," Paramel sighed. "It must've sensed a pain growing inside our young friend and convinced him to relieve himself of the worry."

"But how?"

Paramel sighed, stopping to see a dense patch of Harken Lilies growing around the base of a Hearthwood. The beast went toward the tree, stirring up the lilies' sparkling blue lights.

"He knows better than to listen to the lilies at night," Paramel murmured.

The beast turned around to face them, giving Marian another chance to see its awful attempt at reproducing a human face.

"The boy is resting," it creaked.

Paramel grabbed the beast and made the air swirl around it so fiercely that slivers of bark began to break off. The beast screamed and Paramel loosened his grip and let the wind die down. The beast pounded its head on the base of the tree until a small opening appeared. Then it pulled the tree open as if it were a curtain, revealing Ian's figure resting in its tight confines, branches beginning to wrap around his body, sap slowly rising above his feet.

"Release him at once!" Paramel shouted.

The beast roared and the Harken Lilies burst with light. Marian covered her eyes as she fell back against Benson, her mind going blank. She heard voices screaming as if in terrible pain. Her knees went weak, and her body tumbled to the ground.

"Enough!" Paramel raised his hands and whipped up the wind around the beast again, forcing the creature violently in two directions until it snapped in half with a loud groan.

The lilies went quiet, but the screaming still poured through Marian's mind. She pressed her palms against her ears, her body writhing.

The darkness began to swirl, and Marian felt like she was falling. She was in a cascade of water plunging toward a chasm filled with a green light.

Marian! a voice shouted. She could see no one in the torrent of water. Marian! the voice shouted again as she crashed into the chasm of green light.

She forced her eyes open as she landed in the chasm, her body engulfed by crashing water. There was something here, something pulling her deeper, and she was determined to see it. Her lungs filled with water as she sank. Then she saw it: two piercing eyes in the murky green water, a green fire burning bright within each pupil. The creature roared as it lunged toward Marian. She wanted to be afraid, but she wasn't. What should have been fear was overtaken by recognition. Marian knew the creature and opened her arms to embrace it.

Marian! the voice shouted again, rousing her from the vision.

The world came back to Marian. She took in her surroundings, the smells and sounds of the nocturnal forest, and found herself in Ian's arms, pinned tightly to his body as they lay atop the patch of Harken Lilies she had fallen into.

"You know," he huffed, "one of these days you're going to let me be the only one who gets in trouble and needs saving because I'm far too lazy to keep this up."

Benson groaned his agreement, hoisting the two of them off the ground simultaneously, setting them down on a fallen tree near Paramel. The old sorcerer gathered the dirt at his feet, whispering into the mound, sparking a bonfire to rid them of the remnants of Ian's imposter, its light offering a modicum of safety from the night that continued to close in on them.

Marian wanted to rebuff Ian's comment, but she could only manage to spit out mouthfuls of dark, murky water. She tried not to choke as the water worked its way out of her lungs. As she gasped for breath, she struggled to understand the pull she had felt to the creature in the watery depths.

"Where did you go, child? And what did you see?" Paramel's tone was curt.

Marian thought about the vision as Paramel dug in the dirt at her feet, examining it closely.

"I don't...," she fought to find the words, "I'm not sure. There was a massive chasm with water rushing down to it from all sides."

"And?" Paramel studied the dirt sifting through his fingers.

"And I fell into the water and began to drown until the creature came for me."

The dirt dropped from Paramel's hands, and the world went silent. Benson nudged Ian, who gave him a shrug, and they stared at Marian as she tried to figure out what had happened.

"Coming from a guy who just spent some time encased inside a tree, this is starting to get a little creepy," Ian said.

"Agreed," Marian nodded.

"There isn't much to say now," Paramel said abruptly, walking toward the fire. "Rest well you three, and carry on your journey as you intended."

"Wait! Wait!" Ian shouted, leaping up from his seat. "Our journey was to find you and your journal so you could help us. So, you know, help."

"I am no longer the help you need to seek in this battle. I will be there when it is my time, but you need to find my apprentice. She will assist you with what you need to know."

"What do we need to know?" Marian snapped. She had followed the voice in her head in hopes that it would lead her to clear answers, but nothing she had encountered offered any. "We're running blind with a maniac at our heels, and you're just going to abandon us? Aren't you supposed to be a Vorkyre, a protector of this world?"

"Time changes us all," the old sorcerer said with a heavy sigh, his eyes lost in the flames. "Seek out a young elf named Artimus at Hallenberry Halls. She is the savior you need now."

"We don't need a savior, we just need—" Ian was cut off by the roaring of flames as Paramel walked into the fire, disappearing without another word. "We need answers."

Silence drifted between them for a few moments as they fought to grasp the nature of their predicament. It was Benson who broke it first, grumbling with displeasure as he lifted his heavy body off the log to begin the long trek home.

"Right behind you, buddy." Ian turned to Marian, motioning for her to follow and reaching out his hand to help her up. "How are you feeling?"

"Defeated," she said softly, her eyes shimmering with the light of the flames. "Utterly defeated."

# Fifty-Five

Artimus paced the hallways after the Master's message arrived, a reminder to the Elders and scribes that he did not make idle threats. She ran her fingers across the cold stone walls, wondering how long they would be able to stand up to the torment of his flames. She had wanted to find some means of protection for the Halls and everyone inside, but Erin had cautioned against it. They weren't fighters, and they wouldn't last an hour against the punishment their insubordination would spark. "Help will come," Erin had assured her, but nearly a week had passed, and they were still vulnerable and alone.

The Elders had given up hope and begun removing whatever works they could, storing them in an underground cellar in hopes that the Master's forces would not search the entire grounds. It was a heartbreaking sight to see so many generations of work faced with the threat of extinction. Books by authors long dead, whisked away by time, would never be recreated if they were destroyed. In time, if these inscribed words were not protected, even memories of the lives they'd documented would vanish.

"No time for losing our spirits," Erin called out from behind her.

Artimus turned to see Erin sprinting past her. "What's wrong?"

"Follow me," Erin said without looking at her.

Artimus broke into a sprint, too, to catch up with Erin, keeping one hand at her side to make sure Paramel's journal was safe against her body. After receiving the Master's letter, she had refused to let it out of her sight, studying it repeatedly to try and gain any knowledge she could without his help, desperate to avoid the despair its power over her could cause.

Erin cut a corner abruptly, darting into the first stairwell she found, climbing quickly, taking two steps at a time while Artimus struggled to keep up with her. Neither spoke while they ascended to a wooden door and pushed it open, the air rushing against them as they stepped onto the outer walkway. The sky had gone gray, though a few lone rays of sunshine were breaking through the clouds above the meadow in front of the Halls. It would've been a pleasant sight—they had hoped for rain—were it not accompanied by an on-coming horde of troops, which marched toward them with the emblem of Steinigen held high on banners across the front lines, the dragon surrounded by fire whipping in the wind of an impending storm. Artimus's stomach began to ache as she watched them advance.

"Already," Artimus whispered to herself. She felt overwhelmed with fear, hate, and anger. "What do we do?"

"We need to go say hello." Erin's eyes didn't waver from the mass of men marching toward them.

"What?" Artimus spun Erin around to face her, frustrated.

"You are the Master's emissary. If you don't get down there, they will begin what they came here for. If you can spot one creature amongst them that does not kill or destroy on instinct, we can change plans, but from what I see, there is nothing but bloodthirsty wraiths."

"What am I supposed to say? They have direct orders an—"

"And we have a responsibility to do all that we can," Erin cut her off, leading her to the stairwell. "The Elders are still trying to save what they can of this place, and we need to give them as much time as possible."

"And Paramel?" Artimus hesitated at the top of the stairwell as Erin held her hand. Her hope for his return was quickly fading into the fear that he had abandoned them.

"We don't have time to waste. If the Elders start talking before you do, they might earn themselves a quick release from the fight that lies ahead."

She nodded, her mind finding no fault in Erin's logic, but her body still resisting the action that needed to be taken. "You'll be by my side?"

"As long as I can be," Erin smiled, leaning in and kissing Artimus, their lips connecting for a sweet moment before she began running down the stairwell.

Artimus paused as a wave of pleasure washed

through her, cutting her breath short and making her heart pound, her fingers tingling as they sought to caress Erin's form. Then her feet took flight, carrying her after Erin. Racing down the stairwell, she nearly slipped and crashed on the last tight turn into the ground-floor hallway. Through slits in the enormous stone wall, they could hear the stomping of the Master's men just a few dozen yards away.

"I would like to say before I die, that I blame you entirely for this," Artimus said, grabbing the back of Erin's neck and pulling her in for a long kiss. Their passion momentarily overshadowed their fear, and they wrapped their arms each other and pressed their bodies tight. Erin slowly pulled away and smiled.

"Typical elf reaction," Erin said, turning toward the soaring wooden doors.

"At least elves don't turn into dogs," Artimus snapped, refusing to let go of Erin's hand until she had no choice.

Reaching forward, they each grabbed one of the iron handles on the heavy doors and pulled them open. A powerful breeze blew in, almost knocking Artimus off her feet. She and Erin faced the raucous horde of soldiers. In the distance, the trees swayed violently as heavy rain started to fall. Bolts of lightning shot across the sky as if warring with one another. The loud claps of thunder echoed in the vast entrance hall like explosions.

Artimus took the lead and walked out into the rain, holding her head high and straightening her cloak to show her emblem of Steinigen. She had been free for a brief time of the oppressive torment that had come with wearing it and chafed at the notion of pretending to honor its heritage and power, but it was what needed to be done. She stopped after a few yards, the wind whipping her cloak, her emblem in clear sight. The leader of the horde stepped forward from the ranks of men.

"The weather may be in our favor," Erin mused.

Artimus merely shook her head. "The flames of Steinigen will burn through anything." She turned to offer a faint smile to Erin before her expression changed to the one she'd had for so many years when she'd lived under the tyranny of the Master. All of the affection and joy drained from her face as she stared at the approaching man.

"Emissary!" a voice called out through the wind and rain.

Artimus did not answer but bowed before walking forward to meet him, whispering to Erin to stay where she was.

"Is there any word of the Master's daughter?" the man shouted as he got closer to Artimus.

His face was haggard and his eyes hollow, and yet he looked the best of all the men around him.

"None as I've heard," she paused as she looked back at Erin, the Halls towering behind her. "The Elders are ready to live and submit to the Master's command. They will not stand in your way," she said as she faced him. "But may I suggest you rest for a night or two? The Elders would like to treat you to a feast to show their compliance with the Master's orders. If I read his note correctly, the Master wants nothing left of these Halls, but you will have a hard time setting the place ablaze in this storm."

"We do not need pleasantries," the man snarled.

"Agreed. But I can only assume you must need food and rest. Would it not be more appealing to be protected from the storm, staying dry and warm until it passes? If you set your camps now, you'll be exposed in an open field to whatever these clouds choose to deliver."

Artimus seemed emotionless, her body gently swaying in the wind while she awaited the man's response. Of all the creatures in the horde behind him, only the Traskins would find it appealing to stay outside in the wet weather.

"We will accept," he grumbled, motioning for his second in command to come forward to give the order.

Artimus could feel the rain soaking through her clothes. She turned around to look at Erin but found it impossible to return her smile.

"You did well," Erin said quietly as she came up to join her.

"I merely earned us a little time before they attempt to destroy our home."

"A little time is all we need. Paramel will have made sure our reinforcements are on their way by now."

"And you trust them?" Artimus was decidedly unhappy with the notion of trusting anyone from Steinigen.

"I do. We just have to get them here before this storm relents."

# FIFTY-SIX

Sleep seemed inappropriate after Paramel disappeared, but exhaustion defeated their desire to march on. They had intended to spend an hour or two at the cabin to gather supplies for their trek to Hallenberry, only to extend it to two days after a quick nap turned into bouts of long, blissful sleep. Everything felt normal, briefly, as if the world didn't care if they existed, as if they needn't care whether or not the world carried on.

During the two days they gave themselves to rest at the cabin, Ian, Benson, and Marian talked little. Ian nursed his pipe when not sleeping, staring into the woods beyond the porch; Benson feasted on the food they would not be taking, knowing they wouldn't be able to eat it if it spoiled, or if they died; and Marian threw herself into studying the two journals, searching for a connection or answer. She was sure an epiphany lay just after the next blot of ink or curled-up page, but her mind could not assemble the puzzle pieces, and her eyes closed as she drifted to sleep with the journals resting on her chest.

She wandered in her sleep through the passages that

had gotten stuck in her head. The journals frequently described a chasm, a great opening between the worlds of life and death that needed to be sealed to prevent the spread of darkness. Penelope wrote of the disastrous imbalance caused when the cycle of life and death is broken and how the venom seeps in when the continuity of time is lost. She described the darkness looming just beyond the Logi Mountains that longed to be set free.

Marian dreamed of falling through the rushing water, but this time she was not scared. Her eyes stayed open, and her mind focused on the creature that lay beneath the glowing water. "Show yourself," she whispered, her hair whipping behind her. She could sense the waters roiling at the sound of her voice, turning orange beneath the surface of the chasm. "Show yourself!" she shouted.

The water split beneath her and she heard a deafening roar. An enormous shackled dragon lunged toward Marian, flames lapping the sides of its mouth, smoke pouring from its nostrils, and water streaming off its leathery black skin. It refused to submit to the rushing water. It refused to have its power shackled any longer. With a mighty effort, it broke its chains and spread its wings. The dragon stood taller than the fortress at Steinigen, its wings stretching to the horizons, its presence overwhelming Marian's as the ocean would a stone. It spewed fire toward Marian, who fell happily into its warmth, her eyes fixed on its eyes until the flames took hold.

Marian watched the flames burn bright around her

while she propelled herself toward the dragon, desperate to reach out and grab hold of it. The dragon roared at her, its flames white with rage and blinding. She got ahold of its scales and began pulling herself closer. She wouldn't be stopped.

When she woke, Marian was restless. Two days had passed quietly, and now she was eager to fight. She could still feel the singe of the dragon's breath on her skin and the magnificent power it held within its body. All she needed to do was mend her wounds before they left. Most of her swelling had eased, and the bruises would heal in time, but she had what felt like a cracked rib or two that she would need to do something about.

She didn't dare risk a walk down to the river on her own, having fallen prey to the Harken Lilies twice before, so she gathered a couple of bowls that were near the stove and filled them with water Benson had fetched the morning before. Marian felt her skin tingle as she stepped outside. A stiff breeze was blowing in from the west, and the darkening sky offered a disheartening sign of the journey to come.

After scooping a patch of dirt into the bowls, Marian sat on the ground, lifted her blouse, and spread the mud across her sides and chest. The chill brought her nerves to life. Placing her hands under each breast, Marian began chanting, summoning her power, centering it on the damage caused by her father's men. She fought through the memory of her beating, re-watching each blow rain down on her body as the bones began to break.

Sensing the damage caused, she focused her powers

on the minerals of the earth so they would form a protective cast around her bones until they could heal. There were perks to having powers. Unfortunately, many of them were usually accompanied by monstrous tyrannical impulses.

"I'm just going to say it. This looks a little weird."

Marian turned to find Ian behind her. She rolled her eyes and sneered, then realized her hands were still under her blouse, which is where his eyes seemed fixated.

"Rather gentlemanly of you," she sniped, pulling her hands out from her blouse and standing. The mud was still tightening around her wounds, so she decided against swinging at his head, but she did wipe some excess mud on his clothes as she passed. "You look filthy," she said. "Clean up so we can leave."

She could hear him sigh behind her and stifled a laugh. She felt good.

-~-

Her companions' moods soured over the next few days. They'd managed to make quick progress on their journey at first, helped by the cool temperatures of the fierce breeze that blew in, but the storm that followed turned the ground into slop. Their boots began to sink with each step and the hours dragged in the steady rain, but they couldn't stop. Marian's mind was racing, recounting passages from the journals, and she was growing desperate to find Paramel's apprentice and the third journal.

Benson, however, had been grumbling and moaning from the first drop of rain, dragging his paws in the dirt and growling when they passed suitable shelter without stopping. Ian hadn't been much better but had avoided joining in Benson's pleas to stop and wait out the storm.

Lighting flashed across the sky, sending Benson low to the ground in fear, growling at their insistence to carry on.

"No stopping," Ian shouted, walking up beside Marian. "It can't be much farther away, and it'll be a lot warmer inside the Halls than out here in the rain."

"If they let us in," Marian added softly just for Ian to hear.

The two turned back to the trail as Benson lifted himself and kept moving.

"One problem at a time," Ian said as he took a small lead, stepping a few paces ahead of her.

"So," Marian paused, trying to think of something to say. It had been quiet between them the last few days, neither of them willing to address the vague directions and name of a stranger that had been given to them by a sorcerer. "What was Paramel like when you were a kid?"

"Much like I was," Ian offered as he kept walking.

"What do you mean?"

"Annoying, arrogant, and belligerent," a voice called out from the woods ahead of them.

They stopped in their tracks as Benson flung himself behind the nearest tree. They heard the sound of his body crashing, and they sighed and shook their heads.

"Could he not do that so much?" Marian asked, lighting the fire in her palm.

"No. It's pretty much a given. But at least you can still catch fire in bad weather." Ian was trying to appear confident, but he was still in pain. He had shrugged off Marian's offer to help him, an unhealthy dose of idiocy and ignorance clouding his mind while he tried to appear tough. In earnest, he was frightened to think of the moments when he willingly pierced two men's hearts and watched them die.

"The fire burns from the inside, so don't think you can piss me off and then just dump a pail of water on me," Marian said as she stepped in front of him.

"Duly noted." Ian nodded, catching himself counting the freckles on her cheek.

"No need for the fire just yet," the voice called out again.

Marian's head tilted and her eyes squinted, the voice echoing in her mind as she combed through her memories. She recognized the voice, but she couldn't remember why, and it was gnawing at her.

"It's good to know you listen," a golden-haired dwarf said, emerging from the trees and walking toward them. The dwarf stopped several paces away and stared at Ian and the bulk of bear sticking out from behind a thin tree.

"It's good to know who friends are in trying times," Marian said, lighting her other hand, holding the flames down at her sides as a warning. There was too much at stake to just trust the dwarf was an ally after it had abandoned her with such cryptic instructions.

"It truly is, which is how I got to know Paramel so well," the dwarf said, moving closer.

"Doesn't take a friend to know how annoying he can be." Ian took his place beside Marian, grabbing the largest branch he could find, failing miserably at trying to look intimidating.

"And that is how I knew what you were like." The dwarf laughed and its body appeared to melt away, shifting to a shapeless black shadow before rebuilding itself as a human woman.

"Why does it have to be you!" Ian seethed, tossing the branch into the air and storming back to Benson.

"I've missed you, too," the woman called out, unwilling to hide the disdain in her voice as well. She walked up to Marian and said, "We need to keep moving."

"I'm still not sure we can trust you." Marian refused to extinguish her flames even after Ian's outburst. "I don't know who, or what, you are."

"No, you don't. But you do know the people who are ready to burn down Hallenberry Halls along with everyone, and everything, inside of it. And if they succeed, Ephorus will begin to crumble under the weight of darkness."

"What do you mean?" Marian's thoughts wandered to the dragon beneath the water.

"You've seen it, Marian. It's coming, and our world will disappear if we don't stop it."

Marian's fingers twitched, her eyes fixed on the woman before her, trying to maintain her sanity. Images of fire and disaster permeated her thoughts, the horrors she always dreamed lived beyond the Logi Mountains suddenly seeming very real.

"You're still an arrogant prick, Erin!" Ian shouted, grabbing the gear Benson had dropped and coaxed him out of his hiding place.

"It's good to see old friends," Erin answered back, her eyes still locked on Marian.

# Fifty-Seven

Artimus sat alone in Erin's room, staring out the open window while the storm raged on. The Master's mercenaries appeared content to stay drunk through the storm on what was left of the alcohol from the Halls' cellars, giving the Elders more time to remove what manuscripts and scrolls they could. It was a risky gambit, though. Once the storm passed, their desire for fire and blood would increase exponentially in their debaucherous haze.

Sitting idly, she waited anxiously for Erin to return, struggling against the fear and doubt that had started to consume her. Their plan was rushed and had little assurance of success, but it was all they could do. She checked, once again, as she had every few minutes, to make sure the journal was still held tightly behind her back in her corset. She had begun filling the pages quickly after returning from the depths of darkness, her thoughts eating away at her until she wrote them down. Little seemed to make sense, but it was beginning to feel more and more complete. She just needed more time.

Artimus closed her eyes and fought back the swelling fear of failure. Until this moment, she had been able to ignore it, concentrating on the closest threat instead. But now that she was sitting still and waiting, it felt overwhelming.

Her hands rubbed her temples to try to soothe the throbbing inside her head, her fingers tracing the marks etched around her left eye and down her cheek. She could even feel them moving down her arm toward her fingers. It had taken her a long time to peek into a mirror, afraid of her appearance after the looks she received from the Elders and scribes. But she had no fear or repulsion when she did finally manage to confront her supposed deformity; instead, she was intrigued and fascinated. Her bond with Erin had grown even stronger since.

As she gave in to a comforting fantasy of disappearing from the world with Erin, Artimus felt a surge of light move through her body. When she placed her hand on her heart, she could feel it was beating much faster than usual. She opened her eyes: the world was shrouded in darkness before a wave of green light washed over her.

"You have work to be done. Why are you here?" a familiar voice called out.

Artimus stumbled backward, frightened by the voice. She spun around on the shore, her heels digging into the loose rocks and sand as she searched for Cataren.

"Did you forget how to speak?" Cataren called out.

"No. Just wondering if I've gone crazy."

Cataren appeared, standing idly on the shore, her pale skin and hair glowing in the green light emanating from an oar to her boat. Artimus waited for her to respond, but she offered nothing.

"How did I get here?" Artimus asked, gingerly stepping across the stony black sand that began shifting beneath her.

"All things that exist come here eventually. What makes you different is that you left."

The sand beneath Artimus began to sink as neared Cataren, rapidly dissolving in the powerful pull of a riptide. She could feel herself losing control and reached out to Cataren for help, grabbing on to her oar when she extended it.

"This belongs to you," Cataren said before letting go.

Artimus screamed as the sand gave way, sweeping her into the water. Dark waves crashed over her head and pulled her down into the depths. Choking on the water, she forced her eyes open, determined to find her way up to the surface to breathe, and found herself staring at the walls of Erin's room.

She coughed on the water still caught in her throat as tears welled up in her eyes. She was afraid and lonely and fighting to regain control of her mind. She got up and walked to the window, desperate for fresh air and a glimpse of Erin. The rain spattered on her face in a gust of wind. Shivers ran down her spine as cold droplets slithered down the back of her neck, and she turned away from the window. She wasn't going to let herself be covered in water again.

"That's new."

Artimus lit up at the sound of Erin's voice, her smile uncontrollable as her feet flew across the room. She had no idea what Erin's comment meant, but she embraced her anyway.

"I missed you," she whispered into Erin's ear, gripping her tightly.

"Of course you did. But seriously, what's that?"

Artimus pulled away and followed Erin's eyes to an oar gripped tightly in her left hand. The solid wood was light but strong. Its blade glowed green along the etchings of a whirlpool, on its shaft were the runes of a language Artimus had never seen.

"I...I went back, and—" Artimus was cut short as she heard men screaming from the lower levels of the Halls. She rushed to the window. "Erin," she asked. "Did you not express the intricate nature of our situation?" Her frustration was apparent in every word.

"I'm not quite sure." A nervous smile appeared on Erin's face as she joined Artimus at the window. The two watched as a bear charged across the open field outside.

A high-pitched ringing shot through Artimus's head while she tried to comprehend the situation. "I blame you," she said.

"That is not an accurate assessment of the situation."

"Under siege!" voices called out throughout the Halls.

"I definitely, most assuredly, unequivocally blame you."

"Why should I be blamed for their idiocy?"

"Because I'm angry and you're in front of me." Artimus slammed the grip of the oar on the floor, a flash of green light covered the room before going dark. The green lines on her face erupted in light, streaking through her hair and dying the strands from the roots to the tips. "Now, go fix it."

-~-

"How am I supposed to control the weather?" Ian shouted as he broke through the tree line and saw Hallenberry Halls. He stopped to stare at its massive structure. He'd spent his life in the small villages dotting the outskirts of the Aurian Hills, and he had never been around buildings taller than a single level. Benson roared at him in anger, and a look of disgust formed on Ian's face. "I don't know how you sleep at night with that filthy mouth."

"Children!" Marian shouted. "New plan, need it now! There are scores of soldiers and mercenaries between us and the journal. So what do we do?"

"If Erin can be trusted, she should be in there with Artimus now. So maybe we retreat to the woods and hide out until things have cleared up. The Master's men don't know that they're helping us yet, so they shouldn't be harmed..." Ian's words trailed off into despair as he watched another flash of lightning dance across the sky. Benson howled in fear and ran across the field, racing toward the wooden door and the army behind it. "Oh, this isn't going to end well."

There was no time to think. Ian and Marian sprinted after Benson. They would need to improvise their way into victory or death.

"Did you even consider not screwing this up, or is it just in your nature?" a voice screeched at them. Looking up, Ian and Marian saw an owl flying toward them through the storm. It dove and landed on Ian's shoulder, digging its talons into his skin just enough for him to recoil. "Excellent job at destroying our plan and alerting the Master's men to your arrival."

"We were probably going to have to fight them at one point or another, so what's wrong?" Marian asked, her rage burning bright inside her, raring to release itself.

"Now that the mercenaries are under assault, they've decided to go ahead and burn this place to the ground. You know, the exact thing we discussed, saying we were trying to avoid." Even with the storm lashing around them, Erin's barbs were sharp.

They heard shouting on the Halls' upper walkways and looked up to find archers preparing to fire at will. There were still several yards of open ground left for them to cross in the rain and wind.

"Do any of you think before you act?"

"Nope," Ian said, running after his friend.

"I talk to myself from time to time," Marian laughed, following his lead.

"Just try not to die," Erin snapped as she flew off Ian's shoulder and back to the Halls. "Incoming!"

Ian looked up to see a volley of arrows careening across the sky toward them, one nearly impaling Erin. The door was far too distant for comfort.

"If I die from an arrow I will come back and haunt

you both!" he shouted, garnering a roar of disapproval from Benson who was nearing the door and breaking past the archers' line of fire.

Marian dropped back and grabbed the stick she'd put in her bag. She could hear Ian let out a loud, exaggerated sigh.

"What?" she shouted at him.

"How am I," he said between breaths, "supposed to look tough with a stick?"

Marian lit her palms as they raced ahead of the arrows, using the gusts of wind to their advantage, the archers unable to adjust their shots to match its unpredictable flow. Catching up to their lumbering friend, and within yards of the gate, they prepared to charge head-on into a frenzy of very unfriendly enemies.

Marian drew her arm back then propelled it forward with all her might. A bright red flame leapt from the tip of her stick and burst against the tremendous oak doors, blasting them off their hinges to reveal the mercenaries lining up to meet them. Marian let the flames spread across her body, her eyes quickly disappearing behind glowing embers. She pictured the dragon in her mind, the force of ancient power coursing through its veins unwilling to be hindered by this world.

Turning to Ian, she placed the tip of the stick on his face. He couldn't muster a sound as the heat singed the stubble on his cheek, the scent of burnt hair filling his nose as Marian leaned in closer.

"Any questions?" she asked.

# FIFTY-EIGHT

Nance closed his eyes, letting the wind whip around him, swaying back and forth on the roof of the King's Tower; his tower. Now in possession of the two greatest fortresses in Ephorus, he set his mind solely on redeeming his failure from years before. Flush with power and adrenaline after usurping his father's throne and betraying his sister, Nance had charged toward destiny. Undisturbed by his reckless nature, he marched his forces into the Aurian Hills to confront the dragon that lay resting beneath Sorrow Falls. After Maven weakened the beast under the Logi Mountains, ripping Marian, and half its powers away, Nance intended to do the same. The power to control both, the power to control time and the subsistence of life could have been his. But he had not anticipated challengers to his destiny.

It had been a mistake to ever leave Hallenberry Halls standing. The covenant the Vorkyre bound within its walls to protect Ephorus had shackled his powers the last time he'd been there and tried to lay claim to the bridge between the realms of life and death. His mistake would now be rectified. There were shouts and cries in the streets below as the withered flesh of his sister's body burned, and a blackened smoke filled the air with the foul stench of sulfur, fuel for the battle to come.

He grew bemused, watching his sister's insistence to stay in this realm. Her body had been burning for over a day now, and it simply refused to turn to ash; even in death, she had become a force to reckon with. Stretching his fingers, he could feel the power of the Hearthwood surging in his hand, his sister's rib clawing at his skin.

"Why do I always feel like you are breathing down my neck, dear sister?" He spat the words out, staring at her body.

Because you belong to me, now, Maven's voice hissed inside his head.

Nance turned, expecting to see her standing behind him, but instead found Sever ambling up the steps. A strong wind blew, nearly knocking Nance off the tower and down toward the pyre his sister lay burning on. Nance braced himself as he turned into the wind and looked toward the sky. A storm rolling in from the west was racing into a heavy wind spiraling in from the east. There was no word yet of Hallenberry Halls resting in its ashes, but his men would rather die than face him after a defeat; the task would be carried out no matter the weather.

You fear my little creation, or you would've gone yourself, Maven's voice cackled. Time does not take kindly to those who break its bonds, dear brother.

His skin burned beneath the Hearthwood where her bone continued to scrape his skin, but he refused to relinquish its powers. He refused to bow to her. He refused to bow to time. Maven may have made a pact with the creature beneath the Logi Mountains, but the creature would soon learn it must serve him.

"The Old King, at your service," Sever shouted over the howling wind, dragging the shell of a body that once housed the king into the open air.

Nance turned to see the man's broken spirit lying on the stone, thoughts of his sister fading away. The man's eyes were now black, and the venom webbed out from them and covered his face. The stench of death radiated from him. Sir Garrin and his men had done well in adorning the Old King in his finest garments for all to see. The sight of such a pitiful man adorned in such regal clothing was amusing to Nance. The frivolous and paltry aspirations of mediocre Kings were always obvious in the way they dressed. But their jeweled adornments couldn't stop them from being overpowered. Their gold-encrusted crowns were nothing more than targets for a skilled warrior to hit.

"Please, no more."

The Old King spoke so softly Nance had to lean down to hear him over the winds. He laid his hand on the man's head and smiled, letting the Hearthwood drag across his scalp, the wood tearing into the flesh, releasing the venom from beneath the surface of his skin.

"I just have one more favor I need of you, old friend." Nance laughed as he wrapped his fingers around the Old King's throat and hoisted him off the ground.

The man choked and writhed, his feet dangling beneath him. Nance cared little for his movements and less for the pain he was in. As he made his way to the parapet, the voice of the crowd could be heard, shouting at the City Guard who stood diligently blocking the gate under the command of Sir Garrin. The guards had been indoctrinated into the Trofasthet and were no longer a protectorate of the people but a force for Nance to wield.

Standing still, he let the Old King hang over the side. It took a moment for the crowd to quiet as they tried to distinguish the two figures at the top of the Tower. Nance stood in the strong wind and stared at the shocked faces beneath him with joy.

"This is a moment to remember, sir," Sever said, standing behind his Master.

"A moment they will all remember," Nance added as he turned to Sever and smiled.

A cry rang out from the crowd below. "Monster!" the people shouted as they recognized the decaying figure kicking in Nance's hand. Those who had seen his body fall, crashing into the ground, could only see the standing man atop the tower as death incarnate.

Nance huffed, looking at the Old King. "I don't believe they even feel sorry for you, old fellow. What say you to showing them just what kind of monster you are now?"

Squeezing tight, he let the bone pierce the Old King's neck; what remained of Tomas McCordian released a scream as his body writhed. Nance let the power of the Hearthwood surge through him, engulfing them both in a purple blaze. He roared with pleasure as the man went limp.

The Old King's clothes were gone. All vestiges of his royal life were stripped and burned away. The man himself stared lifelessly at Nance, black liquid oozing from his mouth, dripping down to the people below.

"Go and be an emissary to my new kingdom," Nance said with a laugh, letting go and watching the Old King plunge to the ground below.

Cries rang out from the people as Nance stared down, his hand and arm still ablaze. Sever walked up to see his Master's handiwork, his stone teeth clicking in appreciation. It only took a moment, and then the Old King's broken bones realigned themselves and his body stood up. His lifeless shell went toward the crowd while everyone tried to flee. They were met by an advance guard of Nance's warlocks and Sir Garrin's Trofasthet. Trapped between Maven's burning corpse and the walking dead man, they realized what awaited them and screamed.

"I think a few are getting away," Sever said angrily.

Nance laid a hand on his shoulder to ease him. "They will all die in time."

"Oh, wait," Sever said with a stony grin as the City Guard tossed a few people on the pyre with Maven's corpse. "They're dead now too."

The two shared a smile as the storm arrived and rain began to fall, its heavy droplets pounding the stones around them. The howling wind and booming thunder would drown out even the loudest of cries coming from the people awaiting death below.

# Fifty-Nine

The night sky brought a heavy swell of fear over Inibri. Pight was still unable to fly, dipping in and out
of consciousness, which meant they were grounded
and exposed while the storm raged around them. The
world was a much scarier place when trapped among
the rocks and dirt. Finding shelter in a dense thicket of
shrubs, Inibri dragged Pight to it, covering her body
in fresh, dry leaves to keep her warm as the chill of the
night set in. The rain and colder temperatures began to
chase away the adrenaline Inibri had been counting on
to stay awake through the night, bringing a new battle
she would have to overcome if she wanted to see the
sunrise.

Inibri had suffered much of her life, finding loss and
disappointment far more easily than others, but those
who chase their desires, rather than being content with
what is offered, often do. The pixies had retreated from
civilization by the time of her birth, fearing the dangers
that came with the Trofasthet's first expansion into
Ephorus. The pixies were diligent and loyal to their
task of mending and building the forests that covered

the landscapes across Ephorus, but the people had changed. The only beings left that cared for the earth as they did were the gnomes, and they had retreated into the Aurian Hills in fear as well.

Her people knew they didn't have the strength to stop what was coming. They feared the death that fell upon their closest allies, the elves, and chose not to fight. Instead, like the gnomes before them, they built barriers around their remote forest realms. In her youth, when Inibri rebelled against what she considered her peoples' meek isolation, she found herself shunned and exiled. She was given the mark of the wild, her hair turned the color of a rainbow as punishment. Unapologetic and unsure of what to do, she gambled on finding the Vorkyre in hopes that they would convince her people to rejoin the world around them. But the world had changed much faster than anyone had imagined, and by the time she reached the once hallowed grounds of the Vorkyre, there was only one left.

She fought back tears, trapped in her memories of wandering the woods alone, being chased by all manner of predators until she finally found shelter.

"I am to blame for this," she whispered to Pight, stroking her hair and the black marks on her face.

"I see you've found yourself huddled inside a shrub once again, my dear little pixie."

Inibri looked around to see Paramel, sitting beside the shrub, bathed in a soft yellow glow, casting light on her and Pight.

"It happened again," she cried. "I couldn't save her

either!"

Paramel leaned closer, pushing aside the branches of the shrub to assess the damage. Pight lay unconscious at her feet, the venom's web visible around her eyes. Inibri tried to lift Pight into her lap so she could cradle her.

"I should not have let you follow that man," Paramel said, taking Pight into his own hands. "I will fix this."

"How?" Inibri took her place beside Pight. The storm raging around them, the trees blowing wildly in the wind while the rain poured down, but not a single drop landed upon them while inside the glowing orb emanating from Paramel.

"We must visit an old friend of ours for assistance."

Laying Pight across his knee, Paramel rubbed his hands together before grabbing a few leaves from the ground. He pressed them tightly between his fingers and began chanting, eliciting an orange blaze from the tinder before them.

"What do you mean?" Inibri asked, her breath caught in her throat.

"Don't be afraid," Paramel said softly, setting the fire on the ground.

The flames instantly circled them, replacing the soft glow with a burning ferocity. Inibri could barely see the world around her as the light grew ever stronger.

"Did the world end without me?"

Inibri glanced down to see Pight's eyes open, staring up at the flames.

"Ha!" Paramel laughed. "We would not think to let

you sleep through such an important occasion."

"Where are we going?" Inibri shouted. She was not ready to joke or banter while Pight still lay infected, unable to fly.

"We are here," Paramel answered, stretching his hands above his head and swinging them down by his side to make the fire dissipate.

Inibri saw a vast landscape of towering black sandstone cliffs and heard the sound of rushing water. Wildflowers grew everywhere, their vibrant colors shining through the mist from a tall waterfall.

"Welcome," a voice called out from a thicket of trees.

"Hello again, my child," Paramel said with a smile, his eyes lighting up as a woman came into view.

"Penelope." Inibri's voice barely registered above the sound of the water as she became overwhelmed with emotion.

She watched Penelope glide effortlessly through the flowers, her dress changing color to match the petals that brushed against the fabric.

"Inibri," Penelope answered, kneeling on the ground before her and opening her palms.

Inibri tried to speak. She tried to catch her breath and find the words she had wanted to say for years in the wake of losing Penelope and having to rebuild her life in a cold world that cared little for her. But nothing came except the tears she had been fighting to hold back. She collapsed into Penelope's hands, embracing the warmth they once offered.

# SIXTY

Artimus's breath stopped for a moment when her hand touched the door. The shouts of guards were storming through the hallway, echoing off the stone walls, making it difficult to know how many were an immediate threat. When her breath returned, she steadied her fingers on the handle and pulled the door open. Members of the Master's forces tore through the hallway, a cacophony of clanging from their armor and weapons ringing in her ears.

"They've breached the door!" a voice shouted from down the hall.

"I hate your new friends," Artimus said to Erin, turning to glare at her quickly.

"At least—"

"Set the fires!" a voice shouted; a call that was picked up and echoed throughout the hallways.

"At least, what?" Artimus snapped, her hand gripping the oar tight as the light from its emblem grew brighter, the whirlpool swirling on the blade, casting a glow on her blue face.

"At least you still look beautiful." Erin pulled her

over for a kiss before stepping into the hallway, slipping out of the bonds of her human form and drifting into the shadows.

Artimus could not harness her emotions, her lips tingling from Erin's embrace. She grunted while following Erin into the hallway, gripping the oar tightly, hoping she could use it well.

"What do we—" Artimus began to say when a cadre of soldiers came rushing down from the walkways above, eager for a chance to gain glory and fame while burning down such hallowed ground.

No soldier of Steinigen, save for the warlocks the Master kept with him, contained the fire of the Logi Mountains. But each soldiers' uniform could be used to strike a blaze that could withstand any obstacle—not even heavy rain could put out those flames. Their armor was cast with an enchantment devised by generations of Masters, and it protected the soldiers as they went through the fires they cast while everything around them burned to ash.

"Emissary!" the soldier leading the charge shouted. "Begin lighting the fires. We have our orders." The dead-eyed soldiers gathered and brought their wrists together, just above the Steinigen emblems on their breastplates, and flames burst out, sparked from the mouth of the dragon on their breastplate and rising high to the ceiling.

Artimus could no longer bear having the Steinigen emblem on her chest, and she gripped the neck of her tunic and ripped it off, dropping it to the ground, exposing her body free of emblem or mark of servitude.

The eyes of the Steinigen dragon glared up at her from the floor, the ever-watching eyes that had tormented her and taken her childhood. Artimus lifted the oar and slammed it on the dragon's head. A crack opened up in the floor and spread toward the soldiers who were inching forward. Artimus stood firm, eager for their attack as Erin's presence flowed around her like a snake.

"I still hate you right now," Artimus whispered, lifting the oar to reveal the shattered breastplate. She reached behind her back, her fingers searching for the journal held tightly against her skin by a strap under her blouse.

"Oh, I hadn't noticed."

Erin launched herself from Artimus's shoulders, her body soaring through the air, her amorphous form covering the lead man and smothering his screams. Two soldiers broke off and charged toward Artimus, sparking flames on their wrists. She could see that the others were holding back though their swords were raised. They couldn't figure out how to strike Erin's form without killing their cohort as well.

"You are not welcome here!" Artimus shouted, lifting her oar and gripping it with both hands, shining the light of the blade at her attackers.

The soldiers ran at her, jumping over the crack in the floor. Artimus took a deep breath and felt the sensation of water coursing through her lungs again, but this time there was no discomfort. Her body began purging the water; tiny droplets forming on her skin. She swung the oar at her attackers, releasing a torrent of water that swept them off their feet and extinguished their flames.

Her instincts kicked in, and the anger that had been building in her for so many years broke free. She smashed the oar into the breastplate of the man to her right, igniting the fire within his emblem of Steinigen. His armor broken, the man had no defense against the flames. Artimus turned away, ignoring his cries and cracking the oar across the brow of the other soldier. Their body falling limp before her.

The rage was growing beyond her control. Artimus could feel the pent-up aggression from years of servitude, years of torment, all ready to be released.

The remaining soldiers screamed as they turned and began to flee.

"No!" Artimus shouted, slamming the oar into the stone floor. Her body felt free and untethered to the shame and fear forced upon her as a child.

The floor shook violently, causing the men to stumble into one another. Artimus took a step forward, ready to see this fight to its end, and felt the floor sink beneath her.

"Not good," she muttered, turning to see Erin shift into an owl.

The soldiers' screams evaporated as they ran down the hall. The floor was no longer stable enough to hold a fight they were bound to lose. Artimus let her anger seethe as she watched her former tormentors run away.

The Halls were still standing, at least for the time being. Neither Artimus or Erin moved, their ears fixed on the frenetic sound of battle ringing out throughout the building until a familiar voice from Artimus' past carried over the noise.

"Marian," Artimus murmured, her heart skipping a beat.

"Did you know her?" Erin's voice broke through the fog clouding Artimus's mind.

"No. She was never allowed to talk to anyone." There was a wistful sound in her voice, a hint of lost desire, her mind fixated on the girl she'd found covered in lava and brimstone at the base of the Logi Mountains years before.

"Well, now's your chance to say hi. You need to get them to lead the Master's forces out of the Halls before they—" screams of terror followed by the roaring laughter of a bear cut through, "—destroy this place on their own."

"What about you?" she asked Erin.

"I'll clear the upper halls of any stragglers and try to put out any fires they may have started. We need to protect this building."

Artimus carefully made her way over the dipping floor as Erin glided along the wall. The stairwell was still intact and secure, giving Artimus some hope that the damage could be repaired.

"Why is this place so important to Paramel?" Artimus said, grabbing Erin's wrist and pulling her close.

"I'll explain when we have more time, I promise. But right now, we have to fight." She kissed Artimus before turning around and sprinting down the stairs.

"Don't get killed," Artimus shouted, reaching behind her to make sure the journal was still secure in her corset.

"No promises today." Erin gave a quick laugh before

disappearing around a corner.

Artimus tried to ease her mind. She could still hear the storm raging outside the walls, thunder exploding, its fury blending with the sounds of war beneath her. Somewhere in this sanctuary, the Elders and their scribes were cowering in fear. The sound of the floor collapsing could not have been easy to hear as they hid in their rooms.

The whirlpool began to glow once more, swirling in a violent torrent as Artimus's eye lit up, the green streaks running across her face and hair joining in. She could feel her lungs filling with the dark waters again, but this time there would be no hesitation.

# Sixty-One

The fire raged inside of Marian. She had charged the guards behind the door without fear or hesitation, laying each to the ground before Ian or Benson could even muster an attempt to fire off a shot from their twigs of death. The sulfur hanging in the air fed the flames, its stench reminding her only of her father and the hell he had forced her to live in. This was his desire. This was his goal. He wanted all of Ephorus to burn and carry his mark.

Marian could feel him gnawing at her soul, the image of the dragon boring its way into her mind, trying to take over her thoughts, but for what purpose?

"Target practice!" Ian shouted beside her, firing a blue bolt down the hallway into an advance guard. The bolt managed to miss the soldiers and careened into the wall. "Didn't mean to do that?" he whimpered.

The misfire broke through Marian's thoughts, and she turned and glared at him for his lack of aim.

"Would you like to help us stay alive today, or just bring the place down for them?" she snapped.

"Why can't I do both?" Ian flung his arms up in

frustration, launching another blue volley into the ceiling, sending down a rain of burnt embers from the impact as Benson growled beside him. "That one was definitely my fault."

Marian wanted to be angry, but she couldn't stop herself from smiling. "You are so stupid sometimes."

"You're the one leading us into battle without a plan," Ian said, the sound of guards gathering around the corner growing ever clearer.

"And you're the one following," she snapped, stepping close enough for the flames on her palms to lap his clothes.

"Well, you're pretty and assertive, and I just feel like I should."

Benson roared beside them, pointing toward the charging soldiers coming from both sides. They had gotten outflanked and were pinned in the middle. Marian stretched her arms out to her sides and launched a volley of fire in both directions, pushing back the troops.

"I like that answer," she said, leaning in to kiss his cheek. Marian could see him blush as she pulled away, a puff of smoke rising from the heat of her lips touching his skin.

She took his brief silence and put it to use, scanning the hall for their best option. There was a large door a few paces behind them, leading to what she hoped would be easier ground to fight on.

"Shall we?" Marian asked, pointing toward the door, emanating poise and power.

"We shall," Ian smiled, gripping his twig.

Benson grumbled, placing his paws on Ian's shoulder to stop him from moving. Ian paused and looked behind Benson.

"What's wrong?" Marian asked, a tinge of doubt coloring her confidence.

"Nothing," Ian said with a half-hearted smile as he patted Benson on his arm. "This door is as good as any."

"For what?"

"To find Erin and Paramel's little assistant," he said nonchalantly.

Marian paused as she held the door handle, letting the power surge through her body before they entered. "Why does it feel like we never actually have a plan to not die?"

As her adrenaline surged, she opened the doors. The great room had stained-glass windows stretching from the floor to the ceiling. They entered the room slowly, Marian's mind racing. Something was wrong. She glanced at the windows and was distracted by the craftsmanship and beauty. Each window depicted an event in the history of the First Walkers and the Vorkyre, an homage to those who brought life and protection to their world. This was hallowed ground, reserved to keep Ephorus safe and prosperous; the last of its kind.

A sudden pang of fear gripped her, her eyes lifting to the immense chandeliers hanging down from the ceiling. Everything felt ancient and inert in this room. Aisles of books spread out around them, layers of dust resting atop volumes written by long-forgotten authors, all of these memories consumed by time. The place was quiet and still, but the chandeliers were trembling. She realized the guards weren't holding back out of fear. They were trying to corner their prey.

"It's a trap!" Marian shouted.

A flurry of arrows rained down from archers on a narrow walkway, forcing them into a defensive position. They dove behind a long row of books and journals that provided protection, Marian and Ian panting on their hands and knees as Benson seemed to fight the urge to crawl up into a ball.

"This is a little much, don't you think?" Ian laughed nervously as they listened to the Master's forces shouting out orders to surround them.

The walkway circled the entire upper floor of the library giving the archers ample room to maneuver and chase them from their position into the arms of the soldiers advancing from the entrances on the ground level. Marian tried to stand to get a better view but was met with a volley of arrows rushing toward their position. Her eyes locked on the feathers of an approaching arrow soaring straight toward her, and she froze in place.

She'd always imagined that death would come quick, but she was met with a sudden jolt of pain that drove that notion away. The arrow sliced the side of her neck before burying itself in a thick tome behind her head. Ian yanked her down before the next volley arrived. He held her down as arrows stormed through the air, refusing to let her up until they had caught their breath. Benson roared, alerting them to soldiers creeping around the rows of books surrounding them. They were about to be overwhelmed if they didn't act.

Marian pushed away from Ian's arms, her hand finding the wound on her neck. The blood seeped out over her fingertips, but its flow was light and the wound was shallow.

"You okay?" Ian asked, his hands beginning to shake while he tried to ready his twig for the fight.

"Never better." Marian lit the fire in her hand and seared the wound shut, letting the surge of pain break through her lips with a warrior's cry.

The smell of sulfur filled the air, the soldiers sparking fire on their armor and lighting the books and shelves ablaze to pin them in. The fear of death was welling in Ian and Benson's eyes as they sat side by side, waiting out the volley of arrows before the charge.

Their fear was her fault. She had set everything in motion, all the disastrous moments that led them here.

"What do you mean?" she heard Ian shout as Benson grumbled and pointed at the ceiling.

A loud crash came from high above, causing everyone in the room to pause and stare at the ceiling. The room fell silent. A faint green glow took hold of the chandeliers, and small pieces of the ceiling began to crumble and fall. They heard the sound of wood splintering and cracking above them.

"We need to get out of here and find Erin and—" Marian started just as the ceiling buckled, the entire building groaning around them. The substructure was cracking beyond repair. Chandeliers began to fall around the room, crashing through the rows of books they had been designed to illuminate. The ancient masterpiece of architecture, its soaring arches and high stone walls, unparalleled for its time, swayed visibly. Screams erupted from some soldiers who were trapped by a shelf of books; they were destined to be the last to see the chandelier crafted by the able hands of the Vorkyre that came crashing down on them.

Benson began to grumble again, yanking Ian off the floor and pushing at Marian. The archers were hesitant to fire, distracted by the collapse of the chandeliers.

"What's he doing?" Marian snapped, feeling the heavy paw push her into a darkened corner.

"The ceiling—" Ian said. A flash of green filled the room before a wave of darkness took hold.

# Sixty-Two

A cold, nagging fear gripped Erin's heart. She was anxious about leaving Artimus, scared she might not see her again.

Erin tried to displace her worry, taking advantage of the guards who stared curiously at the owl soaring through the hallway toward them. She unleashed her talons before they could sense her attack, shredding one man's face, relishing the agony of his scream while she morphed into her human form. She ducked the swing of the man's counterpart, his sword clashing against the stone wall behind her, his forearm cracking from the reverberations.

His right arm was limp and useless, so Erin grabbed his throat, letting her hands shift into black, her shadow crawling up his neck and into his mouth. The soldier tried to swing hard with his left hand, but he could only manage a glancing blow before she shoved his body against the wall. His partner on the ground lay bloodied and blind, but he screamed in desperation to alert any nearby soldiers of her presence.

Feeling the life slip from the man in her grasp, Erin

let him drop to the ground. Her left hand shifted back to its human form, and she focused her energy on the talon she brought forth with her right.

"It's been some time since I've gotten to do this," she whispered in his ear before piercing his heart. "I should thank you."

The soldier went limp, his eyes bulging while a stream of blood trickled from the side of his mouth. She knelt beside him and felt the last gasp of air seep from his lungs before she licked at the blood. Her eyes went black and an overpowering urge to devour crept into her mind as her human form washed away and her shadow engulfed the two men until only a few drops of their blood were left.

Erin became consumed by a feeling she had suppressed deep inside until she'd heard the clattering of armor. Soldiers were approaching, coming toward the scream, and she flung herself into a crevasse, letting her body meld with the shadows until the soldiers had passed. With little to see but blood on the floor, they didn't even stop to investigate, moving past and leaving Erin alone to think about the horror she had just unleashed.

There was no time to feel regret or agony over what she had done. She could search herself for answers after they pushed back the Master's forces.

Hello old friend, a voice hissed, bouncing off the walls around her.

"No," Erin whispered. She shifted into her human form and planted her hands over her ears.

"Do not hide from the venom you serve!"

The voice snapped through her mind as a jolt of pain weakened her legs, toppling her to the floor. She screamed as she felt her form trying to shift out of her control.

"You may run child. But I will always find you."

A deafening roar rolled through the air, a giant clap of thunder shaking the Halls. Erin pushed against the stone floor and rose. A naked woman was standing in the shadows at the end of the hall, gliding above the floor, her form disappearing with each flash of lightning then returning. The bones showed beneath her leathery gray skin as she came closer.

"No!" Erin shouted, her senses reeling, the stench of burnt flesh becoming overpowering.

Maven appeared in front of her, fingernails digging into her chin as she forced Erin to look into her eyes.

"You will serve the venom again."

"Never," Erin answered, the pain overwhelming, a stream of black liquid pouring from her chin, her legs writhing in agony beneath her as Maven lifted her from the floor.

"You will. And if you do it well, I may even let you keep this new pet you've claimed."

Lightning flashed, striking the Halls and sending shards of a broken window across her body. When Erin looked up, she was alone. She lay on the cold stone floor in shock. She didn't want it to be true, but there was no ignoring the Plaga. Maven was waking, and the Halls were beginning to fall around them. She needed to get back to Artimus before it was too late.

# Sixty-Three

"So," Marian began, her voice barely audible under Benson's thick fur, "new plan, huh?"

"Yeah," Ian answered, lending a hand to Benson to help him get off Marian.

The disgruntled groans of his friend were drowned out by the shouts of archers directing the soldiers on the floor below. The caved-in ceiling had scattered bookcases about the library, turning it into a maze with ample hiding. For the moment they were under cover of a leaning bookcase propped up by a wall, but trying to escape this room would put them back in the line of fire for all the archers.

"Maybe we can just stay here for a little while." Marian pushed her back against the wall, listening to the wind howl outside the building's walls.

"Don't think that's going to be an option."

Benson roared, grabbing a soldier who was sneaking around the corner of the bookcase, hurling the man down to the ground. Ian pressed himself against the wall, his eyes fixed on the sword Benson was desperately trying to free from the man's grip. Marian leapt forward, grasping the man's hand, igniting her flame. The searing pain pried open the man's fingers as the sword dropped to the floor at Ian's feet.

Ian did not hesitate to grab the sword but felt his body quake with terror when he pressed the blade into the man's chest, piercing his armor and cracking through his ribs. The soldier looked at him with fear, frustration, and despair. Then he broke free from Marian's grasp and pulled a dagger from his belt, only to drop it when his body started convulsing.

Standing above the man, ignoring the tumult around them, Ian watched him slowly lose his grip on life, his eyes growing wide as the darkness crept in. The world began to shake around Ian as the man gasped, clutching the blade in a desperate attempt to pull it out of his chest. An awful cry rang out in Ian's ears while he fought against the man's last attempt to survive.

"Ian!" Marian shouted, but he didn't answer. He was watching the man's eyes slowly close, blood pouring through his fingers as he tried to pry the sword free. "Ian!" she shouted again, this time wresting his thoughts from the man before him.

The screaming had stopped, only for Ian to realize he had been its source. His hands were shaking violently, barely able to wrench the sword free from the man's body.

"Ian, we need you here." Marian stood beside him, her hands gripping his shoulders tightly before she wrapped her arms around him in an attempt to stop the shaking.

Benson roared, asserting his power, but Ian could see

fear stirring in his friend. The soldiers had regrouped, and Ian could sense they were closing in.

"I never wanted to kill anyone," he whispered, watching blood drip down to the floor from the tip of the blade.

"That's because you are a good person. But my father, and these men, have taken advantage of that and are counting on the few good people left to not stand against him. I need you, Ian," Marian said. Her anger at their predicament was palpable, and she was growing restless just waiting in the shadows for the attack.

"This whole building is going to collapse if—" Marian was cut off by Ian, who yanked her out of the way as a long, sharp arrow flew within an inch of her heart, the blood-red feathers of the fletching glancing against her chest, ripping the fabric as they passed. Ian countered quickly, dropping the blade and letting loose a blast from his twig, giving Marian time to spark her flames.

Ian stared forward, unable to look Marian in the eyes. He leaned his forehead against hers and pulled her close.

"I think I might have to kill your father," Ian whispered in her ear.

"I'm okay with that," she smiled, taking her place beside Benson.

Peering out from the rubble of the collapse, they could see the library being surrounded; dozens of the Master's soldiers staring them down. The brute force of Steinigen was advancing, taking orders from the few archers left on the remnants of the walkway above them. Ian dared to step out to look for an escape route, and a burning arrow whizzed by, impaling the wooden bookcase at his side. Smoke from the fiery shaft of the arrow crept into his nose. He stared at the iron arrowhead: its serrated edges would cause maximum damage if pulled out. As he turned toward the archer, another arrow was launched, heading straight for his chest. It was too late for Ian to get out of the way, and he closed his eyes and prepared for the impact, but there was only a sickening thud. A flash of glowing green light engulfed his body.

"Try not to die just yet," a voice snapped at him. "I'm still kind of new at this."

Ian opened his eyes to see a young elf, her blue skin shimmering in the light of an oar she'd raised in front of him. The arrow was lodged in its luminous wooden blade.

"You must be—"

"Artimus," she finished his sentence for him as the heavy oar recoiled against his stomach, sending him reeling to the ground. Ian gasped and wondered if he had misjudged her as an ally until a dozen or so arrows started whipping by.

"Oh, come on!" he shouted, his frustration with the archers reaching a breaking point.

"We go now!" Marian shouted from behind him, dragging Benson out of their makeshift refuge.

Ian and Artimus followed closely behind them, ducking arrows and taking whatever cover they could find.

"If we take the fight to them, the archers will have to hold their fire to keep from killing their own." Marian had centered the flames in her palms, preventing any stray sparks from flying about in the coming melee.

"Agreed," Artimus answered, lifting her hand to halt their progress. "I saw them pushing in when I came into the room and there's a breaking point in their ranks only a few rows over. If we stay low, we can draw them in as we advance, taking on smaller factio—,"

"Wait," Ian raised his hand while Benson mumbled in his ear. "Were you the one who blew up the ceiling?"

"Irrelevant to the moment," Artimus snapped. "And it was an accident. They happen."

Ian wanted to ask more questions, but the glare he received from her green eye, plus an impatient gesture from Marian as she waved her fiery hands at him, brought his line of thought to an abrupt end.

"Right, carry on." His offer of contrition was met with indifference as Artimus turned her attention solely to Marian.

"Are you ready, Firestarter?"

"How do you know that name?" Marian drew back in surprise, staring at the elf whose skin was covered in tiny droplets of water that were glistening in an array of colors.

Before Artimus could answer, another round of arrows came crashing around them, skewering the tops of the wooden bookcase they were sheltering under, forcing the conversation to a close. The tips of these arrows quickly sparked fires in the books and shelves; the whole of Hallenberry Halls was sure to follow.

"Behind me!" Artimus shouted.

Marian followed Artimus as they leapt out from

behind the bookcase and charged straight toward the Master's forces. There was no more time to draw them in and pick them off. Arrows continued to fly throughout the library, but none were aimed at them. Calls to burn it down began ringing from the walkway above.

Marian could feel the heat rising in the room. The soldiers of Steinigen knew how to start a fire. They knew well how to burn their prey out from hiding and watch them suffer amongst smoke and flames until they were ready to pounce and finish their work. She could only imagine the countless horrors these minions of her father had caused, and the fury it brought forth in her drowned out their calls, her scream piercing the air as the flames on her palms burned even brighter.

They made quick work of the soldiers they crossed paths with, and Artimus and Marian refused to stop, plowing into their front line. The close-quarter combat took the soldiers by surprise, and the first two in line were scalded by Marian's palms, her hands crashing into their chests and shattering their armor. Her fingers pierced the iron plates of their armor and then their skin, the heat unrelenting until she pulled back to finish them each with a blow to the head.

Artimus matched Marian's body count in turn, making use of her small frame to maneuver the oar, spinning it in her hand and striking them with ease. She had no memory of learning to fight in such a manner, but the oar responded to her thoughts, carrying her body along with it. Skulls cracked and armor shattered under the weight of her blows.

The soldiers began running into the messy rows of bookcases near them, trying to find a way around the wreckage to flank their abrupt assault. Benson grumbled with displeasure at their current predicament as flaming arrows continued to rain down around the library from the walkway, threatening to trap them inside the burning walls.

"We're gonna be fine," Ian said, wishing his words hadn't come out an octave higher than his normal tone. "We always are."

He raised his fists at the sound of pounding footsteps. Benson slapped his paw against Ian's head and waved a twig in front of his face as a reminder.

"Probably right." Ian reached for his twig, his hand brushing against a vial in his pocket. He had one last potion left, and potentially no other chance to use it. The vial was filled with an opaque potion he used to sort his study at home. "Screw it. Why not?"

Benson rumbled in agreement, dipping his twig into the vial when Ian popped the cork, letting the potion seep into the wood in hopes of the best. The twig began to vibrate ever so slightly in his paw as he raised it, and with a roar he let loose a spark that flashed when it struck the body of a charging soldier, sending the man flying through a bookcase screaming while his body folded neatly in on itself.

"Well, alright." Ian grimaced as he watched Benson fighting off the notion to vomit. He took his time letting his twig soak in the potion before pulling it out and corking the remnants left in the vial, placing it back in his pocket.

Standing in a circle with their backs together, the four began parrying the attack of the Master's forces together, hammering anyone who dared charge forward with a flurry of blows. They kept pushing forward. Marian and Artimus in the lead with Ian and Benson close behind, leaving no openings in their circle for anyone on the ground to break through. Their power was overwhelming to the soldiers, but their inexperience in battle quickly showed. They had been coaxed out of the last row of bookcases left standing, and they found themselves with no cover.

The remaining soldiers stopped their forward press and held their guard while the archers unleashed a new volley of arrows, pushing the four up tight against one another. There was no cover, there was no safety. They had been pulled into a trap. Each way they turned a fire was raging and the emblem of Steinigen stared them down en masse.

Marian's scream caught everyone off guard, shattering the stained-glass windows around them and sending Ian and Benson to their knees.

"You're not taking me back!" Marian screamed. Fire seeped out from her lips, scorching her cheeks. "I'd rather die!"

Burn it down, child. Burn them all down! a voice shouted, their words echoing through her head, triggering a power deep inside her.

Marian lost control of her powers and flames erupted across her body and broke out on the floor around her. Artimus tried to tamp them down with her oar, amazed to find that she, Ian, and Benson were sealed inside a bubble while the flames surged all around them. Flaming arrows flew through the air, slicing through the fire, unchecked by her power.

Ian looked up and saw the concern growing in Artimus's eyes. She wasn't going to be able to protect them for long and, even if she did, the library was covered in flames that had spread to every corner of the room and were now clawing at what remained of the ceiling. Hallenberry Halls was lost. The covenant made between the Vorkyre and humans was broken by the fire of Steinigen and the Logi Mountains.

"Can you help me get closer to her?" Ian asked Artimus.

"I can try."

Artimus pressed ahead, pushing back the flames with her oar. Benson helped by leaning against her back, helping to push her forward. Their bubble went with them. Marian hung in the air, her eyes faded into the fire that had taken control of her, smoke billowing from her mouth and nose.

A green glow emanating from Marian's body when Ian grabbed her hands. Her palms burned his skin. "Marian!" he shouted, pulling her close so he could stare into her eyes. The fire faded briefly and he saw the girl he first met. "We nee—"

An arrow pierced Ian's back, puncturing his lung, leaving him gasping for breath. Words were no longer an option, and he could feel his legs giving out beneath him. With a smile, he tried to pull her close one last time, but he lost his strength and collapsed at her feet.

Marian's eyes flashed with fury and filled with fire

again, and her scream was matched only by the roar booming from Benson, who was fighting to reach his friend. The arrows continued to fly, but they disintegrated, unable to break through the fire coming from Marian as her anger began to consume everything around them. Her arms stretched wide and her head rolled back while the scream continued to surge from within her, adding heat to the flames.

Ian stared at her from the ground, blood trickling down from his lips, and wondered what death would be like. He felt a quivering underneath him and thought maybe the world was preparing to open up and invite him into eternity, but his mind was still sharp enough to realize that the vial in his pocket was shaking violently. Its remnants were reacting to Marian, desperately trying to break free of the container to reach the power it felt surging around it. Ian managed to slip his hand in the bag and pull out the pink liquid to see it boiling within the vial. He tried to laugh, but he only managed to cough up a little blood before he muttered to the others, "This should be a fun way to go."

He could see Artimus and Benson's eyes widen when he opened the vial, the potion streaming into the air and bursting to life in the fire, forming a vortex as it encircled Marian, rushing toward her outstretched fingertips. A crimson wall of fire formed around the four of them, the heat near unbearable as Ian tried to shield his eyes.

"I can't hold this back any longer!" Artimus cried out, her feet slipping against the pressure of the fire.

"Erin!" she screamed before she lost her grip and the oar slipped to the floor, sending her and Benson flying out of the bubble, neither able to see into the wall of fire shielding Ian and Marian.

Ian watched helplessly as they disappeared. He could feel the heat from the raging fire, but the light was dimming, and the world was washing away with the sound of rushing water.

"I'm sorry," he whispered, his body falling limp, "but this sucks." He tried to force a laugh, his last breath forcing its way out with a gasp before he closed his eyes.

# Sixty-Four

The howls had carried on outside the Tower's walls throughout the day after the Old King had been set loose upon the people. Phillip had watched, mortified, while the possessed being grabbed whatever form of life was in reach, piercing human flesh with his fingers and infecting it with the very venom the Master had poured into him. Those that had the chance to flee the city did so at their peril; the warlocks had taken their places on the roads and left blood-stained trails wherever they went.

All these horrors he watched were worsened by the sight of Maven's body refusing to burn atop her pyre. The awful stench that billowed out from the flames clung to the air, forcing its way through him. He had spent the first few hours gagging, desperate for a breath of fresh air until his lungs had begun to adapt to the burning sensation. It was ever-present now. Even after the Trofasthet removed her corpse from the flames, returning her to the darkness of the dungeon, no matter where he crept in the Tower, Maven's scent stayed close. It gnawed at his thoughts, pulling him deeper into the darkness.

Time was increasingly indiscernible. Phillip's feet continued to carry him down the stairwell in the dark; the burning embers of the torches left untended by the Trofasthet offered little light. The Master had locked himself in his chambers after his sister's stubborn corpse ruined his moment of victory. The Trofasthet were busy among the people of Crescent City, welcoming those who wished to avoid the fate of the former king into their ranks demanding devotion to save them from the terror. The world had reverted to chaos, and everything seemed inconsequential.

What power did life truly hold? What nature of existence was meant to reign supreme? he asked himself, tortured by the ease with which the venom spread, devouring the fragile life they had all once known.

"She's alive," he whispered to the walls around him, his knees growing weak and his stomach turning sour. The stench of sulfur grew more pungent by the moment as he realized he was closing in on the cell she had occupied.

The farther he walked the less light his eyes could find. There was a single torch lit just beyond her cell, but it offered little more than elusive shadows dancing on the cold stone walls. He paused, a deep desire to run away gripping his legs, but his mind refused. He had seen the power of the Hearthwood, and he knew its rightful owner was the Plaga.

He was taught her song when he was just a child, and it was a reminder of the demons that lurked behind the emblem of Steinigen he was meant to fear forever, the terror that awaited all life beyond the Logi Mountains. Though he tried not to, Phillip couldn't help but sing aloud when he reached her cell. His hands grabbed the bars and pushed the cell door open, his feet shuffling forward while he sang:

Dancing dragons flying by, Tales of fire burn the night.

Little children run away, for your mother's come to play.

Phillip watched Maven's corpse begin to glow, the pale red embers of a dying flame, the gray, leathery skin that refused to burn away. Smoke wafted out of her mouth as her stomach began to slowly rise. He continued to sing.

She sings a lullaby of fear while pulling your soul ever near.

Your time has come o' little one, the darkness it has overcome.

Tears streamed from Phillip's eyes as he watched Maven sit up on the stone slab. Her gray skin shimmered from within. She slipped her legs over the side of the slab and slid down, her feet hitting the floor without the slightest of sounds. Her naked form shone against the dim light outside her cell, and she walked effortlessly toward him as if unaware she had ever been dead. Phillip was frozen in terror, his mouth agape, his thoughts transfixed. Maven stopped inches away, her hand flying up and grabbing the back of his neck, forcing him to look down at the open wound of her stomach. Fire flowed freely in the gap where her rib had been removed for the Master's Hearthwood.

"I want it back," she hissed, her nails digging into his skin, clutching his vocal cords.

Phillip tried to respond but couldn't.

Maven pulled him in close as she pressed her cold body against his. "Remember, child, that when I speak," she hissed in his ear, "you listen."

Her nails dug deeper into his neck as he began to choke on the blood rushing to his mouth. Phillip longed for death as a burning sensation tore through his body.

"We should let him work now, Master," Sir Garrin's voice called out from the shadows to Maven.

She closed her eyes, a look of ecstasy crossing her face at the sound of his voice. "You've returned."

"And you have risen," Sir Garrin said, walking into the cell, his eyes focused on Phillip's body dangling from her hand.

-~-

Nance stood hunched over, his head tweaking to the sides while he fought the pervasive thoughts stripping away his sanity. Maven's image was ubiquitous, lurking in the dark corners of his mind, taunting him, mocking him, devouring him.

There had been no word yet from his soldiers of the fate of Hallenberry Halls, or his daughter. It mattered little at the moment, though. If Maven had been able to corrupt his thoughts and put her miserable remains of an existence into his mind in such a manner, the Halls must have fallen, breaking down the Vorkyre's covenant and earthly protection.

Desperate to contain her laughter rolling through

his mind, Nance turned toward a map on the wall of his chamber. He ran his right hand across his brow, not thinking of the Hearthwood, which had become second nature to him. The wood and bone scraped him, searing the flesh where it touched, causing steam to rise from his skin. The burns were a mere nuisance that would heal in time, unworthy of distracting him from his target. Deep within the Aurian Hills lay the entrance to Sorrow Falls, where he had failed in his last attempt to bring forth his inheritance, the true nature of Ephorus, the destined path of existence.

It was all he wanted, all he craved, all he would kill to have. Laughter rippled through his body, breaking free from his pinched lips and bursting to life in the Old King's former chamber. He had not heard such a high-pitched sound coming from his body before, but the craven desire for destruction would not relent, nor would the laughter; the Jesting Master was breaking beyond control. A loud knock interrupted his thoughts and brought him back to a fleeting sense of sanity.

Nance lifted his head to stare at the door. "Enter!" he shouted, making no attempt to hide his irritation at the interruption, his laughter dying out.

"We have word, sir," Sever shouted, his silicate feet scraping against the floor and shaking the furniture as he rushed to his Master's side.

Nance looked from the map to his old friend standing patiently, hand on his sword, ready to slay whoever he was asked to. "Speak."

"The Halls have burned and are decimated," he

began as he walked closer to his Master to hand him a letter.

"But," Nance started to fill in the report of failure for him.

"It was at your daughter's hand."

"Intentionally?" Nance asked.

"No, sir. It would appear they were near death in battle when she lost control of her powers and brought it down."

Nance looked at the cracks in the floor left by Sever's eager and hurried steps while he began to pace around the room. "When she fled, did she run to the Aurian Hills?"

"Yes, sir."

"Ready Muspelheim. We will ride at the break of dawn. Send word to the remainder of our forces there to stand their ground until we near, but not one of their fellow soldiers is to be buried. I want them to seethe over their deaths and fuel the anger we'll need for all of existence to tremble at our presence."

# SIXTY-FIVE

The void came on quicker than Ian expected, time evaporating while he floated aimlessly. He began to wonder if he would be trapped in this nether region forever. Falling deeper into the darkness, he began to leave behind his thoughts and memories, what was once his life slipping into the abyss. If this was death, then he would welcome it; he would give himself over to the nothingness of eternity. A feeling of peacefulness washed over the few remnants of shame and disappointment left clinging to his mind. Death would be fine, he thought, exhaling what he imagined would be his last breath.

With his lungs empty, Ian drifted farther away, watching a faint green glow hover on the horizon before he crashed into murky black water. His mind began firing again as he sank deep. Ian thrashed at the dark water, clawing his way up and breaking through the surface, sucking in as much air as he could.

"How many times do I have to die in one day?" he shouted, slamming his palms on the water.

A sudden rush of fear filled Ian's body as the water

began to roar behind him. The urge to look won out over his feeble hope of avoidance, and he turned to see a massive wave surging toward him.

"Nope," Ian mumbled before turning around and thrusting his arms forward, desperately trying to outswim the crushing wave bearing down on him. "No, no, no!" he shouted, feeling the water dip underneath him as the wave began to crest over his head.

The green glow on the horizon disappeared as Ian was absorbed into the wave. He fought to hold his breath until he realized there was nothing left in his lungs. Desperation began to break his resolve, his lungs and body beginning to burn with a sensation he couldn't withstand. His mouth opened on instinct, refusing to understand that there was nothing for him to breathe.

The black water began to pour into his body, rushing down his throat and filling his lungs while he convulsed. Ian tried to fight it, but it was just too powerful. His legs stopped kicking, his arms stopped paddling, and he lay motionless within the wave, staring helplessly at the oncoming shoreline.

For the second time he was being ushered by darkness to an unknown destination, and it was beginning to piss him off that he hadn't just died already.

"Come on!" he shouted, amazed that he had air in his lungs to verbalize his displeasure. "What the...?" he began again, realizing the burning sensation had stopped and he could both feel his heart beating and his lungs rising and falling as if all were normal. He was so focused on this feeling that he forgot he was in the confines of a great wave. He pulled his shirt up to find the wound of the arrow that had pierced him; it was sealed shut and covered by a green web. He was about to touch it when the wave broke against the shore and his body crashed down on a black pebbled beach.

His sudden departure from the water left him reeling on the smooth stones. The faint glow reappeared on the horizon, offering dim light by which he watched the water slowly fall back into the sea that had cast him out. He was stranded and alone.

"Ow!" he shouted into the void, giving voice to his growing exasperation with death.

Pushing himself to his knees, Ian groaned, pulling at his drenched clothes as they clung to his body. The idea of spending an eternity in drenched clothes was unacceptable, so he began to disrobe. If he was going to be forced to stay in this realm while dead, he was going to at least try and be comfortable.

He made quick work of his shirt and trousers, laying them out on the stones in hopes that they might dry out even without any heat from the light of day. Is there a day here? he asked himself, staring toward the horizon while the subtle breeze from an incoming wave brushed against his bare skin. That breeze was the only thing he had enjoyed since his eyes had opened on the darkness. Ian turned to face the open water and groaned again as he came face to face with a woman standing by a small boat, oar in hand.

"You ever step in horseshit?" Ian called out. He protested his perceived maltreatment from death by not reaching for his clothes. "This," he said, waving his hand emphatically at his surroundings, "all of this is like stepping into one big pile of horseshit!"

Content that he had made his point, Ian reached down for his clothes and struggled to slip his legs through the still soaking wet trousers, grumbling loudly so the woman would hear. His tantrum continued after he'd pulled them up and laced them tight at his waist, and he grabbed his shirt petulantly and walked toward her.

"Maybe if I'd had a ride the first time I wouldn't be—" his defensive statement was cut short by the blow of her oar, sending him onto his knees. "Ow! What the hell was—"

"You don't belong here," the woman's voice was curt and uncaring of the pain.

"Didn't choose to come here on my own," Ian seethed, rubbing the knot forming on his head.

"The elf does not have the strength to do what is needed on her own."

Ian's memory sparked, and an image of Artimus flashed in his mind, the green glow of her oar matching the one that just sent him to his knees. "You know Artimus?"

"Do not force me to enter your realm. You will not find my approach suitable. Take this and fix what you have failed at before you return to me again."

"What the hell does that—"

A flash of green light broke through his mind as the oar struck him on the right temple. The light around him instantly faded into black as he fell on the pebbled beach, drifting deep into the growing darkness.

# Sixty-Six

The sun never set, Inibri noticed. No matter how many minutes or hours passed, the light stayed the same, shining down on them from behind the canopy of trees and reflecting off the pool of water at the base of the waterfalls, resting before the towering cliffs carved out by the water over time. A plethora of butterflies swooped through the air, their colors exquisitely illuminated, their wings flapping in rhythm. It seemed wondrous and beautiful but completely unreal.

"What is this place?" Inibri asked.

"It is the place between. This is Sorrow Falls." Penelope was walking along the banks of the water with Inibri resting on her shoulder. "It was lost generations ago when the last Vorkyre left it to try to save the First Walkers' creation."

"This is Paramel's home." Inibri turned to see the old sorcerer giddily sharing a few more raunchy jokes with Pight, her smile as bright as the light around her.

"It *was* his home." Penelope's somber tone commanded Inibri's attention. "After he and his brethren left this place, they were excommunicated, abandoned by the forces beyond time; that which awakened the First Walkers into existence. The Vorkyre may enter here, but they have no dominion."

"Who has the power here now?"

"Whoever is powerful enough to claim it. We studied relentlessly...," Penelope's words trailed off as she walked into the shallows of the water, her fingers tracing an image of Ori in the ripples.

Penelope hid her pain well, but Inibri could still feel it. She knew of the sacrifice Penelope and Ori had made in the waning moments of their fight against the Master of Steinigen. She had wanted to help them confront him, but Paramel wouldn't let her come. She waited weeks for their return, despair over losing her greatest friend increasing with each sunset. Finally, Paramel returned alone. His grim stature and tattered clothes told Inibri that neither would be coming home.

"Are you alive? Can you come back with us?" she blurted out her questions to Penelope, her tongue acting on its own agenda.

Penelope smiled, kneeling down on the banks of the waterfall. "I am tied to this place now. What we accomplished required sacrifice, and this was mine. The power we subdued and trapped beneath the falls must be cared for. I cannot leave without consequences."

"I don't understand."

"It's hard to describe," Paramel's raspy voice chimed in. His face looked tired and sad. Pight fluttered from his palm to Penelope's shoulder and pressed her body as close to Inibri's as she could without pushing her off.

"Life, or better spoken, our creation, has but one inherent inevitability—death. There exist beings who control this path to ensure life finds its way throughout its course in time. These beings are not able to be killed by our power, but the First Walkers found a way to contain them."

Inibri and Pight could not take their eyes off Paramel, watching as he walked on the water, spreading ripples in his wake.

"What's behind the Logi Mountains?" Pight asked. "Why does no one travel there?" Her voice was trembling.

"The venom. It extends everywhere, encircling everything but Ephorus," Penelope answered for him.

"But what about the sea? I've seen fishermen sail out and come back with their boats filled with fish. That is not an illusion." Inibri's puzzlement was overtaking her while she fought to make sense of all that she knew to be true.

"They bring home fish, but never a tale of new land. Never a sighting of any home to be found other than Ephorus." The joy that had filled Penelope's voice earlier was gone. She stared across the water, defeated by her knowledge of the truth.

"What is it that's here? What are you watching over?" Inibri asked, flying off Penelope's shoulder and landing on a rock protruding from the water.

She tried to peer through the ripples to see into the deep, hoping something below the surface would make sense to her, but there was just darkness.

"There are two creatures that keep the universe in

motion, dragons formed from the cosmic dust of an existence before our time - Skopun the Creator and Verowest the Destructor." Paramel peered down at the water, "Skopun rests in wait beneath me, its rage tempered by Penelope's enchantments."

"Where is the other?" Pight asked, gripping Inibri's hand.

"Verowest rests in chains beneath the Logi Mountains. The Master is trying to conquer both."

Inibri continued to stare into the depths of the water, trying to catch sight of whatever was in there. She got impatient and dove in, swimming down through the water with her eyes open. She could feel that she was not alone. She saw two burning green eyes and they started to bore a hole in her chest as the water began to boil around her. Her head pounded and her wings ached. She couldn't close her eyes.

She felt a sudden pull from above, and her eyes finally closed. When she broke free from the water, she was resting in Paramel's hand.

"What did you see?" he asked, pulling her close to his face.

Her words unable to break past the fear, she stared into his eyes in silence. His gaze grew cold and bitter. His eyes drifting to the water beneath them.

# SIXTY-SEVEN

The rain continued to fall, pooling in the pits of stones that had crumbled when the walls began to give. Hallenberry Halls was in shambles, its once great edifice a ghostly aberration of its former self. Marian stood alone in the center of the library, continuing to search the rubble for any sign of Ian, any sign he might still be alive. The few of her father's men who had survived the blast had retreated toward Cosen, unwilling to die after their mission had been accomplished.

"Please be here," she muttered to herself, prying back another slab of fallen stone, the loose rock rolling to the side as she peered into a small crack.

"You won't find him here." Erin's voice was flat as she made her way through the rubble to stand beside Marian. "You can lift every stone, search every crevasse, but you won't find him."

"You don't know that!" Marian's shout caught the attention of Artimus and Benson, who were resting under a small bit of ceiling that remained, offering a little shelter from the storm.

"Yes, I do, and so do you." There was no malice in

her words, nor was there empathy.

Marian stared at Benson, hoping he would support her, but the bear refused to make eye contact. When the vortex had dissipated and the battle had ended, he had nearly attacked her when he realized Ian had vanished. Now he sat quiet, puffing on the toy pipe he'd refused to leave behind at the cabin, holding Ian's twig tightly in his paws.

"If he's gone, then I killed him." Marian choked on the words as she spoke, her voice catching in her throat, her tears blending with the rain pouring through the broken roof. Her eyes darted back and forth across the ruins beneath her feet, strewn with the scars of battle. "I killed him."

"No one goes to war knowing who will live and who will die. There is no guarantee any of us will survive what is left to come, but we need to keep fighting, no matter the cost."

"It's my fault!" she said, her voice ringing above the storm, catching in Benson's ear as he roared in return before storming away. "He thinks so, too," she cried, falling to her knees. "I took his only friend away."

Marian knelt and hunched over, lost in the pain of doubt and failure. She had left her home unsure of what the cost would be for her to succeed, and she was now faced with the cost of failure. The abstract threat of death that hung over her father's intentions was becoming real and was breaking her, eating away at the resolve that had given her the strength to challenge him.

"Do you remember me?" Artimus's voice broke

through her thoughts.

Marian looked up to find her sitting on the rubble beside her, the oar resting across her lap, its green glow dormant. She glanced at the elf's face, staring at her eye and the green web of lines that trailed back into her hair and down her neck, and shook her head.

"Should I?" Marian's voice was cold, a growing sense of despair overtaking her concern for the world around her. She bobbed back and forth, trying to remain calm.

"There was an eruption in the Logi Mountains two decades ago that created a small fissure. When the ash settled, there was a challenge for all the kids who lived in the dwellings outside Steinigen to see who could get the closest. I imagined it was my chance to be accepted, to stop being shunned because I was an elf.

"I wanted to be ready for my chance at redemption, my chance to win approval, so I snuck away from my home one night to see the fissure. I was curious to see it and feel the heat against my skin. I thought I'd be alone, but when I arrived, you were there, resting on a rock and staring down into a pool of lava at your feet, your body still dripping as you stood naked, covered in brimstone."

Marian fought to place the memory, to recognize her face, but nothing would come. All that came was the memory of darkness. Her eyes tightened on Artimus, unaware that the storm was finally breaking and the sun was coming through the clouds above the Aurian Hills.

"I can't recall how long I stared at you until I walked forward to say hello. You were beautiful, and you were still shedding the lava, kicking it off your feet as if the immense heat and burning meant nothing to you."

"What are you talking about?"

"You," Erin chimed in, taking her place beside Artimus.

"I am not in the mood to be toyed with!" Marian shouted, her arms igniting as she planted her hands in the rubble, pushing herself up from the ground.

"Nor am I in the mood to pretend this is funny," Artimus snapped back. "I took you home with me that night to my parents, and when I told them where I found you and what I saw, they left us both at the gates of Steinigen, refusing to have anything to do with either of us. They wanted nothing to do with whatever power tore you from the grips of the Logi Mountain, bringing you to birth in this world. I spent the next several years inside those walls as a servant to the Master. I was beaten, tormented, and scarred because I knew you were special when I saw you as a child, and I will die for a chance to help you defeat him now. Ian must have felt the same."

Benson roared from across the destroyed room and came over, the bag slung over his shoulder. Marian could see the pain in his eyes, but he stood tall beside her before wrapping her in his paws and pulling her tightly to his fur. He nuzzled her ear, grumbling gently when she relinquished the flames and wrapped her arms around him.

"The creature that rests below the Logi Mountains, the creature your existence was torn from, has powers beyond this world. What rests within you the Master longs to have, to control, and he's not the only one."

Letting go of her hold on Benson, Marian's mind flashed back to the waterfall. "Maven."

"She's returned." Erin's voice cracked, the pain of Maven's touch still reaching through her thoughts.

"She's dead." Marian stared at her in fear, unwilling to accept what Artimus had said.

"Death is a part of existence." Artimus planted her oar in the broken stones, letting the light radiate around her. "It's a fault left open by the First Walkers' misguided notion that can be exploited."

"She's coming for you." Erin's voice was barely above a whisper, her eyes refusing to look at even Artimus. "She pulled you from the creature."

Benson growled in confusion, squeezing his paws against his head while he tried to sort through his thoughts. Marian laid her hand on his arm to try and calm him down before turning back to Erin and Artimus.

"I am my own person!" Marian shouted. "I do not belong to anyone or anything."

"You belong to existence, as we all do. Whatever sense of freedom you wish to feel you owe it to serve your purpose before you can be set free."

Artimus let her words hang in the air. Marian glared at them, her mind raging from grief and anger, her body riddled with pain.

"I just want this to be over." Marian's words came out broken and barely audible as her body sank to the rubble at her feet.

 Somewhere running in the woods or tucked away during the early morning hours at my desk, I indulge in the fanciful images that materialize in my mind and beg to be brought out into the light and written down on the page. Is it magic? Maybe. Is it a good or bad habit that I will never escape? Possibly. Only other writers will know the truth. Thankfully, I have the support of my lovely wife, Jennifer McCaslin, who lets me humor my whims and curiosities throughout the day to make my dream of being an author come true.

Keep up to date with all my past, present, and future work at www.minorflock.com. And feel free to follow along on Twitter at @minorflock.

www.ingramcontent.com/pod-product-compliance
Lightning Source LLC
Chambersburg PA
CBHW021223060726

47590CB00005B/1606